INTERITUM

INTERITUM

Latin for life after death

Abena Malcolm

Library of Congress Control Number:		2023903580
ISBN:	Hardcover	979-8-3694-9015-0
	Softcover	979-8-3694-9014-3
	eBook	979-8-3694-9013-6

Rev. date: 03/28/2023

To order additional copies of this book, contact:
Xlibris
AU TFN: 1 800 844 927 (Toll Free inside Australia)
AU Local: (02) 8310 8187 (+61 2 8310 8187 from outside Australia)
www.Xlibris.com.au
Orders@Xlibris.com.au
849675

ONE

DEATH

My heart throbbed in my chest. Working twice as hard to get the blood I needed to my vital organs. Even taking a shallow breath was difficult. The oxygen my body craved did not reach my lungs; instead they deflated as the air slipped past my parted lips. No matter how hard I tried, they would not allow me to take another breath.

White tiles and bathroom fixtures swam as I moved my head. I wasn't supposed to be in this room. Where was Mary?

The darkness started at the outskirts of my receding consciousness — engulfing me. My grip on this world loosened as the last vestige of my life slipped away. The time had come. My body had given me the signals for death.

Suddenly, there was nothing. More than nothing. No sense of 'self'. I did not exist. No air. No atmosphere existed around me. There was just my essence floating in pure nothing — less than nothing. Numbness and loneliness coursed inside me. Yet, at the same time, it felt as though a peaceful blanket enveloped me. This would be my last peaceful moment. I didn't know what lay ahead of me, I just hoped I would be able to get through it in one piece.

A familiar wave of panic spread through me. If I had had a body, it would have started at the back of my throat and worked its way to my extremities, making my fingers and toes tingle in the aftermath.

The familiar sensation panicked me further — why did I do this to myself? Why would I be so stupid? What if it didn't exist and my consciousness floated in this vast emptiness, forever thinking?

I have made a mistake.

A distant, muted 'thump,' 'thump,' 'thump' thrummed in my ear; a sound which I vaguely recognised. The panic turned to fear as the sound became louder and louder; seemingly originating from nowhere. It surrounded and vibrated through me, and with a sharp jolt I remembered what it was. My heart, the beat of my heart.

One by one, my other senses came back to life. The tangy scent of dank, stale air — different from the air I was used to, but not unpleasant — drifted my way. A freezing ground soaked up my body heat, and stars sprouted behind my eyelids, creating intricate kaleidoscopic patterns. As these renewed senses came flooding back, I worked out I was lying on my back on the metallic floor.

My lungs inflated, prompting me to take several deep breaths and inhale the life giving source. I realised the thumping wasn't just the beat of my heart, but the throbbing in my temple pounded to the same rhythm. The pain was unbearable. I scrunched my eyes up even further, but it only worsened the pain.

Knowing that I must do something, and I couldn't stay in the freezing cold much longer, I eased my eyes open. A strange pitch blackness greeted me and I lifted a hand from the floor and waved it in front of my face. The air rippled from the movement, but my hand was invisible in the darkness; only stars sparkled slightly out of reach. I kept my eyes open, petrified to close them again and prayed they would adjust to the complete darkness.

A small smile crept across my face as the deep black faded enough for me to see a muted rectangular outline far ahead of me. A door.

My instincts told me to reach that door and face what lay beyond it; no matter how unpleasant. It was the path for me; the next step. I couldn't go back if I tried — no one in my position could turn back.

I sat up and goose bumps pricked my skin and I realised I was naked. Embarrassed by my state of undress - even though no one was around to witness it - I hugged myself in an attempt at modesty.

The semi-darkness engulfed me as I sat for a moment, thinking about the life I led, and concluded it was too short. I didn't truly live. I was never given a proper childhood and my teenage years flew by in a cloud of unremarkable incidents. My familial upbringing and supposed 'path' took over my every waking hour, and freedom was never time-tabled. My days were spent in prayer and homework - "Playing is for children," was the only explanation I was given. He was the only thought in my mind. I wasted hundreds of hours sitting in my room reading the Bible, bathing myself in His words and teachings. Thinking back, I think I wasted my time on Earth and now... I can't think of it. What was done was done, and I needed to be ready for the next stage.

When I summoned the courage to stand up and make my way to the door, I found that my limbs had turned to lead. I struggled to move, stumbled but regained my balance, and when I finally found my bearings, I realised with a shock that the outline of the door had disappeared. My only way out.

The skin at the back of my neck prickled alerting me to a presence behind me, but when I spun around, I faced nothing. The oppressive darkness — which had come back with full force — successfully hid the being lurking inside it.

I took a deep, steadying breath — which burnt my throat and lungs — and exhaled. I watched as a cloud of mist emerged from my mouth, giving a clear indication of the room's extreme temperature.

"Shit," I whispered to myself, my voice hoarse from lack of use.

Suddenly, my legs moved of their own accord. They were guiding me to my predetermined destination, as though I had made this journey before and the steps came back from a deep-rooted source. With my renewed sense of purpose, the darkness receded, the temperature increased noticeably, and the hazy outline of the doorway appeared again far ahead of me; in the direction my legs were already carrying me. My speed increased with my noticing. I found myself jogging, running, then quickly sprinting to the door, clearly desperate to reach it and escape this unnerving place which I had awoken. The further I ran, the lighter the room became. The doorway became clearer and more inviting, and the bright lights pulsed around the doorway hypnotising me. I needed to go towards the light. This is what I had been working towards my entire life. I hoped this is where it would begin.

I stretched my hand out to grasp the doorknob, but before I reached it, the door swung open. A pure white light blinded me and I stopped in my tracks. I lifted my right hand up to shield my eyes at the same time as an eerily disembodied voice intoned: "Welcome to Purgatory, please keep to the left."

My eyes adjusted to the bright light, and the details of a long, straight, white, windowless corridor materialised. Divided in the middle by a thick red line, the corridor faded into the distance but did not end. A distant memory jolted in my mind, but was too intangible to form.

Mounted at regular intervals on the ceiling were naked fluorescent tube lighting, reminding me of my old high school hallways. The only things missing were the metal lockers which lined them and the hormonal teenagers which filled them.

"Welcome to Purgatory, please keep to the left." The female voice repeated, making me jump. I started forward. I touched the left-hand wall, afraid of what might happen if I strayed even an inch across the red line. After ten paces, I glanced back towards the doorway, but it had vanished. The endless white corridor and red line stretched behind me much in the same way as it formed in front of me. The scenery did not change as I walked further away from my starting point. No twists or turns, and no markers gave away the distance which I had travelled or an end point.

The silence in the hallway took me aback, the soft 'slap', 'slap' of my bare feet was the only sound in it and it echoed unnaturally around me. A feeling of loneliness sprang forth from an untouched corner of my mind. All my life, I had been surrounded by people, and without my other half, I was not complete.

I took this time to examine my body and assess the results of my earlier actions. My veins had expanded and rose above my skin. A tangled web of swollen arteries, veins and capillaries covered my entire chest, but it looked the worst above my heart. The blood vessels had turned blue from the lack of oxygen and bruises patterned my ribcage, displaying where my heart had pumped hard against it. I touched my skin with my fingertips, afraid that even a light touch would be too much, but no pain came. The bumps the blood vessels created tickled my fingers as I traced each path until they disappeared again under my skin.

"Welcome to Purgatory, please keep to the left," the voice repeated.

I sighed at the repeated mantra, rolling my eyes at the unnecessary reminder. My father had ingrained the unpredictable nature of this place into me, so I wouldn't dare cross that line. I could not jeopardise my mission for a simple case of curiosity.

I gasped when a black smudge loomed in the distance, on the right hand side, giving me a welcome break from this monotonous walkway. The female voice echoed in my head reminding me to stay on the left but natural curiosity overtook me. The smudge soon materialised into a black door and when I came level to it, I turned to face it. I stared for a long moment, pondering the obvious test and wondered what lay behind it. Would it hold the same room I had just escaped, or something different altogether? I longed to turn the handle, desperate to find out what lay beyond.

As I reached out, the voice said: "Keep to the left." It had become deeper, more menacing and threatening. The speed at which the tone changed drove home that I was in an alien environment and anything could happen or change without notice. I walked on, glancing back occasionally until the door faded into the distance.

I estimated around ten more minutes passed before I encountered another black door on the right-hand side. A bleak shadow crept over me, warning me of a possible danger behind it but unlike the other door, this one was ajar. Curious, I craned my neck to peer around the crack, but stopped short when a menacing growl issued from the space next to me. I froze and looked to my right. Seeing nothing, I hoped my imagination and isolation had manifested a hallucination, but when the growl came again, accompanied by two more, I panicked. The putrid smell of wet dog and dog breath floated up from where the growls had issued from, and I wrinkled my nose against it. A whimper issued from the doorway, when I looked back at it, a set of eyes, wide with fear, stared at me through the crack.

"Run," it whispered.

I stood frozen for a moment before my brain registered the warning and then I took off at a sprint. As I ran, black doors appeared, right in front of my eyes, each on the right-hand side of the corridor. Each had a pair of frightened eyes behind the crack, issuing the repeated warning:

"Run."

"Run."

"Run."

Each voice added to the last until the shouted refrain echoed around the enclosed space, and the snarls and growls faded into the distance. I ran faster than I had ever run before, trying to put as much distance between the invisible threat and myself. My heart beat against my damaged chest. My breath left my lungs burning and a searing stitch developed in my side. The clamour the voices created was deafening. Then the voices suddenly quietened.

I slowed my pace to a jog and cocked my head into the eerie silence, puzzled. It didn't take long to figure out what quietened them. A huge, grey, skeletal hand grasped a door frame ahead of me. Its long and nimble fingers clutched the door frame — gouging marks deep into it — and the other braced itself on the floor. The creature was so tall, it needed to duck under the door jamb to extricate itself from the small opening. As it pushed itself to its full height, its left hand cratered the floor, leaving a deep, manhole cover-sized hole in the ground.

The creature looked peculiar, I never thought something so grotesque could exist. The rest of its body was just as grey and skeletal as its hands, and its bones jutted out through its mottled skin. It wore no clothing, its shoulders were broad and its pectoral muscles were well defined, giving it a male physique even though it had no visible sex organs to confirm. When it stepped away from the doorway and faced me, I noticed it had no facial features.

Only a blur of protrusions, depressions patterned its face, and a small hole lay where its mouth should have been. It stood sentinel-like staring straight ahead, ignoring my presence.

When I drew level with the grey creature, I caught a glimpse inside the open doorway behind it. I stopped short. As with each other doorway, a pair of frightened eyes peered at me, but this time I was allowed to see the creature in its entirety. It looked similar to the grey creature which had emerged from the doorway but a less developed version. An unseen force seemed to be sucking its eyes into the back of its head. One of them had been covered by the surrounding skin creating a familiar depression into its face, and the other one was well on its way to being completely covered. Its nose had fallen off long ago, leaving only two tiny holes as evidence of it. Shiny scar-like tissue covered the lower half of its face, and its lips looked as though they had been burned off. Tattered clothing hung around its emaciated, grey–beige body. Half of its skin looked mottled and dead and the other, scaly and reptilian. It looked malnourished and in the later stages of decay. During the obvious transformation into the tall grey creature in front of me, one of the creatures in the room arms had grown faster than the other, with the hand dragging against the floor. Whereas the other clutched at its rags in a white-knuckled grip.

Its skin stretched apart like glue between fingers, when it opened what remained of its mouth. "Run." It croaked, from a disused voice box.

At the sound of its captive, the tall creature's head snapped towards me, finally noticing me. I sprinted away from it, but it started after me at a loping run, its long limbs flailing wildly as though the creature wasn't yet used to their length. I smelt the putrid breath and wet fur a moment before the phantom growls resumed. The grey creature's deep panting breaths issued from a few meters behind me, drawing nearer at each exhale. I chanced another backwards glance and stumbled, almost falling. Out of every entryway which had appeared since I started running, similar creatures emerged, each at different stages of development, but each one as tall as the first, as grey and skeletal, and each was loping towards me. My face paled at the sight.

When I faced forward, a door materialised ahead, this time on the left-hand side. So, following the female voice's instructions, I kept to the left and watched as it drew nearer and when I reached it, it swung inwards. I skidded to a halt at the threshold, and beyond lay a black abyss identical to what lay inside the other doorways. I stood in front of it for a moment, contemplating my next move. Nothing emanated from within. The emptiness reminded me of the black void which I fell into when I first died. I did not wish to go back to that state. My breath caught in my throat when I glanced to my right, back towards the creatures. Hundreds of them loped towards me, as though, in slow motion. A sound to my left, made me snap my head around. More black doors had materialised, and I gulped when more grey creatures emerged and made their way towards me. The white tiles had all but disappeared, the grey creatures instead engulfed the entire space.

A sharp pain stung at my leg and I clutched at it. Three, deep claw marks had appeared. Blood oozed from them, dripped down my leg and pooled at my naked foot. I remembered the invisible creature's growling and my fear peaked. Left with no other choice, I leapt into the abyss. Praying what came next would not be as frightening as what I had just experienced.

TWO

PURGATORY

A thin membrane in the space beyond the doorway vibrated as I dived through it. Instead of free-faking, I floated in the pitch black plane. It felt different to the vacuous space I found myself in when I first arrived, but it still felt familiar, as though I had been in it before. At first it was comforting, floating through nothing, only vaguely hoping to reach the other side; but when I tried to breathe, I realised my lungs had frozen in a half-inflated state and refused to work. For the second time, the lack of oxygen was panic-inducing. An unseen force had pinned my arms to my side, paralysing me. It floated me through the blackness, as my body shut down for the second time in so many hours.

My body suddenly plummeted, as though made of lead. I gathered speed as my heavy body ate up the distance between my starting point and the inevitable end. As my speed increased, the air woke around me. The wind whistled by from my right, sprouting goosebumps along my arms, which were still pinned to my side. I squeezed my eyes shut and prayed my suffocating body would hold on until I reached the end.

Everything happened at once, my arms sprang free from their confines, I drew in a deep breath into my lungs and my eyes flew open in relief. My back arched and my short black hair stood up on end at the sudden change in the atmosphere. I started free-falling. My arms flailing and my body somersaulting in the air into my next destination.

I broke through another rippling film and I fell hard onto my hands and knees, skimming off the top layers of skin. My face then collided with the floor. Bitter clumps of dirt invaded my mouth and metallic blood mingled with it. I balled up my hands, grabbing fistfuls of the compact dirt, spat the foreign matter out of my mouth and gritted my teeth hard against the pain. I pushed myself up off the ground, wincing at the myriad of injuries which I had accumulated since I arrived here.

I looked around at my new location; a circular room made of exposed bricks and not a door in sight. Several leaks came from the ceiling, discolouring the bricks in paces and moistening the walls allowing lichen and moss to grow in abundance. Sconces, mounted in groups of threes at regular intervals, burned brightly in the circular room and thick drips of candle wax caked the sconces and walls, creating metre-long, pearly wax stalactites. The candle's flickering light played havoc with my eyes, and the subsequent shadows seemed to take human form and come alive before my very eyes. Frightening figures escaped from their walled prisons and danced around the room. As this happened, I heard faint whisperings and a strange scrabbling sound echoing around me.

I span around on the spot, searching for an exit. I heard an odd sucking sound come from the ceiling, and looking up, I found the source. A black trapdoor, which I had obviously just come through, was merging back into the brickwork. Patches of wood still showed through the liquified brick, but in seconds the ceiling swallowed it with a final gloopy pop. My only escape had disappeared in front of my eyes. What was happening?

The whisperings grew louder, drawing my attention back to the shadowy figures in the room. The space where their eyes should have been, glowed red as they glided noiselessly across the dirt floor, surrounding me. I took a scrabbling step back, but something clutched at my left arm impeding my progress. It felt as though it had just been plunged into icy water. Clamped on my arm was a hand made of pure shadow. I looked up to an elongated face. Its pulsing red eyes stared right into my soul. My heart started in my chest. The shadow bent its head, its mouth open to reveal an even deeper black opening. I screamed long and loud, but this only seemed to excite the shadows. The grip on my arm tightened, the red eyes pulsed faster, and the whisperings grew to unintelligible shouts. I suddenly realised they were communicating with each other but I couldn't understand what they were saying.

I desperately looked for another exit but I could only see a wall of rippling black surging towards me. I heard another gloopy popping sound, the same sound as when the trapdoor had disappeared into the ceiling. Sure enough, through a small gap in the shadows, I saw an archway materialising — in the same manner as the trapdoor. It pushed the liquified brick aside, making room for its wide opening. Inside the archway was an ill-lit tunnel. A way out.

I struggled free from the shadow's ever-tightening grip on my left arm and ran through its freezing cold body straight into the tunnel. It turned pitch black before I took five steps into it. When I looked back, I realised why. A wall of black with a dozen pairs of red, pulsing eyes stared after me, blocking any light which would have penetrated into the tunnel. The shadows didn't cross the threshold with me, leaving me to find out what would happen here in peace.

I limped through the wide passage, eager to get far away from the shadows. As their whisperings died down, the scrabbling sound (which I heard upon my arrival into the circular chamber) sprouted up again. I realised — when prickly fur brushed against my legs — it was the sound of many clawed feet. As I distanced myself from the humanoid shadows, the walls narrowed and brushed against my shoulders, creating an extremely claustrophobic space. Many furry creatures wound around my legs in figures of eight, taking up too much of the space and forcing me to squeeze and stumble sideways through the too-narrow passageway. They bit and licked at the claw marks on my right leg, breaking through the skin anew and allowing more blood to flow. As their bloodlust increased, more of them clawed and bit excitedly at my other leg creating another fresh blood flow from which to drink. I couldn't fight them off. There was no room in the ever narrowing tunnel. The mere thought of those icy humanoid shadows was enough for me to grit my teeth and push forward despite the pain. I couldn't turn back. I had been warned.

After five agonising minutes, a crack appeared up ahead, and a tentative breeze drifted by, cooling the cuts on my legs, giving them a moment's reprise from the constant attacks. Faltering streams of light tried to pass through the crack, but I was too far from it for the light to impact the darkness around me.

The draft became steadier and stronger, and fresh air overpowered the dank and foetid air which I had been breathing in in the claustrophobic tunnel. As I neared the crack in the wall, the furry creatures fell back, seemingly afraid of the light. A nasty thought crossed my mind. Maybe they were afraid of what lay beyond it. At every turn, I had encountered menacing creatures which had tried their hardest to impede my progress through a Purgatory. I knew deep down that nothing good lay beyond that crack, but I couldn't stay in this tunnel much longer, as if I turned back my legs wouldn't be able to handle another attack by those bloodthirsty creatures.

I stopped at the crack, closed one eye and turned my head this way and that to peer through it, trying to get a glimpse of what was to come, ignoring the throbbing pain in my legs for the moment.

Something pushed hard against my back and shoved me forward. I screamed and I put my hands out to brace myself against the impact of the wall, but instead, I slipped easily through the crack, which widened just enough to let me pass. I staggered a few steps and spun around to face the crack. I glared at it, hoping to see what had pushed me through it but saw nothing. I only heard a sinister voice titter as the crack stitched itself together.

"Good luck, Violet," a squeaky, laughing voice sneered as the crack finally closed. I rushed back to where the crack had been just moments before, but faced a brick wall identical to the brick back in the round chamber. I hammered my fists against it. "How did you know my name?" I asked the unyielding rock. "Who are you? Where the fuck am I?"

Nobody responded. The squeaky voice didn't speak again. The brick wall didn't yield to my hammering. I was trapped in yet another unknown location.

"Fuck," I whispered. "What have I done?"

My hands, throbbing from pounding the wall, fell to my sides. I turned to my new location and prayed I had arrived at my final destination. I had stumbled into the tallest and widest room, bigger than any cathedral I had ever been in. A white staircase towered in front of me. It rose high into the ceiling, with an innumerable number of steps. It came to a pinpoint several hundred metres above me, but I had no way of knowing whether that was where it truly ended. On either side of the staircase stood empty wooden benches — much like the ones you see in courthouses — and between the wall and the benches was a narrow walkway, made of rough cement, not even a metre wide. Every aspect of the room extended so far on all sides of me I couldn't see the ceiling nor the side walls.

I didn't move from where the crack had been and thought about my next moves. I looked to my left and right, and then up at the gleaming staircase. Which direction should I take? In the other rooms, either a literal or figurative guiding hand showed me where to go next, but nothing presented itself here. I waited a moment hoping the strange woman's voice would return and guide me, or even a neon sign would appear, but nothing came. I was alone in a deafening silence.

With little other choice, I took the directions the voice gave me when I first arrived. Turning left, I marched along the walkway between the benches and the wall, keeping a hand on the cool brick as I did so; praying this was the right way.

After five minutes of walking, the monotonous scenery didn't change and my resolve faltered. Had I made the right decision? I started to panic and my chest tightened; an early warning sign of an oncoming panic attack. I felt as though phantom eyes had been following me since I had walked away from the staircase and the feeling had only gotten stronger the further I walked. I heard the sigh of an exhaled breath. I thought it was me, but a chill ran down my spine nonetheless. But it was the rustling of fabric which made me stop dead in my tracks. I wore no clothing, so the sound couldn't have come from me.

My started running, bare feet slapping hard on the concrete floor, sending loud echoes around the room. Through those echoes, a stifled cough issued from behind me. I spun on the spot, my wide eyes darting around, searching for the source of the cough. No one was around me and I was sure the cough couldn't have come from anywhere further than five metres away. I stood rooted to the spot, listening out for another phantom cough, but nothing came.

As I turned away, a voice whispered. "You're going the wrong way." The phrase echoed around the cathedral-like room a couple of times before fading away.

I clapped a hand over my mouth to stifle a scream and stared at the spot from which I was sure the voice had issued. Tears sprung to the corners of my eyes — no one was there. A tear escaped and fell down my cheek into my hand.

Another sigh and rustle of clothing issued from the same spot. I backed away from the sound until I collided with the stone wall behind me. To my right, a loud 'slap', 'slap', 'slap' of bare feet ran towards me, gaining speed as it drew nearer, but there was no physical body to accompany the sound. The dam broke and fresh tears puddled in my palm. The footsteps sprinted past and a rush of air wafted past me, making my short black hair sway in the aftermath. I squeezed my eyes shut and covered my mouth with both hands, trying not to let out a sound.

When the footsteps didn't return, I took a deep breath and opened my eyes, hoping to see something to make my delusions tangible. I stared at the spot the noises had issued from, and sitting on a bench, third row from the front, was an old man with scraggly grey hair which stuck up at odd angles. He wore nothing but a dirty piece of cloth tied over his body, he uncrossed and crossed his legs and the fabric rubbed together creating the familiar rustling sound; but what shocked me the most was that he sat right next to the staircase I had just walked away from ten minutes ago.

"I told you you were going the wrong way." He perched on the edge of the bench, his hands folded on his knees, staring at me with deep, soulful, brown eyes and a ghost of a smile upon his lips.

The footsteps came back towards me on my left–hand side. I snapped my head around to the sound, fear coursing through my body.

"Don't mind him, he loves to scare the newcomers." The old man smiled at me showing pearly, white teeth.

"Who are you?" I asked, not taking my eyes away from the source of the footsteps.

"I am not quite sure," he replied.

"Oh," I said. I turned to him, frowning. An invisible hand touched my arm and my heart jumped in my chest. I leapt back, screaming and jerked my arm away from the touch.

"Hey," the old man called to the empty spot beside me. "Leave her alone," he looked back at me. "Sorry about him," he added, shaking his head and sighing.

"Th–thank you," I waited until my heart rate had slowed before I spoke again. "How long have you been here?"

"Too long." He said sadly.

I didn't respond straight away, not knowing what else to say. His answers had been vague so far, so I settled for another simple question, hoping to get more concrete answers: "What's your name?"

"I can't remember," He slumped on the bench, defeated. "Take the steps. Everyone I have seen come through here, have taken the steps and left," he grumbled, gesturing to the staircase.

"What happened to those who stayed?" I asked, afraid of the answer.

"I don't know." He shook his head. "I have never seen them again."

'He wasn't helpful,' I thought to myself. "Thank you for the information." I thanked him nonetheless. I had started up the steps, when a thought formed. "Why don't you come with me?"

"I can't."

"Why not?"

"I have tried many times. I can never reach the top. I've stopped trying now." I sighed, turned and headed up the steps, knowing there was no way I could help him if he didn't want it.

"Good luck." His voice drifted up to me, but it sounded more like a warning than a sign of encouragement.

I tried to shake off the conversation with the strange old man and focused on the mountain of steps ahead, but I couldn't help but wonder about the people who hadn't come this way before me. What had happened to them? I stopped climbing, my foot hovered above the next step — the old man had clearly stayed. I could have ended up like him, existing in this white room for so long I couldn't even remember my own name. I guess it wasn't a coincidence that the steps had materialised again when I thought I had left them far behind me; someone was clearly showing me the way. I took a steadying breath and planted my foot onto the next step and vowed to reach the top even if it was the last thing I did. I also vowed to meet whomever was helping me through this ordeal.

My adrenaline took me further up the steps than I thought it would, but I knew it wouldn't last and as I predicted, my energy levels plummeted. Sweat dripped from my brow and my legs shook, forcing me to stop and catch my breath. I surveyed my surroundings and from this altitude, I could no longer see the floor or the old man, and the brick wall was just a smudge in the distance. Each step I had taken was left with a bloody footprint, making it easy for anything to follow my path. I just hoped there wasn't anything in this room which would want to catch me.

I turned to look back up at the never-ending staircase and sighed before starting back up them. They became steeper and deeper, and coupled with the fact that my energy levels had depleted from the loss of blood, the second round up the stairs was more arduous.

My next break came sooner than I intended. My legs shook more violently and every breath I took burned my throat. The stitch I developed in the white hallway came back with full force and my resolve to reach the top faltered. It was just too far. I crouched on the step I had stopped on, glanced up at the innumerable steps I had still left to climb and sighed once more.

"Hi, what's your name?" A childish voice asked in my left ear. So close its breath brushed against my skin.

I jumped back against the bench behind me and stared wide eyed at a short, hazel-eyed girl standing a foot away from me. She cocked her head to the side and her blonde hair, which hung in clumps to the middle of her back, swayed with the movement. Her hands twisted in her dirty blue dress, her frayed edges fraying further still in the movement. I didn't respond.

"What's your name?" she pressed, seemingly forgiving my rudeness.

"V–Vi–Violet," I stuttered, stunned by the sudden appearance of this young girl.

"That's a lovely name. My name is Mary-Jane," she declared, giggling. At least she knew her name.

A smile stretched across her face causing a flake of dead skin to crumble and float away on a playful breeze. I recoiled further away from her, disgusted.

"Do you want to play?" she asked, bouncing on the balls of her feet.

"I would, but I have to get to the top," I gestured heavenwards, still panting from my exertions and fright.

"You don't," she said. "Stay and play with me. Those steps are tiring, so just stay here." She smiled innocently at me, still playing with the hem of her dirty dress. More skin broke free and floated away in bigger clumps so patches of her shiny skull showed.

"I am sure I have to take the steps," I replied, standing from my crouched position. "Someone told me I needed to go this way." I took a further step up away from her and even though she was smiling at me, it didn't reach her eyes.

"You have to stay," she shouted, stamping her foot. "Stay and meet my friends." She turned and beckoned behind her. I followed her gaze. A dozen people I hadn't noticed before moved quickly to flank her. Their skin flaked freely away much like Mary-Jane's. Half of them wore tattered clothing whereas the other half wore nothing at all. When she turned back, she reached out her hand to grab a hold of me, but I took a dancing step away from her.

"You don't want to touch her." A deep, panting voice said behind me. I whirled around. A naked man knelt on a bench staring at me. His face was grey and flaking in places much like Mary-Jane and her friends, but he seemed friendlier. "I made that mistake and now I am stuck here." He paused for breath.

"What is wrong with all of you?" I asked in revulsion, batting away flakes of skin that, when on impact, crumbled to dust like a moth's wings.

"She has trapped us here, forever," he panted, his skin flaking away in larger clumps. An outstretched hand pointed at Mary-Jane. "Leave..." Each breath seemed to pain him and he doubled over clutching at his chest as all his skin flaked away leaving every bone exposed. "You have to–" His breath gave out before he could finish his sentence. His fleshless jaw hung open in a comical manner and he moved no more, but the reality of what had just happened was not funny in the slightest.

A skeletal creature emerged from the distance behind the man. Its bony limbs clattered on the wooden benches as it crept on all fours to the strange, but nice man, like a cat stalking its prey. Mary-Jane's breathing came in excited gasps behind me as the skeletal creature approached. When it reached what was left of the man, it bent low on the ground and sniffed around the man's body. A tongue darted out of its own skeletal face and it licked the naked skeleton. It then licked its exposed teeth, savouring the taste and stared straight at me with a hungry look in its protuberant eyes.

"You might not want to listen to Gary, he doesn't know what he is talking about. Many people come and go, but only the stupid ones turn out like Gary. I can save you, teach you; come with me," Mary-Jane said, holding out a hand.

I turned to her, her skin had flaked away, and she was, herself, in no better a state than Gary was. "You mean they all end up like you and your friends? I don't want your-" Mary-Jane didn't give me a chance to finish my sentence.

"Creature, get her." The rest of her skin had crumbled away, so it was a command issued from a skull. A skeletal hand grabbed my elbow and with surprising force, dragged me back towards the benches. I wrenched free of its grip but stumbled forward onto my already scuffed knees. A sharp pain stung my elbow and when I looked, the skin looked identical to Mary-Jane's and her friends — grey, mottled, cracked and flaking away — I clamped my hand over my elbow hoping to stem the flow of the decay.

I glared up at Mary-Jane. "What has it done?" I spat out flecks of spittle flying from my mouth.

"It has turned you into one of us," Mary-Jane replied coldly and she folded her skeletal arms across her chest. Most of her skin had flaked off by that time, leaving only stray strands clinging to bare bones.

"Why can you still walk and talk? What the fuck happened to Gary?" I asked, trying not to think about my flaking arm.

"When you are the Keeper of the Halls, the rules don't count for me." She replied. "I transcend the rules of this room, but you don't."

My limbs became heavy and my vision blurred, the decay had started to spread over my whole body, and my skin on my arm cracked beneath my fingertips.

"I see you died of a heart attack, but so young," Mary-Jane's voice pierced into my pain-addled brain, taunting me. "I have seen those marks before, the way your veins pop out; it must have hurt."

"Shut up," I whispered, trying to keep my sanity together.

"I hear it takes up to five minutes to die from a heart attack, and you are in agony the entire time." She laughed and the way her lower mandible hung limply and her tongue danced in her mouth as she did so, was disturbing.

My breath came in gasps, and I tried to regain control of my failing body. "Shut up," I said, with more gumption.

"I–" she started.

"I said shut up. You don't know me, you don't know what I have been through," I shouted, interrupting her and with renewed energy I staggered to my feet. Both of my legs and my elbow throbbed — the fall made the wounds on my legs open and blood flowed freely again. I hobbled up the steps, leaving more bloody footprints in my wake.

The pain started receding, and the decaying ceased as I made my way away from Mary-Jane and those creatures, but not before encompassing my whole arm. I looked at it and prodded the dead skin. The pain had disappeared, but my arm hung useless and limp by my side.

THREE

HELL

My body ached from its exertions. Every single muscle, most of them I hadn't used in a while, screamed for a reprise; but the top of the steps turned out to be closer to Mary-Jane and her band of followers than I expected. I crested the last step, crawling on all fours, wanting nothing more than to rest but knowing, deep down, this wasn't the end. I stood up, but my shaky legs could barely bear my weight. I hoped I would have time to rest later.

A huge, glinting archway clouded by a thin mist loomed ahead. The three claw marks and other smaller cuts oozed blood and my skinned knees and palms throbbed from the fall; swollen and red. Instead of the leisurely stroll which I had planned, the pain forced me to limp over to the archway.

The mist grew thicker as I neared the archway and the acrid scent of burnt hair filled the air. My tastebuds protested and my eyes stung and watered violently. I lost all sense of direction. Whipping my head around, I squinted behind me. I hoped to catch a glimpse of the top of the stairs, but the mist was so thick and it obscured it. I faced forward again, caught sight of a glint of gold ahead of me and I limped over towards it. The first tear fell from my eyes, as I made my way towards the glint; I shut them tight so I was forced to wave my hands in front of me to catch an obstacle before I slammed into it.

The atmosphere gradually changed, the air became lighter and bright spots danced behind my eyelids. I blinked my eyes open and two spear tips were pointed right in my face, eclipsing the bright light. I took a couple of steps away from them and waited a moment. If they were going to be used to hurt me, it would have happened already. I looked from the spear tips, to the wooden shafts attached, to the two enormous men holding them. They each loomed over me, standing at around ten feet tall and stood beneath the archway I had glimpsed earlier. They took the weapons away from my face and crossed them over each other, still barring my way through the archway. I continued to stare at the giants in front of me, wiping the mist-induced tears from my face. They stood unmoving, the spears held in hands the size of manhole covers. They each wore sink-sized helmets with a visor, and each was decorated with a crest of red feathers. Long greaves covered both legs, they carried a small round shield on their left arms and a short sword hung from their leather skirt on their left-hand side; they looked identical to Roman Gladiators.

After another minute, I relented to the fact they wouldn't use the spears to hurt me and I focused my attention on the archway above them. Peering through the thin mist and glowing lights, I saw that the archway was made of marble, carved with ancient symbols and imagery which looked completely alien to me. I took two hesitant side steps towards the archway and when the Gladiators didn't move to stop me, I took the remaining three steps to it. I laid my palm flat against the cool textured stone, someone had inlaid gold in the marble, adding texture and depth, and I fingered it in awe. The archway looked ancient, cracks and fissures ran through the marble, but the gold still shone as though it were laid only a day ago.

"Violet Deneuve, congratulations on making it this far, many have not had the courage to overcome the challenges you have faced. Please make your way to the processing area to the right and welcome to Hell." The same eerie voice, which greeted me in the white hallway, rang out. The words echoed around me, bouncing back off the walls before dissipating. After the words faded away, the Guards snapped to attention, holding their spears to their sides, and clearing the way for me to pass.

I tip-toed underneath the archway, craning my neck skywards. The top of it was fifty feet above my head and it was, at least, twenty feet deep, my mouth gaped open. I paused beneath the arch way, lost in the sheer size of it and momentarily forgot about my surroundings. I tried to soak it all in, capture every detail of this, never before seen, work of art. It was the spear butts banging on the ground which brought me back to the present and urged me forward. Adhering to the instructions given, I tried to steer myself towards the right, but once I crossed the archway's threshold and distanced myself from the intimidating Gladiators, the mist returned, but this time thicker and heavier. I looked back just in time to see it envelop the archway, shrouding the bright and gold off it and the Gladiator's armour.

The mist forced me to close my eyes again, but this time I knew what to expect. My eyes still itched, but I controlled my breathing so the mist didn't burn my throat as much, but I could do nothing about the burnt hair smell which hung in the mist. My outstretched hands detected the change in the atmosphere before my lungs did and I opened my eyes. Through my blurred vision, a wide, white corridor with a makeshift wooden conveyor belt running along the left-hand wall, quivered in and out of focus. I took two tentative steps towards it, and as I did so, the exposed gears underneath it turned, moving the ancient leather belt with an unseen power. At regular intervals, along the length of the conveyor, hung shoots stood around three feet above it. They were named after different items of clothing — 'T-shirt', 'Trousers', 'Underwear', etc.

I walked along the conveyor examining the crude craftsmanship and the wear and tear which betrayed its age, when a loud clunk sounded behind me. I spun around and at the start of the belt. A small brown package had fallen out of the first shoot marked 'T shirts' and it trundled along the belt, making its way towards me. Five-seconds later, another package fell out of the second shoot marked 'Trousers'. Every five-seconds after that, and as the belt turned, more packages fell out of shoots, adding to the pile on the belt. The wood creaked on the verge of collapsing, but it held up, even under the strain of the added weight. Half a dozen packages stood at the end of the conveyor and one by one they fell to the floor in a heap, some scattering across the hallway so I had to scramble to gather them together.

After the tumultuous activities of my journey so far — the adrenaline rushes, injuries and near misses — I had forgotten about my lack of clothing; as though it felt natural to be naked after such an ordeal. I didn't have time to look through all the packages I had gained. Instead I tore into two of the flimsy tissue paper packages - tied closed with thin twine - labelled 't-shirts' and 'trousers'. I winced at the various injuries over my body as I dressed and cursed my useless right arm as I tried to shove it through the small armhole. The t-shirt was see-through, exposing my tortured body and displaying my pinkish areola, and the cotton trousers were unflattering, clearly designed to be unisex. I gathered the remaining packages in my working arm and stumbled down the corridor, weighed down by my cumbersome load. The tissue paper and twine, from the previously opened packages, lay forgotten at the end of the conveyor.

The disembodied voice rang out in the corridor. "Here in Hell, we would like to make your stay as comfortable as possible. Please adhere to your previous lifestyle to make the transition easier," she paused. "We have assigned you to bunk 1,962, Dorm C. To make things easier, we have now installed a shoot to take you to your bunk, as we have had many complaints about Souls getting lost."

I stopped short. The packages fell from my arm and fell to the floor. Souls. Souls.

"Souls, souls... Souls." I whispered to myself. The word lost all meaning the more I said it — much like any word said one time too many — and I let go of a breath I wasn't aware I was holding.

I bent to pick up the fallen items, still dazed by the woman's choice of words, and when I looked up, the corridor had come to a sudden dead end. Upon closer inspection, I could see a clear tube camouflaged against the back wall. The tube stretched from the high ceiling to the floor, dwarfing me. I stopped in front of it, unsure of how to get inside it. My good arm was still full of my newly-acquired packages, and the other still hung uselessly at my side. Then, as though it read my thoughts, the glass slid apart at an invisible seam, allowing me to enter. Afraid of what might happen, but deep down, knowing I had to blindly follow instructions, I stepped inside the glass and turned back to face the still moving conveyor.

The tube sealed itself shut, hummed to life, and began to sink into the ground. When the conveyor belt was out of sight, the tube shot off into the ground like a rocket. Attempting to brace myself against the sides of the tube, my packages flew out of my hand to the top of it, hitting every available surface on the way up as they did so. The journey only lasted a minute, but it felt like ten. I went through many twists and turns, sudden directional changes, and at one point I found myself upside down. The tube remained underground during the entire journey, sinking deeper and deeper into it, skimming against the myriad of different types of stone.

When the shoot slowed, and the packages fell sadly to the bottom, the tube emerged up from the ground and I found myself at my final destination - an enormous single room. I looked up but could only see the vague brown smudge of the ceiling towering far above my head, but the longer I looked at it, definition appeared in the colour. Wooden beams materialised in the murk, much like a barn's ceiling. I looked back down to ground level and saw a sea of simple, metal bunk frames, filling almost every available space in sight. Each had a thin mattress, a single white pillow and white sheets, with a wooden night stand at its side. A thick white line separated each set of bunk and nightstand, signifying the boundaries between each set and creating makeshift walkways between them.

The doors hissed open, allowing me to escape its claustrophobic confines. Gathering up my packages for what, I prayed, was the last time, and hurried out of the shoot, eager to be free of it. It sank into the ground, and the disembodied voice said quietly: "Congratulations again, Violet..." It trailed off, leaving a sinister, unfinished end to this stage of my adventure.

I stumbled over to the bed which I exited next to, dropping two of my packages, but managing to dump the majority of them on it. My right hand banged hard against the floor, when I bent to pick up the dropped packages, but the resultant pain didn't come. I hadn't had time to come to terms with the loss of my dominant arm. I fell to my knees and cradled the liquid-like limb in my good, but equally useless left arm and cried. The salty tears flowed like a river down my face, fat droplets fell into my lap and soaked through the thin material of my white trousers, making them more transparent. Time ran away from me but soon, the sounds of people around me penetrated through my melancholic brain, and their whispers and stares stabbed deep into my flesh.

My semi-dried tears stuck to my cheeks, and I wiped them away, angry that I had let my guard down so many times since I had arrived. I had had no way of knowing what I had gotten myself into, but, so far, it had been much worse than anything I could have imagined. Taking a deep breath to calm myself, I stood up and gathered the remaining fallen packages. I perched on the edge of the bunk, sighing and glared down at the floor; adamant not to meet the curious eyes of those around me. Was this the end of my journey or the start of another trial? I thought back to the wooden conveyor and what the voice told me — it said I had arrived in Hell. So this must be it.

I turned to the packages I dumped on my bunk and opened them one by one, making a mental note of the remaining packages' contents. I had several more white t-shirts and trousers and a couple pairs of white shorts, a white jacket, and two pairs of white socks; a thin pair of slippers — much like the ones given in hotels — and some underwear. They were each cheap, flimsy and transparent, and I didn't think they would last long. The mundane activity helped me keep my mind away from my current predicament.

The air was heavy with whispered words and the dreadful smell of masses of bodies cramped in an enclosed space; it reminded me of the many locker rooms I had been in in my life. I looked up and my eyes glided past my new surroundings. Blurs of white uniformed people swam past, but no distinguishing features stood out. It was as though the stressful journey had caused my brain and body to shut down, to stop taking in any new information, and I only hoped I would be able to gather new information once I had the time to rest and restore my energy.

I rubbed my left hand on my tired legs, the blood had stopped seeping from the claw marks and scabs had appeared at the edges of them. The haphazard cuts on my other leg — from the furry creatures in the tunnel — looked to be already healing too. My hand travelled from my legs and massaged the dead skin on my right arm. I raked my fingernails over the dead skin and small flakes crumbled away when I touched it. I snatched my hand away, scolding myself as I knew the skin would disintegrate to the bone if I carried on playing with it. It hung uselessly at my side, and no matter how hard I tried, the muscles within it would not move. I could not entice even a finger to flicker. I picked it up in my left hand and let it flop back down, it thudded hard against the bed frame, and swayed in the aftermath of the movement, but again there was no pain.

I sighed again and rubbed my face with my left hand and looked up straight into the brown eyes of a tiny boy standing in front of me. He was silent in his approach and my arm had taken all of my attention, so I recoiled away from him, stifling a scream. "Oh, you s-scared me," I stammered, putting my hand to my chest, to calm my beating heart.

He wore the same white t-shirt as I did but it hung to his knees and a dirty pair of white shorts just poked underneath it. His knees trembled as he stood, and his skin was so pale, it looked translucent. His cheekbones and eyes protruded from his face, reminding me of Mary-Jane and her followers' skeletal faces.

"Sorry," he said, in a small voice, bowing his head, and taking a hesitant step back away from me.

"No, I mean, it's okay..." I trailed off, not wanting to upset him any more than I already had.

He gathered himself and looked back up at me, his dirty-blonde hair falling into his eyes and smiled. "My name's Nigel Baxter. What's yours?" He glanced quickly at my right arm, but quickly shifted his eyes away from it; his face flushing.

"Violet Deneuve," I replied, thankful for the end to the awkward silence. I wanted to hide my arm behind my back — embarrassed at its limp form — but the process of doing so would have attracted more attention to it, and I didn't want to give him a chance to openly stare at my deformity.

"Do you want me to show you around?" he asked, biting his lip, glancing every couple seconds at my useless arm.

"I would love that," I replied, bringing my left arm up to stifle a yawn. "But not right now, I need to rest. I am so tired," I said, stretching. My right arm hung as my left arm rose into a huge stretch, and when I looked back at Nigel, he was staring avidly at my right arm, which had stayed at my side during the stretch. I brought my left arm around my body to hide it as best as I could.

"Oh, okay," he said, wrenching his eyes away from my injured limb. "But can we have a walk when you wake up?" he asked, bouncing excitedly on the balls of his feet. Longer sleeves; "Sure," I nodded, clutching my arm to my body and cursing myself for not wearing longer sleeves; I vowed to myself to wear one of the jackets that I had received tomorrow.

"This is my friend, Victor," Nigel gestured towards an old man with long white hair, held in a low ponytail, sitting two bunks away from mine.

I waved at the old man and he smiled and nodded back.

"I am staying here." Nigel pointed at the bunk between Victor's and mine. I nodded, stifling another yawn. "I will let you sleep." Nigel said, shuffling away and smiling. As he walked to Victor's bunk, he glanced back at me. I watched as he clambered up on his bunk — which was too big for him — and talked with Victor, glancing at me every few seconds with excitement in his eyes. Victor put a hand on Nigel's shoulder and smiled at him. It seemed to calm him, but I could still see the excitement in his eyes whenever he glanced around.

I was so tired, I didn't even climb under the thin duvet cover. I lay on top of the bunk, rolled over to a foetal position, with my right arm cradled between my body and the bunk, and drifted off into a disturbed sleep.

FOUR

THE OTHER SIDE

"Let me get this straight Sophie, people don't need to sleep here?" I asked puzzled, rubbing my eyes with one hand and twisting my waist-long black hair with my other.

"No, Mary, I told you, people here don't need to eat, sleep, use the toilet or any facilities we used when we were alive," Sophie replied. "Well, that's what I heard."

"But what do people do here?" I asked Sophie. I sat cross-legged on top of a simple bed, with thin white sheets and a single white pillow, facing her. She sat in a similar position on an identical bed, opposite me.

"Nothing," she replied. "These bunks are assigned to you and you do, well...nothing."

"But have you seen any clocks, toilets, or food here?" I asked, looking around for said items.

"Someone told me they took the clocks away long ago, but the food and washing facilities remain, but you will have to look for them." Sophie replied.

"Have you found them?" I asked.

Sophie nodded. "Yes, but I avoid them as much as I can. They're disgusting. I'm never going back to them."

I took a moment to piece together the information she gave me. "But why would they do this? We were supposed to meet our salvation here."

"Because they want us to adhere to our previous lifestyles to make the change here more comfortable," Sophie replied robotically, clearly quoting a speech. I remembered an eerie female voice saying something similar on my journey here, but that voice had said so many things, so I may have been wrong.

"Yes, but who are 'they'?" I slammed my hands on the mattress in frustration, but the soft material dampened the sound. "And, why are they manipulating us?"

Sophie shrugged, she ran her hand through her shoulder length brown hair, and remained silent, staring at a distant point above my shoulder. Frustrated by the lack of concrete answers Sophie had provided, and by my uselessness, I sighed. I couldn't blame her, she was in the same position as me. She could only know what others have told her and she may not be as interested as I was to find answers.

I looked at my surroundings and a sea of metal bunk frames — identical to the bunks Sophie and I sat on — faced me. Simple wooden tables, with two drawers, sat beside each bunk. The only space to accommodate the flimsy white clothing which we were each given upon arrival; they had been packaged in flimsy, brown paper and tied shut with a thin cord.

A thick white line separated each bunk, creating designated walkways between them, and on, or near, each bunk, a person — be it man, woman or child — lay or stood around it; clearly no one had created an organisational system to this place.

Millions of people were crammed in this one enormous space; more people than I have ever seen together at one time. The subsequent racket and scent which emitted from the crowd was dreadful; if you let it penetrate. I tried my hardest to block out the noise, but the occasional shout, cry or scream infiltrated my mental blockade and jarred me to the bone; I was not used to such a large crowd.

The smell was noxious when I first arrived, but now that I had spent a few days here, I did not register it anymore. It was an unusual smell, something I never thought of experiencing; by no means Sulphurlike, but more like stale, sweaty bodies left to rot, but not quite dead yet.

I looked up at the ceiling at least two hundred feet above my head, a blur of light brown with deeper brown stripes — which I assumed to be wooden beams — criss-crossed each other creating intricate patterns, but were too far away for me to see any intricate details. Walls should have presented themselves, where they would inevitably meet the ceiling, but I couldn't see them.

Sophie lay back on her bunk and closed her eyes, her mousy, brown hair fanned out on the pillow beneath her head. A deep frown furrowed her brow, and she rubbed her stomach in circular, soothing motions. The subject had been too sensitive for me to broach, for I had only met her two days ago, but it disturbed me to see a heavily pregnant woman here. My heart ached for Sophie, as I tried to imagine myself in her shoes, but even the thought of being pregnant brought up such a deeply-rooted fear, I shuddered. I was too young and the consequences… I shook my head, trying to displace the dark cloud of negative thoughts which had formed in my head.

I twirled my long hair in one hand and with the other, again, rubbed my tired eyes. Even though Sophie said no one needed to sleep here, many of those around me slept. My entire body ached after the strenuous trials which I had battled and I felt as though I needed a week of sleep just to recover. I shuddered with fear at the thought of the trials and the strange scenes I had encountered. The tall, grey creature's shadows haunted me. Whenever I shut my eyes, I saw their featureless faces, heard their strained breathing and smelled their putrid breath, as though they were right behind me again. My body and mind had been through everything it could take, but, somehow, I knew the worst was yet to come.

I rubbed my right ankle, which throbbed painfully, with one hand and my chest with the other, trying to soothe the aches and pains which had developed over my body. The blue-black bruise right above my heart sat stark against the translucent, white t-shirt I wore. I traced my swollen blood vessels with my fingertips, hypnotised by the intricate patterns they created.

I tore my gaze away from the horrific aftermath of the injury I sustained which brought me here and raised my head to look around the room. The bed on the other side of me was empty, and it had been since I had arrived. A curiosity burned inside me, I needed to know why it was empty as people occupied every other bed around me.

"Sophie?" I asked, she turned her head to me in response. "Who used to stay at that bunk?" I gestured at the empty bunk with my thumb.

She raised herself up onto her elbows to get a better look, lay back down and nodded to herself. "Her name was Sarah," she started. "I never found out her last name as she kept to herself and spoke little. She was always crying and complained often of a headache."

"Why?" I asked, confused.

"I don't know," Sophie continued. "Whenever I went over to comfort her, she shrank away from me. She never met my eye, nor acknowledged my presence. One morning she was gone, no one knows why or where she went and no one has spoken of her since. It's as though she never existed." She shut her eyes. "I am ashamed to say I had forgotten about her until you mentioned the empty bunk."

I said nothing for a moment, knowing Sophie didn't need me to respond, nor did she need me to excuse her behaviour; even though I could understand her position. I wondered what happened to Sarah. Why did she disappear, and if it happened to her, could I be taken, but where to?

Glancing around the room, a dark-skinned man caught my eye. He was sitting on a bunk around thirty feet away, seemed to be in his early thirties, and was rocking back and forth, muttering wildly to himself. He clutched one hand to his chest, his white-knuckled fingers entwined in his white t-shirt and the other groping at the empty air where the bottom half of his right leg should have been. His eyes rolled to the back of his head, and a deep moan escaped his lips, which carried over to me through the din. He wrenched the hand away from his chest to meet the other underneath his knee to grope at the empty air as though the missing limb still existed. The white cotton trouser leg — much like the trousers I wore — had been hacked off just above the knee, exposing stray strands of muscles, sinew and shattered bone. He rolled his eyes back to stare at the middle distance, and they held such pain, that it took everything inside me not to go to him to try to take it away. Instead, I watched from afar as a myriad of different emotions flashed across his face; ranging from pain, to resignation, and lastly to happiness. His ghostly smile transformed his face from a haunted one, to one which might have been happiness, had he been anywhere else but here. When he smiled, his handsome face stirred a deep longing inside me. I blushed at the improper thought and brought my fingers to my lips to block the sinful smile which threatened to come forth. 'I wasn't supposed to think this way,' I scolded myself.

My eyes travelled from his face to his torso. He had ripped off the sleeves of his t-shirt transforming it into a make-shift vest, displaying well–hewn muscles on scarred arms. I wondered what his life had been like before the injuries, what the circumstances were which had led to his death, and if he remembered anything other than the disturbing thoughts he experienced.

My eyes wandered from the intriguing dark-skinned man and roamed around to my neighbours. Every face was either filled with pain, or tear-filled, there was no inbetween. There were no happy facial expressions. I wondered why everyone looked this way and when I would descend into this inevitable depression.

I looked back over at Sophie. She was staring glassy-eyed towards the ceiling, tears glistening in her eyes and her lower lip was trembling. It didn't take a genius to predict what she was thinking of, as her hands worked overtime, rubbing hard on her swollen stomach. She shut her eyes, and a tear leaked out and travelled down the side of her face until it disappeared into the pillow beneath her head. Guilt rose inside me. How could I be feeling sorry for myself, when I knew other people here were suffering more than me?

"Sophie," I whispered, getting up from my bed, but stopped at the last second when she didn't immediately answer. She lay instead, with her eyes closed, allowing the tears to stream down her face. I didn't know what to do.

"How did you die?" A soft voice said. My head snapped around in search of the errant voice, desperate to hear another person's story. Two women sat on the edge of a bunk, three rows behind mine. One woman comforted the other who covered her face, sobbing.

"Come on, it can't be that bad." The first woman said, trying to coax the other's hands from her face.

The sobs grew louder, drifting over along with the other woman's murmurings. I sat up straighter on my bed, straining to hear the muffled words from the sobbing lady, but I couldn't understand what she was saying.

The two women sat huddled together for a long time, saying nothing and their closeness fascinated me. They were the first people I had seen who had spent more than ten seconds together, as everyone else here avoided each other's gaze, touch, and never even spoke to one another; only to themselves.

Finally, the woman lifted her face from her hands a little, and I gasped, recoiling in shock. The woman's head snapped up and her eyes locked menacingly with mine. She glowered at me for half a second before dissolving into tears and putting her head back into her hands.

Half of her face and hair had been burnt away, the skin stretched taut on her face. The puckered and discoloured burnt skin had several open sores which oozed pus, and several patches of shiny bone peaked out between the burnt skin. Her left eye was missing, the only thing remaining was a blackened socket and the remnants of her burst eyeball stuck to the back of it. The other woman brought her closer to her body and glared at me. I turned away from them, ashamed at my reaction. I squeezed my eyes shut, trying to block the image that floated to my mind, but it only sharpened behind my lids, highlighting her horrific facial disfigurement. I, too, wondered how she died. It must have been awful.

"I know, I had the same reaction when I first saw her," Sophie said.

I lifted my gaze to her and her expression mirrored mine; a combination of pity and revulsion. She rubbed tears from her face, still staring at the ceiling.

"What happened to her?" I asked, fighting the urge to turn back to stare at the disfigured woman.

"No one knows for sure. She almost never speaks. Only cries," she replied. "But I think she died from an acid attack. I have seen burns like that before when I was alive and helped people with similar injuries."

"Why don't you help now?" I asked.

"There is nothing I can do." She shrugged.

"What? Have you tried?"

"Believe me, I have tried, but she doesn't want my help. She doesn't want anybody's help. I am surprised she is allowing the other woman to be so near her." A hint of bitterness sounded in her voice.

"I–," I was at a loss for words. Pain and misery seemed to be the main emotions which lived here. I was unsure of how I would handle it in the long run.

"I am sure you come here in the same state as you die in," Sophie whispered.

I stared at my chest examining the spider-web of swollen veins, arteries and capillaries covering the majority of my torso. I heard a sob and glanced back at Sophie. Her hand was kneading patterns onto her stomach.

"I can still feel her," she whispered, breaking into a flood of tears.

I leapt off the bed and strode over to her. I hesitantly reached out a hand, unsure of whether she wanted me to touch her. She grabbed my hand and squeezed tight, I took this as my cue and knelt beside her bed, holding her hand tightly as she sobbed.

"I am so sorry, Sophie." My throat closed against the tears, choking off my words. She shook her head, the tears flowing faster. "I will do everything in my power to get justice for you, to get you what you deserve." I whispered.

After half an hour, Sophie stood up and rummaged around underneath her bunk, she pulled out a tiny stove and two wooden cups.

"Where did you get that?" I asked her.

"That doesn't matter," she said, waving away my question, but she seemed nervous, furtively looking around as she set up the equipment. She fiddled with the stove and a small flame erupted. She grabbed a pot filled with water from beneath her bed and set it on the stove. A brown cloth tied closed with a thin hempen rope also came from beneath her bed and she sprinkled leaves into both cups. The water in the pot boiled, and she poured it into the wooden cups.

"Seriously Sophie, where did you get this stuff?" I asked, my eyes wide with surprise.

"I can't tell you," she whispered fervently. "But it will help you."

She waited a few minutes then handed me a cup. I took a sniff of the liquid and then a tentative sip. The liquid filled my body, and the effects were immediate. A calming wave came over me, a headache I had pushed to the back of my mind, cleared, and I didn't bother questioning her again. I simply allowed every sip to sharpen my senses and heal my body. Sophie cleared away the stove and bowl, and grinned at me after her first sip of tea. She closed her eyes and seemed to melt as the calming effects of the tea coursed through her.

FIVE

THE WALL

The candles gutted out one by one, darkness creeping closer to my hiding place in the crevice of a rock wall. Blistering heat from the stone seeped into my skin as a sweat broke out and a bead slid down the back of my neck.

Fur rustled against fur and the claws of the huge creatures scratched against my naked body. They climbed over my arms, legs, my abdomen, and even scuttled over my face. The piquant scent of oiled leather mixed with lavender — my favourite scent — drifted over an instant before the vague outline of two human legs, wearing sandals and greaves, stood before my hiding place. The creatures squeaked in fear and scrambled over me and out of the niche to escape the imminent threat. I held my breath, praying my assailant wouldn't notice but a hand shot into the crevice and wrapped around my neck in a vice-like grip, crushing my windpipe.

I thrashed around, suffocating from my constricted windpipe; my face reddening from the lack of oxygen. A second hand grasped my shoulder in an unyielding grip and shook me. A featureless face entered the small space, blocking out the light which filtered into the crevice I had taken refuge in. Its mouth split open, displaying a black cavern and it whispered indiscernible phrases. Odd words pierced into my oxygen deprived brain, but it took a while for me to realise it was a repeated phrase. My assailant shook me harder and faster so my whole body writhed on the dirt floor. The phrase became louder and more insistent until the words sharpened.

"Wake up, Violet!"

The horrendous smell of perfumed sweat, blood, piss and shit penetrated before any other sense awakened. My eyes snapped open, and I brought both my hands up to my throat but only my left hand obeyed. I clawed at my throat trying to pry away the imagined fingers which choked me. My breath came back in gasps when I realised I was in no danger, and a curtain of white hair, eclipsing deep grey eyes loomed over me — Victor.

"Are you okay?" he asked. "You were having a nightmare." His hand gripped my shoulder, it had been his hand and voice in my dream. I couldn't speak, my throat still sore as though the nightmarish hand had been real.

"Thank you for waking me," I swallowed hard but regretted it, as that simple act burned my throat.

"Is she going to be okay?" Nigel's small voice whispered next to Victor.

Victor looked over to Nigel and smiled. "I think so," he replied.

Nigel shuffled over to my side, his head bowed and dirty-blonde hair hid his eyes. "I thought you died," he said. "I couldn't wake you up. You were asleep for ages." When he looked up at me, his blue eyes glistened with unshed tears.

"It's fine Nigel," I paused. "How long was I asleep?" I asked, sitting up on my bed and attempting to stretch. My limp arm forgotten, I blushed when I realised it had not lifted in the air with the other when I stretched.

"Three days," Victor replied.

"Three days?" I choked out, my eyes bugging out of my head. Both Nigel and Victor nodded sagely.

I balled my left hand into a fist, rested my head on it, and I closed my eyes, taking deep calming breaths. When that didn't work to calm me down, I banged my head against my fist. A hand clasped my shoulder, and I lifted my head to see who it belonged to.

"Don't do that," Victor said soothingly.

"How have I lost so much time?" I asked in a small voice.

Neither Victor nor Nigel replied, their eyes bored into me, but I refused to meet their gaze. I grabbed the jacket which I had shoved at the end of the bunk before I fell asleep and tried to dress myself. Victor helped me manhandle my arm into the tiny hole and between the two of us, we got myself dressed.

Nigel sat crossed legged, on the floor, with his back against my bedside table. Victor made himself comfortable at the end of my bunk — amidst my scattered belongings — and they both looked at me, waiting for me to speak.

"I didn't expect it to be like this," I said lamely, gesturing around the room.

"Nor did I," Nigel piped up, happy to have something interesting to talk about. "I thought that it would smell really bad."

"Do you mean you thought it would have smelled of sulphur?" Victor asked.

Nigel nodded. "Yeah, and I thought that there would be a lot more fire..." He trailed off, looking around for the absent fire.

"I, for one, am glad there's no fire," I said, looking over at Victor, who nodded in agreement.

A silence lingered, during which our own dark thoughts occupied our minds. This didn't seem like the Hell I had always read or heard about. I expected Hell to be covered with dirt walls and floors with ceilings so low you had to bend low to get around; sharp stalactites and stalagmites would be growing through the floor and ceiling, creating intricate mazes. I expected lakes of fire and people hanging from entrapments — sexual or otherwise — and little red cherub devils floating around everywhere on tiny wings carrying tiny pitchforks and cackling evilly. The floors were instead made of beige tiles and no walls, dirt or otherwise, were in sight. I thought I had been prepared, but no one can be prepared for the afterlife. Nothing in my former life described Hell in this way, it had all been speculation and I stupidly believed it. I frowned, how could anyone predict what the afterlife was like if they hadn't been to it? How could anyone stipulate that the actions of your life determined where you went when you die? They must have gotten something right though, because here I was, in Hell.

A reference from the Bible, which I learnt years ago, sprung to the forefront of my mind. The Book of Revelations, verse 21:8, says:

"But the fearful, and the unbelieving, and the abominable, and murderers, and whoremongers, and sorcerer, and idolaters and all liars — shall have their part on the lake which burneth with fire and brimstone: which is the second death."

I took another look around and thought Hell was nothing as the Bible described it, no lakes of burning sulphur bubbled and popped. I looked at the people around me and they didn't look evil; they didn't look like murderers, or vile, or even sexually immoral. They all looked normal, if sad.

"What happened to your arm?" Nigel asked, restarting the conversation.

I had, again, forgotten about the injuries I sustained through my adventure getting here. I rubbed the skin on the back of my hand and more dead flakes fluttered away.

"I don't know," I paused, thinking of the creature I encountered at the steps. "Something touched me. I don't know what it was. It was a humanoid skeleton, but it crawled around on all fours like an animal." I licked my lips nervously.

"You don't have to carry on," Nigel whispered. Victor said nothing, and had a far away look in his eyes.

Recollecting what had happened to me made me feel anxious, but I carried on regardless. "On my way over here, I met this little girl," I continued. "And she had some friends with her. One of her friends — this thing — it touched me here," I pointed to my elbow where the decay was the worst. "My skin immediately turned grey and started to flake away. Whatever it passed on to me, travelled up my arm, from my elbow, and only stopped its course when I got far enough away from the girl and her friends."

"That's horrible," Nigel said in awe, and Victor said nothing, still having not broken away from his internal thoughts.

"I know," I nodded.

"How did you die?" Nigel asked. My heart skipped a beat at his words and took me back to a foolish place.

"I think we should drown ourselves." My sister suggested.

"I can't bear the thought of that," I replied. "Can we do something less painful?"

"What about taking daddy's gun?" she asked

"No, never," I scolded. "He would freak if he found out."

"Then how?" she asked.

"I am thinking, Mary."

I shook away the memory. "Wow, that's a forward question, Nigel," I said, trying to keep my voice neutral, but I gave him a piercing look, not wanting to talk about my death just yet.

"Sorry, I am just curious," Nigel said, scratching his nose.

"Well, how did *you* die?" I countered, raising an eyebrow. He squirmed uncomfortably, twisting his huge t-shirt in his hands. "See!" I exclaimed, pleased at his reaction. At my exclamation, Victor seemed to snap back to reality, smiling at the contrite look on Nigel's face.

"Would you like us to show you around?" Victor asked me, trying to ease the tension in the air, and rightly guessing that a distraction was in order.

"You read my mind," I said, getting up from my bunk and stretching. I blushed again, still unused to the lifeless arm which I carried with me.

"Can I come?" Nigel asked. He still sat on the floor, looking up at us with a hopeful look on his face.

"Of course you can," I said smiling. "It was your idea, remember?" Nigel's face split into a wide grin, and he leapt up and ran off.

"Come on," he called back to us in a whine when he realised that we weren't following him at his desired pace. He was clearly impatient to show me Hell and its occupants.

We followed the makeshift walkways — devised by the painted white lines separating the bunks — and wound our way past a variety of different people. As we walked, my ears pricked at a steady rhythmic 'thump', 'thump', 'thump' which pierced through the cloud of constant chatter. I turned and my attention was drawn to a tall, blonde man, lying on his bunk, his feet dangling over the edge of it. His bare foot banged against one of the bed's spindly legs in the same rhythm as the thumping I had heard. His left arm draped over his face, blocking out the light, and his right hand played with one of those hotel slippers you were given upon arrival. I stopped and stared at him for a moment, but then turned away, my curiosity having peaked when he did nothing else of interest.

I quickly forgot about him with the new and interesting sights and smells, but then the skin on the back of my neck prickled. I turned back towards him. He had leant up on his elbows and was staring after me. Our eyes — emerald green to moss green — met, but he didn't look away like any normal person would when caught staring. He, instead, continued to stare, his eyes x-raying through me and penetrating my innermost being.

Someone grabbed my hand and tugged at it, distracting me from the impromptu staring contest with the blond haired man. I looked down, and Nigel stood next to me, staring up at me with adoring eyes.

"That's Mrs Scott," he whispered, pointing into the crowd. I followed the line of his outstretched finger, and saw an ancient woman sitting on a rocking chair next to a pristine bunk. Her eyes were closed, and she looked to be asleep, but then her mouth soon twisted into a small smile, stretching her dark, leathery, wrinkled skin which hung off her body as though she was melting away.

"She has been here forever, and she has powers..." Nigel said, trailing off ominously. I tore my gaze away from her and glanced back at Nigel; he was looking at Mrs Scott with wide, fearful eyes.

Nigel, Victor and I stopped for a moment to take her in. A sense of deja vu passed over me. I had seen that old woman before, but I couldn't remember where. One of her eyes squinted open and stared right at us. Nigel squealed and darted behind my legs, his tiny fingers digging into my knees. I put a comforting hand on his head and I smiled at the old woman, my cheeks tinging pink with embarrassment, at having been caught staring. I looked away from her but chanced a sly glance back towards her. She had sat upright in her rocking chair and was staring intently at me. A large red birthmark on her palm caught my eye when she lifted a wrinkled, liver-spotted hand in farewell, but she folded her hand away when she caught me staring at it. A wooden cup was cradled in her other hand and she lifted it to her mouth, winking at me, as though we shared a secret. I didn't know what to make of the exchange. Her gestures were so familiar, but I couldn't figure out why she struck a chord with me.

Nigel tugged at my hand and I turned away from her. We wound our way again around the walkways, deciding which way to go at each turn, but I couldn't get Mrs Scott's birthmark out of my head. For the second time in two minutes, a sense of déjà vu overwhelmed me; I had seen that birthmark before. My left palm tingled and burned. I gasped in pain and looked at it but there was nothing visible on it which would have caused any pain. I tried to shake off the painful sensation and assumed that I had just imagined the pain. I clenched and unclenched my hand several times to dispel it.

After five minutes of spontaneous decision making, meandering through the sea of white beds, a long trestle table, laden with a variety of food appeared in the distance. A raised platform held the trestle table in the middle of a clearing empty of bunks, and my eyes lit up with delight. Piled high on one end of the table were breads, cheeses and several different types of cooked meat; some were cold but some were hot and visibly steaming. A mountain of fruits and vegetables sat at the other end; meeting in the middle of the table. Everything gleamed in the light of three candelabra standing equidistance on the table.

Blurred bunks swam past me as I ran towards it, and the people on and around them stared after me. My ears fell deaf to the warnings from Nigel and Victor, and the sniggers from those around me. I leapt on to the platform, but when I reached the table, a wave of pungent smells hit me like a slap in the face. Mouldy cheeses, rotting fruit and vegetables replaced the fresh looking produce which had stood on the table not thirty-seconds before. Flies hovered over the mountain of rot, and maggots crawled in and out of every piece of food, creating a maze of tiny tunnels wherever they went. I gagged and stumbled backwards away from the awful stench and as soon as I reached the bottom step of the raised platform, it disappeared.

"What? Why didn't you warn me?" I choked out, coughing into my left hand.

"We tried," Victor said smiling. "But you didn't hear us."

"What is this?" I asked, between coughing fits.

Nigel grinned up at me. "I don't know why, but we call this the 'Unholy Mountain'."

"What is it doing here?" I asked, shaking my head in disgust and glaring at the deceiving food.

"I heard that it has been here as long as Hell has been around. Mrs Scott told me the food on there was once eatable, that someone put it out to help the 'souls a-a-c-c-climate'." Nigel said proudly. I smiled at him and he beamed back.

"She also said when people tried to eat the food they kept falling ill, but the food remained regardless." Victor added.

"Why did they fall ill and why didn't they take it away if it made everyone ill?" I asked, still glancing at the now non-threatening display of food. From this vantage point, the food looked delicious once again.

"She doesn't know, she said she heard this from someone else," Victor explained. "We tried to get more out of her, but she can be a bit temperamental."

Nothing they told me shed any light on this puzzling exhibit. I needed to sit with Mrs Scott and pick her brain myself. First, I needed to find out why the tall blonde man was staring at me. My mental to-do-list was growing. I glanced back to his general direction, but we had travelled further than I expected and I could no longer see him.

"Come on, let's get away from here," Victor said, shepherding us away from the confusing display.

"Are there more of those?" I asked.

"Yeah, loads," Nigel shouted back at us. He skipped ahead of us and was chattering happily to people near him.

"They are dotted around the place, supposedly to make it easier for the 'souls' to get to them," Victor said. "It would have been foolish to only have one of them, when there are millions of people here."

'But why would they have so many if they are useless?' I thought to myself, but decided not to ask it out loud, knowing Victor would have no answers.

I shuddered at the word 'soul', still unused to the terminology.

"It takes some getting used to, but we are souls," Victor said, noticing my shudder.

"It's just scary. I never thought it would be like this. Never," I said, closing my eyes and taking a deep breath.

"Nothing can prepare you for this. Nothing in my previous life even hinted to Hell being like this," he admitted. "But look on the bright side, at least we are not swimming in fiery lakes, being whipped by evil demons or lying on beds of nails. This isn't so bad for Hell."

I was so caught up at the sight of food, I didn't see the shower stalls right next to the platform. I frowned and cautiously made my way over to them. A few feet away stood five stalls. Surrounding them were walls only around two feet tall and around three feet clear of the ground. They made it impossible to get any privacy in them. I walked into the first stall and found I was tall enough to look comfortably over the walls and at the surrounding people, each staring humorously at me. A crude metal shower head hung above me, which, upon closer inspection, held a layer of rust and mineral deposits, so thick you could not see the individual holes in it. A distant, 'drip', 'drip' issued from deep inside the single pipe which fitted the faucet to the wall.

"Do people still use these?" I asked to noone in particular. I stood on the tips of my toes to get a better look at the rust.

"No," It was Victor who responded. "They have been here as long as the food has been here, but no one has used them in a long time."

"Hmm," I murmured, still enthralled by the shower head. I reached out a hand and tried to turn the knob. It was stiff but after a little jiggling, I loosened it enough for a trickle of brown, stagnant water to dribble out of the shower head. I quickly shut it off, avoiding the flow of water and remaining clean and dry.

I stepped out of the stall, walked to the others, checking if they were in the same state as the first; they were. I walked around to the other side.

"What the–," I muttered when I turned to look at the back of the shower stalls.

Five equally rusting and decaying toilets backed onto the shower stalls. They were each falling apart in one way or another. Only one of them had the broken remains of a seat but the others were devoid of such comforts. Each cistern had no lid and when I walked up to the nearest toilet and looked into it, the water inside was brown, murky and moving of its own accord. I gagged at the offensive smell and put a hand over my mouth to block the noxious fumes from entering my body.

Slow footsteps came up behind me. "Had your fill?" Victor muttered, a hand covering his nose and mouth also.

I nodded, unable to take my hand away from my mouth for even a second. I turned to him and rolled my eyes at the mirthful glint in his eyes.

"What?" he asked from behind his hand, not attempting to mask his mirth.

I shook my head at him, saying nothing, and walked away. I followed the line of toilets, turned the corner and found myself back where we started. I could see the 'Unholy Mountain' — as the guys called it — and the shower stalls. Nigel sat cross-legged on the floor near the stalls, his chin in his hands, waiting patiently. When he spotted me, he leapt up and ran to me.

"Are you finished?" he asked.

"Yes, I have had my fill of stinky water for the time being," I winked at him, grinning.

"Are we ready to go?" Victor asked, appearing at my other side.

"Yes, please. Get me out of here," I muttered.

Nigel again tugged at my hand, eager to get going again, but when I didn't keep to the fast pace he wanted, he ran off ahead, weaving through the bunks. I glanced back at the shower stalls, the toilets and the 'Unholy Mountain' and shuddered, but not smelling anything from them from this distance. I wondered what other useless facilities they had here for us. Deep down, I was unsurprised that Hell had something so sinister disguised behind something innocent looking. It brought home the notion that nothing was what it seemed here and I would have to be careful in my future investigations.

The three of us walked on in amicable silence and occasionally Nigel pointed out people he thought would interest me, or run ahead and disappear, only to reappear behind us again, panting from his exertions. I watched him as he spoke to the people around — he was sociable and they each knew him by name — but when he looked back and urged us to catch up, his eyes held love for us and I knew those people were not as important to him as Victor was; or I was becoming.

"How long has Nigel been here?" I asked Victor.

"Not much longer than I have. We arrived at around the same time, he–," Nigel interrupted Victor, he had come back to relay a seemingly important piece of information.

"That's Günter, I don't know his last name, but he was a German scientist in World War II," Nigel whispered, raising his eyebrows conspiratorially.

"He was a part of some atrocious experiments," Victor added when Nigel ran away again, distracted by someone calling his name. "He got away with it and loves to brag about them to anyone who will listen. Steer clear of him."

Günter was an ancient man, older, even, than Victor, his short hair was translucent and wiry, sticking up at odd angles, as though someone had just electrocuted him. Intelligence sparkled from his bright, hazel eyes, even if his body betrayed his years. He wore the same clothes as the rest of us, but he had an air of superiority about him in the way he held himself. His voice drifted over to us and the tone of it and his choice of words showed his high standing in society. A group of men sat cross-legged on the floor around his bunk, enraptured by his words. They each looked brainwashed, staring gormlessly at him, with glazed over eyes and mouths agape.

"Smith is the man in red," Victor murmured in my ear. "He was a carpenter. He made that rocking chair for Mrs Scott. He can make anything, but I don't know where he gets his materials." The man in the red shirt, stuck out like a beacon, sitting at a desk, working on a piece of wood. He had a young boy who looked to be about eight years old, sitting beside him on a hand-made stool, handing him various tools occasionally.

We walked aimlessly for another half an hour and a myriad of different people came to attention for various reasons. Some we spoke to, and some we gave a wide berth. Some of the soul's states were shocking. One half of a man's face was burned off, exposing an eye dangling out if its socket and skull bone showed beneath blackened and burnt skin. A young woman had taken some of the food from a nearby trestle table and gorged on it at her bunk. She kept on wrinkling her face in disgust as she tore off huge chunks of bread and stuffed them into her mouth. She bit into pungent cheeses, and swallowed them along with huge pieces of unidentified meat. When she finished eating, she collapsed on her bunk, as green, foaming vomit seeped out of the corners of her mouth. Her eyes rolled back inside her head so only the whites showed.

Two men in gladiatorial clothing appeared out of nowhere, and strode over to the vomiting woman and hauled her away from her bunk by her upper arms; her feet dragging along the floor behind her. I watched as they marched her away, but after a few feet they disappeared into thin air. I clutched Victor's arm in shock.

"Did you see that?" I asked, staring wide-eyed at the spot where the gladiators just disappeared from.

"That happens," Victor answered, shrugging. "They come and go as they please."

I continued to stare at the spot where the gladiators disappeared, willing them to reappear. My mind went back to the huge marble archway I had crossed under to get to here and the two huge men in gladiatorial clothing, each holding spears, which guarded it. They wore the same clothing as those two here, but had been twice as large, in every sense.

"The souls here call them 'Guards'," Victor added.

"Why Guards?" I asked.

"Because they guard Hell, they patrol from time to time, but mostly keep to themselves, unless they need to interact with you, like that lady."

"Look, another one," Nigel said beside me. I followed his finger to where he pointed. Another man wearing gladiatorial clothing, paced back and forth, three bunks away. He put a hand to his temple and disappeared. I gasped again, still unused to the magical elements of Hell.

"No need to be surprised Violet, they do this all the time," Victor said, shaking his head and smiling at me. "You will get used to it."

"I don't think I could ever get used to it," I replied.

"Trust me, the Guards disappearing and reappearing at will is only the tip of the iceberg," Victor said.

"Nothing makes sense here." I sighed.

We continued to meander through the bunks and just when I got bored with the monotonous scenery, a brown smudge appeared up ahead.

"What's that?" I asked Victor, pointing to it.

"You will just have to wait and see," Victor replied, winking at me, picking up his pace a little at my words.

The brown blur sharpened, and I realised it was made of stone. As I neared it, different shades of brown materialised, with the deep black pockets dotted here and there. I gasped when I realised what it was. It was a wall.

"I knew it." I whispered to myself and my heart leapt, excitement coursing through me. I looked at Victor and his knowing smile was the only confirmation I needed.

When we arrived within metres of the wall, my pace quickened. I strode ahead of Victor, weaving clumsily around the bunks, bursting with excitement. When I reached it, I turned to look back at Hell in all its majesty. A sea of men, women and children placed haphazardly around the large enclosed space.

I turned back to face the rough stone wall with nooks and crannies pitted through it, some of them so deep I couldn't see the stone at the back of them. My heart lurched as I peered inside a particularly deep one and traced my fingers along the warm stone, which seemed to thrum with life. A dull beat thudded inside it as though it had its own heart. We walked along the wall for a little while. I ignored the people around me and focused solely on the only life I cared about before me. I kept my left hand touching the wall the entire time, soaking up its unnatural warmth through my fingertips. I closed my eyes and the first semblance of happiness since I had gotten here bubbled forth.

I knew something was amiss when my hand, instead of touching warm brick, touched nothing but air, but the air had a different quality to the air here in Hell. I could no longer feel warmth coming from the stone, and upon closer inspection, nothing appeared to have changed. The stone was still present but I could feel nothing beneath my hand. I snatched my hand away from the wall and turned to face it full on. A dark imperfection marred the smooth stone, which looked different to the other nooks I had encountered. The space beyond flickered unnaturally. I wouldn't have noticed anything amiss had I just been looking at this spot in the wall. I placed my hand flat against the stone and pushed it into it. I gasped when my hand disappeared inside it, creating ripples in the stone as though it had become liquid. I pulled my hand out of the stone and watched as the ripples faded away and the wall turned solid again. I squinted into the wall, turning my head this way and that, trying to get a better look into the imperfection, but to the naked eye, it looked to be normal stone.

I turned to Victor and Nigel, who had stopped walking in front of me and turned back to stare at me, each giving me puzzled looks.

"What's down here?" I asked them, turning back to the wall.

"Down where?" Nigel asked, comin over to me.

"Something's here," I muttered, turning my head and squinting to get a better look.

"We can't see anything Violet," Victor said gently, putting a hand on my shoulder to steer me away. "Just the stone."

"Something is definitely here," I insisted, pulling myself away from his loose grip. "Come and look for yourselves." I beckoned them over and positioned them so they faced the wall right where I was looking.

Once Victor had crouched to my eye level, his eyes widened with disbelief. I thought I was going crazy but witnessing his reaction affirmed my beliefs.

"You're right," he breathed. He, too, saw a dark tunnel hidden behind the stone.

"See," I exclaimed. "I told you and look at this." I pushed my hand into the stone and watched as the stone liquified and rippled outwards away from my hand.

"What the—?" Nigel squeaked out in terror.

"How did you find this Violet?" Victor asked, staring at my hand imbedded into the stone wall.

"I don't know," I replied. "I was just walking, and I felt the atmosphere change. My hand was no longer touching the stone, and when I looked back, my hand had disappeared into it."

"What have we found?" Victor asked no one in particular.

"I don't know, but I'm going to check it out," I proclaimed.

"I don't think that's a good idea," Victor cautioned, Nigel, transfixed on our discovery, said nothing.

Taking a deep, fortifying breath, and ignoring Victor's warning, I strode into the wall.

SIX

THE GUARDS

A tentative breeze wafted over my face and it carried with it a light and airy scent – different to what I was used to here in Hell – and the sleeves of my thin jacket rippled as I crossed the threshold. I hesitated for a heartbeat, no longer, and took my second step inside the imperfection but Nigel yelled out in surprise, stopping me in my tracks. When I spun around to see what had happened, two Guards — in their Gladiatorial uniform — had appeared beside Nigel and Victor. I strode out of the hidden tunnel and stood next to Victor. The change in the air was unmistakable. As I emerged back into a cesspool of crammed, unwashed bodies, the air stood heavy and stagnant, but just underneath, the scent of oiled leather penetrated through, taking me back to this morning's dream. A cold sweat broke out on my brow and coated my entire body before I had the chance to take in the situation before me. The two Guards had appeared from nowhere – as they were wont to do – and one of them was brandishing his long spear in our faces. I sidestepped out of the sharp spear tip's reach and bumped into Victor.

"Ouch," Victor cried out, rubbing his foot with a frown on his face.

"Where did you come from?" I asked, hoping to get some answers from them. I threw an apologetic look to Victor. The image of the other Guards dragging the comatose woman away from her bunk wavered in front of me. The ruthless way in which they dragged her away rang mental alarm bells — if they were so cruel to her, then they could be just as cruel to us.

"What are you doing here?" The Guard with the brandished spear asked, ignoring my question. His blue eyes gleamed with fury behind his visored helmet. When we didn't answer, he grabbed Victor by the scruff of the neck and shoved his spear tip under his jaw. "I asked you a question. Answer me Soul." Victor's body trembled in his grip, but his face was a hard line. He stood staring into the Guard's piercing blue eyes. I stood frozen on the spot, unable to move or speak to help Victor.

"We were just having a look, Mister," Nigel said fearfully, from behind my legs.

"But you weren't here a moment ago," I said before the Guard could speak again. He turned to glare at me, still holding the spear against Victor's chin, but didn't respond. "How do you appear and disappear at will?" I didn't for a moment think he would answer me, but I had to ask.

"I don't care what you were doing," he said, ignoring my question. "You are not allowed to be here. Get back to your bunks, Souls." He said, taking the spear away from Victor's throat. He shoved Victor away and jabbed the spear in my face. I took a step back away from him scowling. Those who occupied the surrounding bunks did not move to intervene, instead they averted their gaze away from the commotion we had caused as though we did not exist.

"We were just looking, no one said we couldn't do that," I said, once my heart rate had slowed. Victor stumbled over, stood in front of me and I put a hand on his shoulder.

"There is, if we have something to say about it," the blue-eyed Guard retorted, the skin on his neck reddening in anger.

"That doesn't even make any sense," I cried incredulously. "How did you arrive so quickly? You weren't here a second ago? Answer me, dammit!" I shouted in his face.

The second Guard remained still and silent during the exchange. He stood neutral-face, holding his spear at his side rather than in our faces like the other guard. His glazed, coal-black eyes peaked beneath his visored helmet, staring straight ahead.

"We do not have to answer such insignificant questions, Soul. I said, 'Get back to your bunk'." The blue-eyed Guard shouted in my face, taking a threatening step towards me; his eyes gleaming furiously.

"Make me," I hurled back.

He lunged his spear at me, but I dodged underneath it, my eyes widening at my speed. Dancing between the two Guards, I tried to dive back into the tunnel, but a strong pair of arms wrapped around me and lifted me from the ground. I struggled to extricate myself out of its grip but he was too strong. My legs flailed in the air and the guard spun me around to face Nigel and Victor, they were both rooted on the spot, too shocked to move. To my surprise, the dark-eyed Guard didn't move to help restrain me. He didn't even acknowledge my presence in any way.

I raked my fingernails across my captors hands and he let go of me with a yelp. I took off running into the imperfection in the wall, but before I took two steps inside, a wave of nausea and dizziness swept over me. The tunnel spun, and a pressure rose in my brain as a headache brewed in my temple. I collapsed to the floor, turned over on my back and glanced at the low stone ceiling shimmering above, before raising myself up on my elbows to stare at the scene out in Hell.

"You had better take her back to her bunk." The blue-eyed Guard said to Victor and Nigel. "And if I ever catch you here again, the consequences will be much worse."

The two Guards turned on their heels and marched back towards the bunks, leaving Victor, Nigel and I alone. The silent, dark-eyed Guard looked back once before they both disappeared on the spot, around twenty yards away. Victor stared at the spot from which the Guards disappeared, his face contorted in rage. My energy levels dropped drastically, and I flopped back down to the ground, eyes squeezed shut.

"How did they know where we were?" Victor asked.

"I don't know Victor, but we have to get Violet out of here. She's hurt," Nigel pleaded, trying to heave my dead weight off the ground, but was too weak to lift me even an inch off it. I heard Victor's footsteps coming towards us and watched, through half-closed eyes, as he shuddered when he crossed into the tunnel. He hauled me up, wrapped an arm around my waist and draped my left arm over his shoulder, supporting the majority of my weight. I was surprised by his strength.

"Let's go," he said to Nigel.

Even in my deluded state, I felt the atmosphere change when we crossed back into Hell. A distinctive smell encompassed the tunnel, which I had liked — lighter and fresher than in Hell — and as soon as we left the confines of the tunnel, the hot, heavy air returned and draped over us like a heavy blanket, seeping into our skin. As we walked away from the Wall, my brain became foggy and I felt a change shift deep inside me. I couldn't put my finger on it, but it was as though a film covered my eyes and I couldn't think or see clearly. My head throbbed and my thoughts shuffled themselves in my mind so I couldn't think clearly.

Our walk back to the bunks was unpleasant. The jovial mood had dissipated and a heavy, dark cloud loomed above our heads — partly from the run in with the Guards and partly from the general atmosphere — dampening our mood. Nausea and dizziness made it impossible for me to walk unaided and the headache worsened the further we walked. The people around stared openly at us. They jostled each other, pointing and whispering behind their hands as we weaved our way between them. Come stood on top of their bunks to get a better view of the strange thruple. If I had had the energy, I would have wept.

We took twice as long to get back than it had taken to get to the wall, and when I reached my designated bunk, I collapsed onto the soft surface and curled up to a foetal position. Every part of my body ached. I clutched at my now sensitive stomach and kept my eyes squeezed shut to block out the spinning room and bright lights. Victor and Nigel's breath wafted over me as they hovered over me, but I did not have the energy to think, let alone interact with anybody.

"Please, guys, could you just leave me alone?" I pleaded to them through gritted teeth.

They shuffled away. Guilt riddled me at my abruptness, but I was glad I could cope with my suffering on my own; the way I had always done.

"Mary, what's wrong?" Sophie asked, heaving herself off her bunk and waddling over, her pregnant stomach impeding her progress. I collapsed onto the floor next to my bunk with a groan. My bed sheets tangled around me as I lay panting on the ground.

"I don't know, the room is spinning and I feel nauseous," I muttered. "God, my head." Pushing my long black hair out of my eyes, I looked up at her, put one hand to my chest and rubbed my temple with the other.

"But why?" she asked, perplexed. "You haven't done anything today. "She tugged at her shoulder length brown hair and frowned at me in confusion.

"I don't know why it's happened, Sophie," I said, exasperatedly. "But I know it is happening." I took a deep breath. "Please help me up. I need to lie down."

I held out a hand, she grabbed it, and with her help, we lifted myself to the bunk. Sophie took a deep breath, walked to her bedside table, opened her bottom drawer and fumbled inside for a second, but her body blocked my view from what she was looking for. I closed my eyes and willed the room to stop spinning, when a softness covered me. My eyes sprang open. Sophie loomed over me, spreading a colourful, patchwork blanket over me. I cuddled into the warmth and gave her a pained smile in thanks. She smiled back and I watched as she retreated to the safety of her bunk, rubbing her stomach, her brow furrowed in pain, but after a minute she became calm.

I fisted the blanket in my hands and pulled it closer around my body, tucking it underneath my chin. How did this happen? I hadn't even left my bunk today, so nothing I did could have made me feel this way.

The dizziness had subsided and the room had slowed to a whirl, but my head still pounded painfully. My eyelids drooped and through my blurred vision, I spotted two men in gladiatorial clothing standing at a nearby bunk staring at me. The accuracy of their clothing made it seem as though they had been actual gladiators. They held their long spears loosely in their hands and their visored helmets left only their eyes visible. One of them mumbled something in the other's ear and pointed in my direction. They turned to each other with grim, knowing looks on their faces. I blinked once and when I opened my eyes again, the gladiators had disappeared from view. I surmised that I had closed my eyes for longer than the fraction a second it took for me to blink. Assuming I was right, they would have had the chance to move away at a normal pace and must have simply walked away from my eye line. If I had been in my right mind, I would have realised something strange about the Guard's sudden disappearance, but I was still nauseous and light-headed, and I had no energy to spare for rational thinking.

I drifted off into an unsettled sleep, but strange images plagued my dreams. Images of stone walls with deep niches carved in them; some were large enough for a grown man to sit in comfortably. Sharp spear tips were being jabbed in my face and body, and were shallowly, but painfully piercing into my skin.

Rivulets of sweat coated my whole body and plastered my short black hair to my face. I thrashed around in my bed as psychedelic and hallucinogenic images floated in my brain.

"Violet, come to Daddy." A burly man with cropped salt and pepper hair, crouched and held his arms out. I instantly recognised his sparkling hazel eyes and squealed with delight.

"Daddy! Daddy!" I cried out rushing into his arms and snuggling into his embrace. "I missed you, Daddy." A delicate waft of lavender drifted over and I frowned, Daddy didn't wear that, Mummy did.

I looked up, expecting to see my mother's face, but recoiled in shock when coal-black eyes, eclipsed by a visored helmet, looked back at me instead.

"You aren't Daddy. Where's Daddy?" I was surprisingly unafraid of this strange man.

"Daddy's not here right now." His voice was deep and sinister, sending chills down my spine, and when I looked back up at him, his eyes had turned bright blue.

"Who are you?" I asked, taking a step back away from the stranger. "Where's Daddy?"

"I told you, Daddy's not here right now." He grinned down at me sinisterly.

A sharp pain exploded on my side and I screamed.

"What's going on?" I asked the blue-eyed man, holding back tears against the pain. He laughed at me and behind him a sea of helmeted men stood, laughing maniacally and pointing at me.

Another sharp pain exploded on my other side. I looked to my left and the tallest man I had ever seen hovered over me, holding a blood covered spear. I looked from the spear tip to my side and gasped as a blood stain spread rapidly on my white t-shirt. What was going on?

More delirious visions and a 40-degree temperature coursed through me. My whole body would be on fire, but in the next moment I became freezing, clutching at my meagre blanket, desperate for some warmth to drive away the cold which penetrated to my very bones.

Coming in and out of consciousness was the worst part, as I never knew whether my visions were real or a subject of my hallucinations. Guards, in their visored helmets surrounded me, they whispered and pointed at me, sometimes they looked normal but other times they smiled at me revealing strange, pointed teeth between their lips and black tongues. Sometimes the Guards morphed into Victor and Nigel, or into my sister and father, confusing me further. A particular Guard — with coal-black eyes — stood out to me in all my visions, but it was hard to get a good look at his full face as he chose to remain in the background, not coming near me at all. It was impossible to tell which of my visions were real or imagined, as the pain I felt felt so real in either state.

"Violet." Someone whispered and shook my shoulder gently. I fluttered my eyes open and stared into the wide, brown, scared eyes of a small boy standing beside my bunk.

"Hi, Nigel," I croaked out. My mouth felt full of non-existent cotton and I was immensely thirsty. "I have a headache," I mumbled, but smiled weakly at him nonetheless, somehow knowing, deep down, that the fevered dreams had stopped and this was real. The familiar face of a person whom I had grown to care about in the few days that I had been here, reassured me after my nightmares.

His face split into a wide grin. "Victor! Victor! She's awake!" He called over to a hazy figure hurrying towards us.

"We thought you were a goner," Victor said, patting my shoulder affectionately, once he reached me.

I jerked away from his light touch. Puzzled, I carefully pulled aside my t-shirt at the neck and revealed a myriad of bruises and shallow cuts covering my entire shoulder. Gritting my teeth, I lifted my t-shirt up from my torso and gasped when a similar array of bruises and cuts patterned my abdomen. I didn't dare look at my legs, but from the feeling in them, I knew they would look the same.

"What happened to you?" Nigel asked, concern etched on his face.

"I don't know," I replied. I glanced at Victor, who was wide-eyed, looking equally as confused as I felt.

"How long was I out?" I asked. I tried to lift a hand to my face to rub my tired eyes and was momentarily stumped when nothing happened. It took me a while to remember my useless right arm, and I blushed, even though I knew my thoughts would not have been broadcast to my audience.

"Three days," Victor said, averting his gaze.

I shook my head, surprised that such a short time had passed. I was convinced I had been dreaming for longer. I took a deep breath and gagged. I had forgotten the stench of the pungent bodies around me and when it came back, it seemed to be more noxious than before.

"Can you help me sit up please?" I asked Nigel and Victor, my body refusing to move on its own.

"I think you had better take it easy Violet. Just until you get your strength back," Victor said, laying a hand on my shoulder, encouraging me to stay flat on my bed.

"No, there is no use moping Victor. There is nothing here that can help me recover and I will not spend my time here just lying around," I said, removing his hand from my shoulder. "Could you just help me up, please?"

In no time, I was sitting up on my bunk, with Victor's, Nigel's and my own blanket around me, recounting my strange dreams to them. From the evil guards 'torturing me with their spears, to my sister and father comforting me, to even the two of them, hovering around me as I slept.

"What do you think they mean?" Victor asked, concerned. Nigel crawled into my lap and looked up at me.

"I don't know," I said, wrapping my arms around his small body. "I just hope they aren't a sign of things to come." I muttered, thinking of the guard's torture. I paused. "I need answers and I can't afford to have any distractions."

"Need answers to what?" Nigel asked.

"Yeah, what–?" Victor asked but stopped mid-sentence, looking off suspiciously into the distance.

I snapped my head up and followed his gaze. A familiar tall blonde man, skulked near us, glancing at us, trying hard not to draw too much attention to himself. I couldn't place where I had seen him before, but a shiver ran down my spine when our eyes met — emerald green to moss green — and locked. He stopped in his tracks when our eyes met and hesitated.

He must have decided what he wanted to do because he strode over with a determined frown on his face. I snuck a peek over at Victor. He had folded his arms and was glaring at the incoming stranger. Nigel glared at him from my lap, but he didn't look nearly as threatening as Victor. I was more curious than wary — I needed to know how I recognised him.

When he drew near to us, he hesitated again. He opened and closed his mouth several times like a suffocating fish, and finally said: "Hi, guys." He tried to smile jovially and gave us a small wave, looking at each of us in turn. He looked uncomfortable as he twisted his hands fervently together. He also had a deep, gravelly voice, which vibrated through me.

We remained silent, watching him suspiciously. He coughed, shuffled his feet, turned away, but in the same beat turned back.

"My name is Curtis," he said. Again, none of us replied, waiting for him to tell us his purpose. "I see you are awake. Are you feeling better, Violet?"

"How do you know my name?" I asked, taken aback.

He shrugged, glancing at Victor and Nigel, then turned his attention back to me. "Do you know what happened to you?" he asked.

"I was ill," I said immediately, without hesitation. I frowned at my knee-jerk response, unsure of why I said that. Curtis didn't seem convinced. He stood at the end of my bunk, looming over and frowning down at me.

"Okay," he said. A heavy silence hung in the air and no one wanted to break it. All eyes were on Curtis waiting for him to continue. Nigel shifted in my lap. I cuddled and drew him closer to me.

"I had a bunk mate," he started. "You looked like you suffered the same 'illness' as him. He had had a fever no human could have survived, and he also complained of a headache at his temples."

"How do you know I suffered the same illness?" I asked, ignoring his comment on the headache.

"I was a doctor when... I was a doctor," he replied. "I tried to help him, but by the time I got what he needed, it was too late."

"Okay," I muttered, confused.

"One day a group of Guards came over and started asking questions," Curtis continued. "What questions?" Victor asked quickly, staring daggers at the stranger.

"Well, they asked me where he had been in the past week and who he had been talking to. Questions like that," Curtis answered, turning to Victor to reply, but turning back to look at me once he'd finished speaking.

I glanced suspiciously at Victor. His reaction to the Guard's questioning caught my attention, but his face gave nothing away.

Curtis carried on with his story and I turned my attention back to him, pushing Victor's reaction to the back of my mind. "I told them I didn't know where he went and as far as I knew he only talked to me," he paused, his face looking pained. "But I lied. I knew he kept on disappearing, but I honestly didn't know where he went," he frowned. "One day I followed him, but I can't remember where we went. I have been trying to remember ever since they took him away — that was months ago and I haven't seen him since."

"Well, what a great story Curtis, but why are you telling us?" I asked, sarcastically.

"It looked like you were going through the same illness he had gone through," he continued. "I recognised the thrashing in the sheets, the extreme fever and sweating. You were muttering quite a lot. I heard you. You looked exactly like my friend when he had fallen ill. I had wanted to come over and see if my expertise could have helped, but I was afraid you wouldn't accept it and that maybe with my presence by your side, we would attract the Guards to us and they would ask unwanted questions. I didn't want to subject you to that. But when the Guards came anyway, I was glad, because it meant it hadn't been me which had gotten David — that was his name — taken away," he finished.

"Wait, what?" I exclaimed. "Guards came here?" I asked, looking between Victor and Nigel. "Why didn't you tell me?"

"We were getting around to it, but then *he* came," Nigel said, glaring at Curtis.

"That's why I am here. I wondered if you needed anything," Curtis asked.

"I don't know if you have anything to help. You were a doctor, but we have no medicine here," I said.

"No, you're right we have no conventional medicine, but I have something that will help. Shall I get it?" He waited for my response.

"It wouldn't hurt to try," I said, shrugging.

"Hold on," Curtis grinned at me, put his hands up in a 'wait here' motion and hurried away. He muttered to himself and ticked things off on his fingers, as he walked away. When he reached his bunk, he glanced around him and lifted his mattress off his bunk frame. He grabbed something from underneath the mattress and put everything back in its normal position — glancing around all the while — being careful to smooth down his sheets so they looked undisturbed. He crouched next to his bunk and lay several mysterious objects on top of his pristine bed, but from my vantage point I couldn't see them clearly. He was too far away. I craned my neck to get a better look, but he shifted, blocking my view.

Sighing, I turned away from Curtis and looked back at Nigel and Victor and they were looking at me with identical looks of confusion on their faces.

"What are you doing Violet?" Victor asked. "Do you trust him?"

"Of course I don't trust him. I don't even know him," I scoffed. "I needed him to leave so I could speak to the two of you alone. Now tell me what has been happening?"

"Well, firstly, we are glad you are back with us," Victor started. I nodded, urging him on. "Erm...," he paused, glancing uncomfortably at Nigel.

"Victor, I can handle it, please tell me," I pleaded, clutching at the surrounding blankets.

"Okay," he relented. "You were unwell, you have to know that," he paused again, taking a deep breath to steel himself. "The Guards were fascinated with you. They were constantly standing around and watching us. They would keep a discreet distance so I think no one else noticed, but we did. They would watch us for hours at a time and after two days they approached us. We could do nothing to stop them. They were brutal."

"Just tell me what they did Victor," I demanded of him.

"They ransacked your belongings, tore everything out of the drawers and ripped everything apart." He paused at the incredulous look on my face. "They wouldn't tell us why they were here and trust me I asked. I don't think they found what they were looking for because when they left, they looked disappointed." He finished.

"A Guard lifted you off your bunk, you were tossing and turning, but calmed down when he picked you up. I don't know which one it was, they all look the same under their helmets. They lifted your mattress away and searched underneath it. They tore the stuffing out of your pillows, ripped your t–shirts and trousers."

"They were especially interested in your rolled up socks, weren't they Victor?" Nigel asked, glancing at Victor, who nodded in agreement.

"Ten came, they took everything and left. I tried to stop them but one of them hit me." He pointed at a healing bruise on his temple I hadn't noticed. They shoved their spears in Nigel's face so he couldn't do anything, but I don't think he would have done anything anyway – he was too afraid." Victor finished. Tears leaked out of Nigel's eyes and streaked down his face.

I put my head in my left hand and rubbed away at the new headache forming in my temples, trying to make sense of what they had just told me.

"They came back an hour later with new things for you," Victor added. "A new mattress, pillows, and clothing. Everything you had before. They put them back exactly as they were."

"But I have nothing other than these clothes with me," I mused.

"We know. We tried to tell them," Victor explained. "But they kept on asking us if you had any contraband."

"Contraband?" I asked. "What contraband?"

Victor shrugged.

I glanced back at Curtis, who was still at his bunk and hadn't moved from his crouched position. Steam rose from in front of him, but I couldn't see the source.

"I think they thought you had stumbled upon something you were not supposed to have," Victor muttered. "I personally know four people here with belongings which were not given to them when they arrived and I have seen hundreds more. New and strange items are passed between the people every day."

"Like what?" I asked, confused.

"Take Mrs Scott's rocking chair or Smith's wooden furniture," Victor replied.

None of the words meant anything to me, I did not know who he was talking about, but I couldn't question him any further because hurried footsteps pattered behind me. I turned towards the sound, and saw Curtis rushing towards us, holding a tray with three crude wooden cups on it. Steam rose merrily from them.

In a small, dimly lit chamber, a group of Guards stood. Each wore a helmet with a plume of red feathers at the top, leather greaves and sandals with thin leather straps which criss-crossed up to their knees. They each held a spear in their right hand, a shield in their left and a short sword hung from a loop on their belts around a pleated skirt. They stood, in attention, in neat rows facing a lone figure positioned at the head of an elaborate altar. Intricate carvings of tiny cherubs adorned it, each wore a set of wings, a halo and horns. Lakes of flames shimmered below and above. A hand reached to them from the heavens through thick clouds. Hundreds of lightly scented candles were lit in the chamber, shrouding the Guards in hazy wafts of smoke. The majority of the candles were set on top of the altar, but others were set on top of short pillars dotted around the room. Some of the Guards shuffled from foot to foot. A cough sprouted in the room, but otherwise it was mostly silent. The only sound was a deep rumbling from the lone figure at the altar, his right hand held against his temple but he seemed to speak to no one in the chamber.

"I have some more information. The new soul who breached security has awakened. What would you like me to do?" The Guard at the altar mumbled. "Yes, Sir." "No, Sir." "I will, Sir." The Guard replied to several unheard questions. The Guard took his hand away from his temple and acknowledged his audience, blue eyes gleaming at them through the visored helmet he wore.

"Okay men, I have more instructions for you," he called to the Guards facing him in a low voice and paused. "We are to not let Violet Deneuve out of our sights. I want to know where she is, what she is doing, and who she is doing it with at all times. Let no one else see Section Eight. Turi will give you more instructions — move out." The group of helmeted men banged the butt of their spears on the ground once in acknowledgement and marched out of the room following a tall Guard with his spear held high in the air. One Guard stayed behind and did not follow. He remained statued to the spot until the last of the helmeted men left the room. He climbed the steps leading to the altar, fingering the smooth wood as he made his way to the speaker.

"What do you think, Macus?" The blue-eyed Guard asked his secondary.

"We will find out whatever she has planned with our men watching her. I, myself, will keep an eye on her too, Astinal." The secondary said, charcoal black eyes glinting beneath his helmet in the flickering candlelight.

SEVEN

THE RECOVERY

Curtis reached my bunk and knelt beside me, grinning, his brilliant white teeth gleaming, and proffered the tray at me. I lifted my left hand from Nigel's body — my right arm still being of no use — and lifted a cup from it. I recognised it, the shape and material triggered a faint memory, but I couldn't put my finger on it. Curtis turned from me and offered the tray to Nigel and Victor, they hesitated before taking a cup. I looked back to the smooth, wooden cup in my hand and brought it to my face; the pearlescent liquid shone in the ethereal light. A long sniff did nothing to identify the ingredients, so I looked back at Curtis.

"What's in it?" I asked.

"I don't know the specific ingredients, but I do know it will make you feel better," Curtis assured me. "I had given it to David towards the end of his illness. It made him feel better for a while, but the Guards still took him away." He frowned at the memory.

I didn't respond, but looked right into his moss green eyes and took a tentative sip. The warmth from the liquid coursed through me, and travelled from my throat to my extremities, relieving the myriad of aches and pains as the warmth traversed through my body. I drained the cup and closed my eyes with relief. The aftertaste was tart but my body felt stronger, so I didn't complain.

A tingling on my abdomen drew my attention to it. I lifted my shirt, and the cuts and bruises which I gained whilst I was unconscious, looked fainter than they had done earlier. "Nigel, can you move for a second?" I asked. He moved to sit on his own on my bunk and I lifted up my trouser legs. The scabbed-over claw marks on my legs had almost faded away, but my stressed blood vessels still strained against my skin. The tea had left my body and mind lighter and happier.

"Would you like to sit with us, Curtis?" I asked him, handing the empty cup back to him, and deciding, in that moment, to trust him.

He nodded and perched on the end of my bed, next to me, laying the tray across his lap and setting my cup back on it. Nigel and Victor handed their empty cups back to him and he set them on the tray. I surmised that Curtis wasn't here to hurt me, but I had never been great at communication so inviting him to stay with us was my strange way of saying thanks. Nigel gasped, leapt up from my bunk and pointed at me, mouth agape. I turned to look behind me expecting to see a deadly creature lurking there, or ten foot flames with bodies writhing in the scorching heat, but only the expanse of beds faced me.

"Violet," Victor cried, the same shocked expression on his face.

"What? You are scaring me," I said, still looking around for what had surprised them.

"Your arm," Nigel whispered.

"What about my arm?" I asked, lifting my left arm up and inspecting it for any abnormalities.

"Not that arm," Victor said. "The other arm."

I lifted my right arm up and inspected it. "But nothing's wrong with..." I trailed off, I looked up wide-eyed, glancing between Victor and Nigel, my mouth hanging open in shock. I flexed the fingers of my right hand and lifted it up into the air. I used it to wave at the guys, then stuck my middle finger up at the world. "My arm." I breathed.

"What is in that tea?" Victor asked Curtis, awestruck.

"I don't know. I get the mixture from Mrs Scott," Curtis replied, grinning at my reaction. "You know her?" he added. Both Nigel and Victor nodded and said something to each other but I paid no attention to anything they said. My attention was focused instead on my newly healed arm. My arm was fully functional, where not even five minutes earlier, it had hung uselessly at my side, only swaying in response to my movements and I couldn't believe the tea could do that. I was so surprised, I didn't speak for the rest of the day, giving the guys a chance to get to know each other.

Over the next few days, Curtis' role in our group solidified as he knew a lot about Hell. He told us stories and brought us what was widely known as contraband; anything from toys to extra clothes. Objects we couldn't have otherwise gotten our hands on.

"Where do you get all this from?" Victor asked Curtis when he walked over with a new white jumper for him.

Curtis tapped his nose in a conspiratorial way and winked at Victor. "I will not name my sources." Victor laughed at his jovial attitude and clapped him on the shoulder in a way of thanks. He didn't seem to want to know the source, but knowing that Curtis wouldn't say, I decided not to push him.

It seemed normal to have him around, as though he had always been with us. Victor warmed to Curtis faster than Nigel did, but once Nigel saw that Curtis wasn't going anywhere, he became friendlier towards him. Curtis would spend all day with us. When we woke up, he came over to talk and sit with us. I guessed he was lonely and wanted company. We never turned him away because I knew what crippling loneliness could do to someone. I loved that we gained a new person in our little group, and Curtis was a welcome distraction to the foreboding thoughts which had been increasing in intensity inside me since I had awoken from my nightmares.

One day, after a couple of weeks of his continuous company, Curtis and I found ourselves alone for the first time. Nigel had wandered off somewhere and Victor was taking a nap. We were lying on my bunk staring up at the blurry ceiling when Curtis whispered: "Mrs Scott and I are good friends."

"Yeah? Who's Mrs Scott?" I responded distractedly, playing with a stray thread on my jacket sleeve.

"I'm sure you know her, anyway, she tells me stories from the old days," he said, ignoring my question.

I didn't know who he was talking about but he piqued my interest, as anything further I could learn about Hell would help me tremendously.

"What kind of stories?" I asked, sitting up on my elbows, trying to keep the excitement out of my voice.

"Well, she told me this one story," he said, sitting up and facing me. "You ready?" I simply nodded, afraid to say anything in case he changed his mind.

"You have to know, she has been here for millennia, and when she first arrived things were…different," he paused.

"Different how?" I asked.

"Well, the Guards were different," he continued. "Greek Princes guarded Hell. They wore togas and carried whips with metal tips to discipline anyone who disturbed the peace. But people continued to wreak havoc, so they would punish them in front of everyone. The Princes loved to make an example of anyone at any time. She told me a podium stood in the middle of a clearing — this place had been much smaller back then — where the Guards hauled up the incendiaries and tortured them in front of everybody."

"That sounds like the Hell I read of," I whispered, disbelievingly nonetheless.

"That's not even the worst of it," Curtis said. "They were out of control, these Guards. They raped women, men, even children on the podium. They claimed it was to keep everyone in check and they were right. Everyone was too afraid to do anything about the rapes. A cycle of fear and suffering trapped everyone. The people wanted to stop the guards, but no one knew how.

"Mrs Scott then led a band of followers who planned a revolt — to take down the Greeks once and for all — but someone exposed their plan. The Greeks didn't suspect Mrs Scott as the mastermind, because she was so old, so they tortured someone else — a young woman — she never told me who," Curtis paused. "They left the woman hanging on the podium for days after her initial punishment. Occasionally the Guards came up to 'play' with her..." He trailed off shaking his head. Victor and Nigel had made their way over to my bunk during Curtis' story and they sat on the floor listening to him.

"I'm not surprised at your reaction," Victor said, as he noticed the shocked expression on my face. "You have become used to this easy Hell, where nothing really happens. The Guards are nicer compared to when Mrs Scott had first arrived. I guess that was what Hell was supposed to be like before it became soft."

"Why are the Greece's not here anymore?" Nigel asked.

"Greek," Victor corrected lightly.

"Well, after the failed plan, the resistance against the Greeks died," continued Curtis. "The woman's torture was so brutal, everyone became more frightened than ever, and mostly kept to themselves. No one talked to Mrs Scott, as the consequences for associating with her had been too dire, but then one day a man arrived. In the beginning, he had been a nondescript man but was terrified, so Mrs Scott took him under her wing. She taught him everything he needed to know about this place and several years later, he took down the Greek army with some of his friends and they took on the role of the Guards."

"Is he still here now?" I asked. A hazy image of manic blue eyes popping into my mind, triggering a faint memory, but it faded fast. I shook my head to rid the shadowy memory and the headache which threatened to form in my temples along with it.

"Mrs Scott says he is, and that he is very influential." Curtis finished.

"I wonder who he is," Nigel murmured.

There was a short silence. "Do you know how the Guards appear and disappear at will, Curtis?" I asked, breaking it.

"No. I've asked Mrs Scott several times, and she claims she doesn't. But I think she does and just won't tell me," Curtis replied.

"It was one of the first things I noticed when I arrived," Victor said. "I asked several people, but no one knew, so I assumed it was something I would never know about," he finished, shrugging.

"There's more to this place, I know it. I need to know everything." I said.

"How are you going to do that Violet?" Curtis asked, raising his eyebrows at me.

"I am not sure yet," I muttered, chewing on my fingernails, looking off into the distance deep in thought. A Guard stood staring at me, around ten feet away. When our eyes met, he looked away and continued on his circuit, but not before I glimpsed coal black eyes underneath his helmet. Another hazy image floated to my mind. The darkness returned for longer this time, but I didn't know what connected the two images, or why my temples throbbed every time I tried to think of it.

"Are you okay, Violet?" Victor asked, frowning.

"Yeah, I am," I replied absently, rubbing my temple and staring after the Guard, who was walking away stiffly.

Dark visions had plagued me since I had awoken from my strange illness, but a true sense of foreboding didn't set in until the day after Curtis told us the story of Mrs Scott's past. We were all sitting at my bunk, when Nigel asked everyone if they wanted to go for a walk; my stomach lurched, and the room started to spin.

"A walk?" I asked, still unsure of why I had suddenly become nauseous.

"Yes, what's wrong with a walk?" Nigel asked. "We have been cooped up here for so long, I want to stretch my legs again."

"Again?" I asked. "But I haven't been away from the bunk since I arrived here?" I looked around at the puzzled expressions facing me. Iit did seem strange that I wouldn't have left my bunk, especially considering the reason I was here.

"Violet, I don't know what game you are playing, but we have definitely been for a walk. We showed you around. Don't you remember the 'Unholy Mountain'?" Victor asked, his eyes twinkling.

I tried to remember a mention of an 'Unholy Mountain' but nothing came to mind. I shook my head at him, my confusion deepening.

"Well, we can show you around, again, now if you like?" Victor added, looking perturbed, but not mentioning my amnesia.

I simply nodded, but tried to wrack my brain for even a distant memory of this walk; nothing appeared. My only memories of this place were the sights, sounds and people from around my bunk. I remembered falling ill, but no matter how hard I tried, I couldn't conjure a memory of how it had begun. All I could remember was lying on my bed, and the more I thought about it, the worse my headache at my temple became.

Shaking off the growing migraine, we set off, following the meandering walkways between the bunks at a slow pace. Disjointed fragments of memories came back, but it was as though the main piece of the puzzle was missing. A particular notch on a bedpost, or an intricate carving on a headboard, stirred something within, but the memories only made me more confused and my headache deepened. We walked past Günter, the World War II soldier, with the troop of men at his feet listening to whatever he said. Smith, the carpenter in the red t-shirt, who had the little apprentice boy sitting beside him handing him various tools.

Nigel kept up a running commentary and tried to remind me who these people were, but I couldn't seem to remember them. This was my first time seeing them. Their faces and stories didn't ring a bell, and I felt stupid and frustrated by my lack of memory. I guess those people were too insignificant to be the key to unlocking my memories.

"That's Mrs Scott," Curtis whispered in my ear, pointing at an old woman sitting in a rocking chair next to a pristine bunk. He picked his way, around the bunks, over to her. She held a cup of tea in her hands in a wooden cup similar to the one which I had drunk from. She rocked backwards and forwards in her rocking chair. Her eyes were closed and a small smile played on her lips. She suddenly opened her eyes and looked straight at me. I met her grey, watery eyes and my heart lurched — her gaze penetrated through me and her smile changed to one of recognition. Her bald, age spotted head shone and her face was wrinkled beyond recognition. I doubted she had left that rocking chair for a long time, but her eyes told a different story. They held knowledge and strength, whereas her limbs looked brittle and weak and her hands struggled to keep the wooden cup steady.

"You don't remember me do you, dear?" She croaked out, after taking a casual sip of her tea.

"No ma'am," I replied, looking at my feet. I was afraid she could read my thoughts if we had any prolonged eye contact.

"You will remember soon enough," she chuckled. "I have something for you dear." She reached over to her bedside table and opened the topmost drawer, taking out a small package and handing it out to me. I hesitated, afraid of a trap.

"Take it, Violet," Nigel whispered next to me.

I had no choice, I tip-toed towards her, still unnerved by her kindness and wondering what lay inside the package. When I reached her, she placed the teabag sized package into my outstretched hand. I stuffed it into my trouser pocket, afraid of opening it in front of prying eyes and backed away from her. I turned to walk away, and she laughed. I chanced a glance back at her and only fleshy gums peeked out from her open mouth. She turned away from me to whisper to Curtis, who was perched on the end of her bunk. I sensed a friendly rapport between them and wondered how they had become such good friends. After some time, they said their farewells. Curtis hugged her long and hard and gave her a kiss on her aged cheek. He walked back over to where Victor, Nigel and I stood, and carried with him a vaguely familiar flowery scent I assumed he had acquired from hugging Mrs Scott. We set off again to see more of Hell, and none of us mentioned the interaction as we walked away. I felt Mrs Scott's eyes burning into me after we walked away, but I fought the urge to glance back.

We walked on for another five minutes in silence – Nigel and Victor taking the lead with Curtis and I following along behind. Our hands brushed once, and I jerked my hand away from his, shocked by the unexpected touch. This happened a second time, but before I could move my hand away, Curtis grabbed a hold of it. I froze, unsure of what to do. I glanced at Curtis, but he was looking straight ahead. After thirty-seconds, I extricated my hand out of his grip, he said nothing. I glanced at him again, but he didn't meet my eyes. The only hint of his embarrassment was the tinge of red on his cheeks.

My eyes roamed the space around me as I tried, simultaneously, to forget Curtis' actions and to memorise the people surrounding me. Who talked with whom, where people congregate. I was trying to get a feel for the people I shared Hell with. I thought I vaguely recognised some of the surrounding people, but I couldn't be sure. The number of memories coming forth was overwhelming, so, naturally, it was hard to filter through the unnecessary ones and find the memories which would help me regain my own failed memory.

A lot of strange people stood out and most of them had disfigurements of some sort; missing eyes and limbs, burns, and growths. I was surrounded by people of all ages and sizes, in all states and circumstances. Some of the injuries showed how they died, but some were vague or hidden.

A flurry of movements caught my eye, and I turned my head towards the commotion. A Guard had approached a woman asleep on her bunk. Another woman walked over to the Guard and tried to push him away from the sleeping woman. He violently knocked her down and grabbed the sleeping woman into his arms, fireman style, then disappeared on the spot. The fallen woman scrambled to her feet, and tried to grab onto the Guard's clothing, but he had disappeared before she had made it to her feet. His disappearance didn't phase me, being used to it now, and I mostly wondered why he took the woman away.

"Why do you think that happened?" I asked aloud to the group.

"I don't know, but I have seen Guards take people away many times since I have been here." Victor answered. He shrugged and turned back to face the way we were walking.

I glanced around again and noticed another Guard standing two bunks away, watching us as we made our way towards him. He did not turn away from my gaze once I had caught him staring — as the other Guard had done earlier — but maintained eye contact. This struck me as odd, as from my previous observations the Guards usually kept to themselves and only interacted with us if we needed 'reprimanding'. The Guard raised his right hand to his temple, and I watched him as his lips moved, but his words didn't reach me. He then turned away from me and disappeared.

"That Guard was staring at us," I said to Victor, clutching at his arm. He had slowed his pace, so he walked in step with me. "He's disappeared now, but he was definitely staring."

"I know, I saw," Victor said from the side of his mouth. "That's the third Guard today I've seen do that. Just act naturally." He finished, looking straight ahead, seemingly in his own world.

I pushed the Guard's strange behaviour from my mind when I spotted a podium up ahead, in the middle of a clearing. At first I thought it was the podium Curtis mentioned – the torture one – but it didn't look like what he had described. From this distance, I couldn't discern what stood in the space, but I needed to find out. An uncomfortable knot sat in the pit of my stomach but I took no notice of it. Adrenaline coursed through me, and my pace quickened as the podium and clearing neared.

When we reached the clearing, a row of five rusting, water-stained toilets stood before me. They each backed onto a short, grey, worn down wall. I stopped in my tracks and the others did so behind me.

"Is this what you call the 'Unholy Mountain'?" I asked Victor, vaguely remembering this sight.

"No, that's on the other side," he replied, smiling.

I walked towards the toilets for a closer look, they had an ancient chain flushing system and the water inside it was brown and moving of its own accord. The porcelain was stained so brown that I couldn't imagine that it was ever once white. I walked around the toilets and a long trestle table stood on a raised platform, laden with a variety of food, which was previously hidden from view by the grey wall. My instincts told me not to go near it, but disregarding them, I ran heedlessly towards it. I leapt onto the platform but a wall of pungent smells hit me. I choked and stumbled backwards off the podium whilst gagging on the foul stench.

"Why didn't you warn me?" I asked, still coughing, when I had run back to the others. My eyes drifted over to the five showers in crude stalls behind them, which backed onto the grey run–down walls, which the toilets backed onto. I watched as Nigel and Victor doubled over laughing, clutching onto a cubicle door for support. Curtis was oblivious to the joke and gave me a sympathetic look.

"I am sorry, Violet," Nigel said between fits of laughter. "We didn't know you would walk straight into it again. You really don't remember this, do you Violet?" Nigel asked, when he regained his breath but he doubled over again, overcome with a fresh bout of laughter, glancing at Victor to see if he was laughing.

I didn't respond, the fumes from the rotting food had triggered a memory, and flashes of stone and darkness flooded my mind. A pair of black eyes swam in front of me, confusing me further. Shutting my eyes to the rest of the world, I concentrated on that one image, trying to connect it to a forgotten memory. The pieces clicked together and my eyes snapped open, they were a pair of Guard's eyes; but where had I seen them before? "Violet, are you okay?" Curtis asked, the others were still doubled over laughing so they hadn't noticed I had quietened.

"Yes, I am fine Curtis," I replied. "Just give me a second."

Shutting my eyes again, I focused on the recent events and smiled when the vision of a Guard popped up; the same Guard who had been staring at me earlier near my bunk. It wasn't the first time I had seen him, but my headache had come back with full force, forcing me to stop thinking about the guard with coal-black eyes for the moment. I decided to talk to Victor about it later to see if he could shed some light on the visions which were plaguing me.

EIGHT

MACUS

I sat in a room in which three rows of five monitors covered the entirety of three of the walls, waiting for my friend and boss to finish his meeting. A different scene encompassed each screen and I glanced at all of them but my eyes kept on drifting to the bottom right-hand corner more than the others. It was trained on an unlikely group of friends lounging about, and around, one of the bunks; they were laughing and joking together. I slid out a control panel — with a variety of complicated-looking knobs and keys — from beneath the middle of the monitors, and tapped out a sequence of keys. The monitor then focused in on the group of people and zoomed in onto the face of a black, short-haired woman, who was laughing heartily along with everyone else. She leant against a tall, blonde-haired, green-eyed man whilst he stroked her arm lovingly. A young boy sat on the floor at her feet, his arms looped around his knees, looking up at her adoringly, and an old man sat with them, his long white hair held in a ponytail at the nape of his neck. They looked comfortable together as though they loved each other's company.

I reached a hand out to stroke the image of the black-haired woman on the screen — ignoring the other male members of the scene — a look of longing in my eyes. A small cough made me spin around on my chair, which squeaked loudly. A stony-faced man stood before me

— the man I had been waiting for — Astinal. He had his arms crossed over his huge barrel chest and he raised an eyebrow at me in question. His bright blue eyes were gleaming in the monitor's artificial light beneath his visored helmet. He leant his spear against the back wall, took off his helmet and pinched the bridge of his nose in exasperation; he wore his full gladiatorial garb, having just come from an important meeting. I had discarded my helmet, spear and greaves once I had gotten comfortable and they were scattered around the room.

"I told you Macus, that is not her, she may resemble her but I assure you they are not the same person. They can't be," Astinal said, cradling his helmet in the crook of his arm and running his hand through his curly brown hair, staring at me with tightly pressed lips.

"I–I..." I faltered, running my hand through my cropped black hair.

"Macus," Astinal said, walking over and putting a hand on my shoulder. "Forget her."

"I thought for sure it was her," I said, glancing back at the monitor. "They look identical."

"You cannot know for sure, and you know the rules, things are different than when we first got here, when we were free to do whatever we pleased. Now that everything is different, it's ultimately better for everyone," Astinal said.

"This situation has never happened before, and you do not know how I feel when I look at her, Astinal." I said, refusing to meet his gaze, instead focusing on the laces of my sandals.

"Macus, I may not feel what you feel, and I never will, but too much is at risk now," Astinal said. "Just let her go."

I didn't speak for a moment, focusing my attention on the screen, thinking of the woman I once knew, and the time we had spent together. Centuries had passed, but the details came back sharp as though I were watching a movie. I remembered her voice and the smell of her hair, the way her emerald green eyes shone with mischief just before she did something silly or daring; she had been my life. I found her here. Why did they have to take her away from me when an eternity together was so achievable.

"What did they say?" I asked, changing the subject. I turned away from the screens and finally looked at him. He momentarily looked morose but quickly masked it with a stern face more appropriate to his character.

"This and that," Astinal replied, vaguely.

"Astinal," I sighed. "You can trust me. How long have we been friends?"

Astinal rolled his eyes and pulled over a second swivel chair, which squeaked just as loudly as its brother.

"We need to get new chairs," he said conversationally.

I waited patiently for him to tell me what had gone on in his meeting, folding my arms and leaning back, getting as comfortable as was possible on such an old chair.

"They told me we need to watch both Violet and Mary. Observe what they do, where they go and especially who talks to them. We stay far enough away from them so we don't draw attention to ourselves and we are taking the watches in shifts."

"Yeah, go on?" I said, boredly, as I had already been made aware of this information.

"They said we didn't need to be discreet in our watches. We are being too lax on them. We need to find out what they are planning. They have approved audio."

"I see, which gives us more freedom to watch them more closely. We will have to tell the others later today," I said, leaning forward and resting my elbows on my knees.

"But first we must see a man about a job," Astinal said, standing up and turning away. He put his helmet back on and grabbed his spear from the corner of the room, waiting for me to dress myself.

I stood up from my chair and grabbed my helmet and jammed it onto my head, I shoved my legs into my greaves and grabbed my spear leaning against the console. Once I was ready, I banged the butt of my spear once on the ground and followed Astinal out of the room. I turned back once to the woman on the screen. She had just spoken and everybody around her laughed. I longed to be with her in the blonde man's position but I knew it would be impossible.

The monitors zoomed out and returned to the standard view of the Afterlife as I turned away. I shut the door behind me with a snap and followed Astinal as he made his way through long white hallways with black doors on either side. We stopped in front of one and it opened of its own accord when Astinal faced it. He crossed the threshold into a pitch black interior and I followed him. After three steps, my surroundings changed, the air became colder and my feet touched hard tiles instead of the soft earthen floor. When the darkness lifted, we found ourselves in a colossal room with simple bunks and millions of people milling around. A buzz of muted conversations filled the room, although occasional peels of laughter or squeals of joy from various children running around bombarded me. We weaved between the bunks, following a predetermined route, passing by men, women and children alike.

I kept my face impassive but my eyes roamed around the room, ready to keep the peace if an argument got out of hand or a fight broke loose. The souls were in high spirits today, so I didn't think I would have to brandish my spear on anyone.

Astinal abruptly stopped in front of a ragged, noxious bunk, I noticed that the surrounding bunks were empty and looked like no one had touched them in years. A thick layer of dust coated everything in the designated bunk area and I could see only one set of footprints had come in and out of the surrounding area. I presumed they belonged to the human-shaped lump which lay on the mattress beneath brown-stained sheets. I fought the urge to cover my hand over my mouth and nose, instead, wrinkled my face in disgust at the stench.

"Get up, Soul," Astinal commanded.

The soul did not get up, but the sheets vibrated and whimpers came from underneath them.

"I said, 'Get up'," Astinal growled, jabbing his spear butt harder than necessary into the lump.

"Ouch!" A male voice yelled, as the soul jumped beneath the sheets. He sat up but kept the covers draped over his body and held them over him with a makeshift hood over his head and tucked the sheets under his chin so you could only see his filthy face. The soul was only distinguishable from its surroundings because of his ability to speak.

"Stuart Willis?" Astinal asked him.

"Yeah, I'm Stu. Who's askin'?" he replied, looking between Astinal and myself.

I banged my spear on the floor once as a warning. Stu jumped and his makeshift hood fell revealing dirty and matted hair adorned with a myriad of living insects.

"We have a proposition for you, Stuart," Astinal whispered to him.

"What proposition?" Stu questioned, leaning forward to better hear Astinal.

"Well, if you do this, we can get you certain things; things you have been craving," Astinal raised his eyebrows at Stu. "Do you understand?"

Stu wrinkled his forehead in deep thought. Astinal sighed, tore the sheet away from Stu's body and dragged him close by the neck of his filthy, brown-stained t-shirt and whispered something in his ear which made Stu's eyes widen with shock.

"I'll do it. Anything. Anything for you, Sir," Stu gushed out, falling to his knees at Astinal's feet, attempting to kiss his toes through his sandals. Astinal kicked out and his foot connected with the side of Stuart's head and he yelped in pain, clutching his head and shaking in fear.

"Listen closely Stuart, as I do not want to repeat this," Astinal said, dragging Stu to his feet. "You see that woman?" He pointed to a long, black-haired woman sitting around twenty bunks away. "I want you to follow her and tell me exactly what she does, where she goes and who she talks to, okay? I need to know everything about her."

Stu nodded. "I understand. I'll follow her..." he paused, licking his lips. "And when will I get–?"

"When you've finished the job. I will come back to you for updates. Do not come looking for me," Astinal spat out, shoving Stu back onto his bunk and without waiting for a response, he turned on his heel and marched back the way we had come. I followed bleakly, glancing at the long black-haired woman as we passed her.

I turned away from her in time to see Astinal disappear. I hazard a guess as to where he went. A second later, I faced a wall of flickering screens, and, sure enough, sitting in front of them was Astinal. I pulled over the second swivel chair and sat next to him. Neither of us spoke for five minutes. I tried to focus my attention on the screens, to keep an eye on the Afterlife, and make sure everyone was comfortable and happy. That was my job, but Astinal and myself's meeting with Stuart Willis nagged at me.

"Do you think Stuart Willis will manage the task you gave him?" I finally asked him, sick of the waiting game and giving into my curiosities.

"I think he will be of use," Astinal replied, cryptically.

"What does that mean?" I asked, frowning at him.

"It means, he is the kind of person who will do what he deems necessary to survive, and if it is to follow our orders, then he will do just that."

"Astinal, how long have we known each other?"

"Long enough for you to understand that there are some things I cannot tell you." He said, finally looking over at me.

"You used to trust me, what's changed?"

He yanked off his helmet and held it in his lap, running his fingers over the intricate patterns on it whilst frowning.

"We needed more eyes on her," he finally said. "I cannot trust all my Guards on this task."

"If you can't trust the Guards, who can you trust? Don't tell me you trust this filthy soul more than your brothers?"

"That's not it, Macus," his eyes turned hard. "I need someone who would do anything for me. Stuart needs something he thinks I can give him, so he will do anything to get it."

"It's not that simple, you cannot trust a soul, do you remember where that led us?" I asked, clutching at his arm.

He pulled it from my grip and had a hand to my throat before I could blink.

"Do not talk of that," he growled.

"Astinal," I choked out. "I am not the enemy." I tried to pry his fingers away from my throat.

He suddenly let go, snatched his helmet from where it fell from his lap and strode to the door.

"You do not have the right to be this angry about what happened," I said coldly. "I am just trying to understand why you would trust a stranger more than me."

"The rules are placed for a reason, Macus," he replied, his hand on the doorknob. "I need all the eyes I can get." With that he strode out of the room, leaving me alone.

I rubbed my throat with one hand and pulled the keyboard out from underneath the console table with the other. Astinal's behaviour troubled me. I needed to know what drove him to seek a soul's help and to not trust in his brothers.

I used the keyboard to manipulate the view of the Afterlife, not looking for anything in particular, glancing at each view once before changing it, but I found that I couldn't switch the screens as easily when the short-haired woman's face filled the screens. My heart ached to be near her. I didn't care what Astinal said. I knew it was her from the first moment she had appeared on the radar. I watched her progress and whenever it looked as though she was faltering — about to fall into the pre-lain traps into limbo — I sent out a helping hand. I shouldn't have, but I needed to see her in the flesh rather than through a screen to believe.

Sighing, I switched the views, so it showed the entire Afterlife. My hands tapped out a rhythmic staccato on the console table. My legs shook in trepidation and I ran my hands through my dishevelled hair twice a minute. My eyes were glued to the screens but not paying any attention. I gave it up as a lost cause and walked out the room. I needed to do something else. I walked the long, lonely, white hallways trying to gather my thoughts. Why did Astinal recruit Stuart? Why did she go to Section Eight?

"Everyone, gather at the Altar room for the midday meeting." A phantom voice rang in my head reminding me of my duties. Sighing, I shut my eyes and visualised the Altar room, and when I opened them again, I stood outside a black door in a white hallway identical to every other one. Out of habit, I reached out a hand to turn the

handle, but the door opened of its own accord before I had even touched it.

"I will never get used to this," I whispered to myself as I walked through the threshold.

Astinal stood at the head of the Altar, he had his hand to his temple, talking to an unknown person, in an unknown location. I was still angry at him for his lack of trust so I didn't make my way to his right-hand side, instead I hung back, leaning against the back wall, near the exit. I couldn't hear what he said, but from his facial expressions it looked serious. I should be by his side, but until he trusted me enough to confide in me, I would stay away.

The room filled up, helmeted men walked in, laughing and joking with each other. I greeted a few, but I ignored most of them and they left me to my musings and gave me a wide berth. A tall Guard walked in, his hazel eyes impassive, I watched as he weaved his way through the crowd, his hand clutched his spear, butting it on the floor at every other step. His back straight as an arrow as he stood in attention in front of Astinal.

Astinal spoke to the room at large, but my mind wandered, and I didn't take in anything he said; this was fruitless. I pushed myself away from the wall and picked my way out of the room. I didn't turn to see if Astinal saw; I didn't care if he did or not. Once I was out of the Altar room everything became lighter, I had more room to breathe and think.

Not wanting to go back out into the Afterlife, or be in the Altar room with a man I used to trust, I didn't know where else to go. The Viewing room held my obsessive, one-sided, staring contest, so I couldn't go back there. I needed to be alone to gather my thoughts. I found myself in my chambers. I undressed, laying my uniform in a pile onto the ottoman at the end of my huge four-poster bed. The fireplace opposite still held the remnants of this morning's fire, and embers glowed in the breeze coming from the chimney. I strode to the vanity, to her picture. I snatched it up and stared at the familiar face. They were the same, and I would prove it.

NINE

THE SPY

I glanced up from the book which Sophie loaned me and through the curtain of my long black hair, I saw two Guards pass my bunk. They walked by at a fast pace but I had the strangest feeling they had just been looking right at me. My eyes followed them as they walked away and disappeared into thin air. I was only mildly shocked, as I had observed the Guards suddenly appear and disappear many times since I arrived. I guessed they needed a way to transport themselves easily as this place was so vast. I just didn't know how it worked and longed to.

I looked back at the battered copy of the Bible which lay open in my lap and snapped it closed, frustrated by its lack of guidance. I once thought it held all the answers. Whenever I had been upset or lonely in my past life, I grabbed the small copy of the Bible I carried with me always and read passages which I knew would lift my spirits. For example, Isaiah 12:2:

"Behold God is my salvation; I will trust and not be afraid: for the LORD JEHOVAH, is my strength and my SONG; he also has become my salvation."

This has been my favourite passage to read. I found the words comforting and repeated them as guidelines, but those words had all been lies.

I had been flicking through it hoping to find passages which could shed light on what might have caused the dizziness and the nausea which had come over me two weeks ago, but no passages helped; I still felt lost. The awful visions which I had endured during my fever dreams flooded into my mind. The sharp spear tips, and the darkened nook in the wall, and to make it worse I didn't know how they started. They had come about with such force, I didn't have the energy to question them when they first started. Now, so much time had passed, I couldn't remember what I had been doing or pinpoint when the visions began. It was as though that information had been taken out of my head by somebody.

My mind still ached from those mental injuries, but something had relieved my body of its aches and pains soon after I had awoken. A warmth had coursed through my body, healing the cuts and bruises which I had somehow gained from the spears in my dreams. I did not know how it had happened, and I was too afraid to ask anybody. I was glad for it though, I wasn't sure how much more pain I could have taken before I broke, inside and out.

"Recite it again," he cried. *"Why do you get it wrong all the time, Mary?"*

"I am sorry Daddy," I sobbed. *"I will get it right next time."*

"It is too late for that." He said, unbuckling his belt. "You know what to do."

Not all of my memories of the Bible elicited positive memories. Shaking the memory out of the forefront of my mind, I let my eyes wander around the people who occupied the neighbouring bunks. I concentrated on each face and memorised those with whom I shared my immediate surroundings. In the short time that I had been here, a little girl had arrived and occupied the previously empty bunk to the right of mine. She sat on her bed with her knees tucked under her chin, rocking back and forth. Her brown eyes — wide open and staring into space — were bloodshot, as though she had only recently stopped crying. I was glad the bunk had been reassigned, but I knew the little girl would never let me anywhere near her, so it may as well have stayed empty for all the company it gave me.

On the bunk right in front of mine, a man hid underneath his covers, shivering; every now and then he let out a loud, ear piercing scream. It startled me when I first heard it. I leapt up and strode over to him to comfort him, but everybody around us shook their heads, silently telling me my efforts would be futile. I longed to go to him and wondered what happened to him to make him behave this way. Most of the time he acted as any normal person would here, keeping to himself but not acting too strangely, but certain days he would assume this position and let out his pent up energy and frustrations. I understood his need for release, I was in the same predicament, but instead of a wild, verbal release, I exercised to release my frustrations. I had gotten into the habit of doing yoga every morning, I still remembered some of the positions I practiced when I lived; the Upward and Downward Facing Dog, the Warrior's one and two, and the Child's pose had been my favourites. I found the ritual calming and it also allowed me time to think.

Several Guards appeared at once and strode over to a bunk across the room. I kneeled on my bed to get a better look and I could just make out a man thrashing around on it, his body entangled in the sweat soaked sheets. The first Guard to reach the man tore the sheets away from his body, but he didn't stop writhing. It took three of the Guards to pick him up from the bed, all the while his limbs flailed as though he was fighting them away. Half of the people around stared at the commotion, and the other half turned their gaze away as though he didn't exist; either way no one helped him. As soon as it started, it was over, the Guards disappeared along with the man and everyone went back to ignoring each other, staring into space.

I sat back down and looked around the room, the lady with the half burned face sat on her bed crying, and the black man with the missing leg sat in his usual position — rubbing at the air underneath his absent leg — but this time he was staring right at me. He nodded at me as though we shared a secret understanding. I frowned at him, confused by his actions, he nodded once more then returned his focus back to his hands.

"What was that about?" Sophie asked, she was sitting on the floor between our bunks. I shrugged, glancing at the spot where the Guards had taken the sleeping man away and back to the black man. He seemed to have forgotten about me and was once again squeezing his eyes shut in pain. "Help me up?" she asked, holding a hand up for me to grasp.

I helped heave her off the floor. By now we were well-practiced, so it didn't take long to get her standing.

"How is the Bible treating you?" she asked, perching on the edge of my bed, tucking a stray strand of shoulder length brown hair behind an ear as she did so.

I shrugged again. "It had always helped before," I said in a small voice, fingering the peeling leather of the spine.

"I find that whenever I read it, it makes this place clearer."

"How?" I asked. "It makes no sense. There is nothing in there that points to this," I gestured around the room. "Take this passage, for instance, from Revelations 21:4:

"And God shall wipe away all tears from their eyes; and there shall be no more death, neither sorrow, nor crying, neither shall there be any more pain: for the former things are passed away."

And, this from Ecclesiastes 9:5-6:

"For the living know they shall die; but the dead know not any thing, nor have they any more a reward, for the memory of them is forgotten. Indeed their love, their hatred and their envy is now perished, neither have they any more a portion for ever in anything that is done under the sun."

Does this place look free of mourning, crying, or pain? Do these people around us look as though they have forgotten their memories? What are we supposed to think when we are dumped here when we were promised salvation?" I leapt up from my bed and paced back and forth.

"That is exactly what we need to question, this book is filled with the predetermined notions of this place. The people who read this book are given skewed expectations of the Afterlife," she said, smiling at the frown on my face. "We will find out what is truly going on here because we will question this and its messages."

"But it doesn't tell us anything," I countered.

"Actually, it tells us everything," Sophie said, standing up and grabbing my arm. I stopped pacing and turned to face her. "We can see the Bible has lied to us about here. What else has it lied about? I used to be a devout Christian, but now I question everything I have been taught; and when we find Him we can question Him. We now have the proof of His lies."

My eyes lit up, finally understanding what Sophie was trying to tell me, and why she lent me the book in the first place.

"Hide that so no one sees it, remember what I told you?" she said.

I nodded and hurriedly stored it in the bottom drawer of my bedside table. I turned back to face her again, but she was frowning at a distant spot over my shoulder. I spun around and followed her eye line. A wide-eyed, raggedly dressed, dirty man, crouched behind a nearby bunk. I wrinkled my nose at his unkempt appearance, only guessing at the stench he carried with him. He ducked down below the footboard but tufts of his matted hair were still visible over it. He glanced above the footboard but ducked back down again when he spotted us still looking his way. He stayed crouched low for another minute until the owner of the bunk strode towards him. Her words didn't carry but her gestures told all. He scrambled away soon after but not before glancing back at us one last time.

"That was odd," I said, turning back to face Sophie, but her eyes were still fixed on the distant point above my shoulder. I assumed she followed the dirty man's path and thought nothing of it.

Two days after first spotting the dirty man watching us, I caught him staring again, but this time from a different bunk. He was, again, crouched behind the footboard, and was peeking over it straight at us. His constant presence grated on me and I was desperate to find out why he was watching us. No one else here acted that way towards us.

"Sophie, do you remember that dirty man who was staring at us two days ago?" I asked. "Well, he's doing it again now," I said, walking over to her and pointing to where he was hiding. When he spotted me pointing at him, he leapt up from his hiding spot and shuffled away. The people around him shied away when he neared them.

Sophie didn't respond. She, instead, stood up from her bunk and reached underneath her mattress. She drew out a tiny notebook which I had seen her use a lot lately.

"Where did you get that?" I asked, reaching out a hand to grab it from her.

"Never you mind," she said, snatching the notebook out of my reach and clutching it to her chest.

"But I want one," I said, pouting, again trying to grab it out of her hands.

"Not now, you can't know anything about this. The less you know the better," she said, clutching it closer to her chest. "That way, if anyone asks you where I got it from, you will be able to safely and honestly say you don't know," she added through gritted teeth.

"You have been spending a lot of time writing in that," I said. "Whenever I look over, if you're not meditating, you are writing in it."

"Yeah," she mumbled, looking around the room and ignoring me.

"Well, are you going to tell me what you are writing about?" I asked.

"No, not yet, I still haven't figured it out myself," she said, still frowning around the room and not meeting my eye.

"Figured out what?" I felt out of the loop and ignored, much like when my sister would have a hair-brained idea and ignore me for hours at a time, leaving me alone with my paranoid thoughts.

"Shh Mary, I am trying to concentrate." She bent low over the notebook and scribbled onto the thick parchment-like paper with a crude looking pencil, occasionally glancing up to squint around the room. She chewed the end of her pencil and spat out the bits of wood which came away with a mildly disgusted look on her face.

"Can I help?" I asked, when she had been silent for a minute.

"No, you can't."

"But I told you about that dirty man," I said defensively. "I told you he was looking at us. You didn't seem to have known about that."

"That's just one observation, Mary," she said looking back down at her note book and scribbling something else. "When I know what's going on I'll tell you, but in the meantime, please," she finally looked up at me. "Please, leave me alone so I can concentrate."

"But where did you get it from?" I asked her. She didn't respond, she stayed in her position — head bent low over her tiny notebook, scribbling — I sighed and left her to it. I spun around on the spot and when I stopped, I walked away in that direction, seething.

Whenever Sophie meditated or wrote in her notebook — which she did more often lately — I took the time to explore the area in which I was living. I walked down the makeshift walkways between the bunks and took in the sights and sounds around me. Most people kept to themselves. No one wanted to talk to anybody else, and they were especially suspicious of anybody who didn't live near them. Everybody avoided eye contact with me when I walked past, which made me treasure my friendship with Sophie even more; even though I was ignored by her a lot too.

I remember when I realised I had a subconscious ulterior motive to my wanderings. I ran up to a familiar looking short black-haired woman, a rush of hope and excitement filled my insides. I spun her around and squeezed her to me, my heart leaping with joy. It continued to beat hard and fast in my chest, pure elation coursing through my veins. I enjoyed only a moment of content before she shoved me away from her.

"Who are you?" She screamed at me and when I didn't respond, she shouted. "Go away, you freak!" She turned away from me, muttering wildly to herself.

I ran away, stumbling a little, my face burning with shame. I hadn't realised I hoped to find my sister here, even though I knew it was near impossible for her to be.

"Sophie?" I said in a small voice.

"Yes?" She murmured. "Where have you been?" She added as an afterthought.

"I was just at the shower stalls," I admitted.

"Why?" she asked, wrinkling her nose.

"They seem like the only real thing over here, they make me feel safe," I replied.

She finally looked up at me. "You know they stink right?"

"I know," I sighed. "I saw someone else get taken away today."

"That happens all the time Mary, forget about it." She said, batting away my misgivings.

"I think it's important, where do they go?" I asked.

Sophie shrugged and bent over her notebook again.

"I feel like I am being followed, that's crazy right?" I asked after a minute, changing the subject.

She sighed and closed her notebook, giving it up as a lost cause. "No, you're not going crazy, I've noticed them too."

"Who do you think is following us and why?" I asked, excitedly. "Every time I look for a culprit, I see normal people, like you and I, but I feel eyes everywhere."

"Well, apart from the obvious," she paused. I shook my head, confused and gestured for her to go on. "The dirty man, the one we see crouching behind th–,"

"Oh yeah, although, I wouldn't count him," I interrupted. "He is not any good at spying. We always catch him. Maybe that's why I forgot about him." I added under my breath.

"I have found out from a friend of mine that his name is Stu Willis." Sophie shook her head in disgust at the name. "But, the other, less obvious spies, are the Guards."

"The Guards?" I asked loudly, shocked.

"Shhh." She flapped her arms at me, motioning at me to be quiet. I glanced around and a Guard, around thirty feet away, stood with his arms folded and glared at us.

"But why would the Guards be following me?" I whispered, turning back to her.

"That's what I am trying to find out," she replied, shaking her notebook and smiling.

I glanced back at the Guard but he had already disappeared. I was about to turn back and question Sophie further when I noticed the black man, with the missing leg, walking towards us. I nudged Sophie and pointed in his direction, and we both stared at him until he drew level with us.

"Hi," he said, smiling. He had a deep, soulful voice with an accent I couldn't place. His dark brown eyes betrayed his pain even if his wide smile tried to mask it. He loomed over us, standing as though he still had two legs, and eclipsing one of the light sources above us, casting us in shadow. I glanced at his right leg to make sure I hadn't imagined the missing limb and sure enough, his hand was clasped onto his right thigh but the rest of the limb was missing. I looked back up at his face, my cheeks flushing red in embarrassment as our eyes locked.

"Hi," Sophie said, breaking the impromptu staring contest which had started between us.

I shook my head, snapping out of the reverie I found myself in. I smiled shyly at his enigmatic smile. It baffled me that his body could be so disfigured, yet he could act in such a normal manner. If I were in his position, I wouldn't know how to act.

"Where are my manners?" he laughed. "My name's Jeff Blake. I thought I'd come over and introduce myself." He paused and squeezed his right thigh again, grimacing slightly. "I've seen you walking around and hoped you'd come over and talk but..." He directed the last sentence at me, trailing off at the end with an implied tease. For some reason, I was surprised by his teasing demeanour and my face reddened further still.

"I'm Sophie, and this is Mary," Sophie said, jerking her thumb in my direction.

I smiled and held out my hand, he grasped it, brought it to his lips and brushed them over it. I snatched my hand away as electric shocks coursed through my arm and up to my shoulder, making me shiver. Embarrassed at my reaction, I held my hand to my face and stifled a giggle to cover it. I sniffed at my fingers, they smelt faintly like freshly laid tarmac. I frowned but didn't have time to understand what it meant.

"I was only joking about hoping that you'd come and talk," he said. "I suspected you'd never have the courage, no one here ever wants to interact with anybody else. May I join you ladies?" His grin widened.

"Of course," Sophie said, moving to make space for him to sit between us on her bed. In the commotion, I composed myself and pasted a sincere smile on my face.

"Well," Sophie started. "I will make tea."

She got up from the bed and rummaged around underneath it. She came back out with the stove, a pot of water and the brown cloth bag.

"Where–?" Jeff started.

"I don't know," I said, interrupting him, exasperated. "She won't tell me. I've asked many times."

Sophie tinkered with the tea and after a few minutes she had three steaming cups ready. She handed one to Jeff, one to me and the last was for her.

"I saw you were unwell a couple weeks ago Mary. I'd wanted to come and see if you were okay, but circumstances prevented me from doing so," Jeff said. He took a sip of tea and turned to Sophie. "Mmm, it's good."

"Oh," I said, surprised. How did he know that I had fallen ill? "Sophie was here to take care of me."

"Do you remember how it started?" he asked.

"No," I confessed, shaking my head and taking a sip of the tea. It tasted just as good as the last batch. "I remember feeling suddenly

nauseous and dizzy, and a throbbing headache started at my temple."
I touched my temple hoping it wouldn't come back. "The symptoms
came on so suddenly and they didn't pass until three days later."

We were silent for a while, each sipping our tea, submerged into
our own thoughts.

"I had a bunkmate," Jeff began. "His name was Joe Brisket, he
was my best friend. We'd talk to one another about our previous lives
and would comfort one another." He paused, taking a deep breath.
"One day he fell ill. I remember, on that day he'd disappeared for a
few hours at the start of it and I hadn't seen him all day. I remember
he came back in the evening and collapsed onto his bunk, mumbling
about nausea, dizziness and a headache. I guess similar symptoms to
your illness." He gestured towards me. "He wouldn't tell me where
he'd been, he said he thought he'd done something wrong." He
looked up at me meaningfully; his look implied that he wondered if
my experience had been the same.

"I'm sure I did nothing out of the ordinary," I said defensively.
Sophie nodded in agreement.

Jeff accepted what I said, nodded once and carried on with his
story. "He was asleep for what felt like a week, and when he woke
up, I tried everything to help him but he refused to accept it. One
day Guards came and questioned me about him."

"What did they ask?" Sophie asked, straightening her back and
leaning towards him.

"They asked me where he'd been in the last week, who'd he been
talking to, had he been acting strange — questions like that — but
I didn't have the answers. If I'd known something I could've helped
him or maybe even lied for him," Jeff shook his head, guilt clearly
showing on his features. "When I didn't answer their questions, they
left muttering, but I couldn't hear what they said. Then they came
back later that day and took him away. I feared for you, I thought
they would take you away as well, but they didn't."

None of us said anything, the implied alternate future hanging
between us like a dark cloud. We finished our tea and handed the
cups back to Sophie. She put them, the stove and the pot back under

her bed. I wondered where she replenished her stock, but didn't ask aloud, knowing she would never tell me. Getting information out of Sophie was like getting blood from a stone; near impossible. I would crack her one day, she will just have to learn to trust me.

TEN

THE PLAN

I sat on the squeaky swivel chair in the Viewing room, watching the familiar wall of screens in front of me. They were each trained on a group of three people; a long black haired woman, a woman with brown hair to her shoulders and a black man with a missing leg — they sat close together talking on a bunk. I noted how identical the black-haired woman looked to my woman, but her energy felt different. Each screen in the room showed a different angle of the trio and in the background of two of the screens in the bottom right-hand corner, the scruffy, dirty, brown hair, forehead and dark brown eyes of a filthy man peaked above a footboard nearby; Stuart Willis. He watched the same trio as I did, but from a different vantage point. Stuart Willis had proven to be a huge disappointment and an even bigger waste of time, he clearly didn't know how to be discreet, as they had both spotted him watching them every day since we bequeathed the task to him. He even drew his fellow bunkmates' attention; Astinal was furious. I had been watching him watch them for the past three days, wondering whether I should relieve him of his duties so no one would uncover his mission. Today would have to be that day.

"Who are you watching?" Astinal asked, walking into the room.

"The Targets," I replied, not taking my eyes off the screen.

Astinal sat down and the chair next to mine squeaked. He took off his helmet and ruffled his curls, attempting to add volume to his helmet hair. He leant forwards, his elbows resting on his knees, his eyes trained on the screens. He reached out a hand and tapped a sequence of keys on the keyboard, and the volume level rose so we could hear the trio's conversation.

"-But they didn't." The man said.

At those words, there was a silence so tense, I could sense it through the screens. They each handed their smooth wooden cups back to the brown-haired woman, and she put them, the stove and kettle back underneath her bunk.

"I dread to think what would have happened if they had taken me away." The black haired woman eventually said, breaking the silence.

"Nor can I," agreed the brown-haired woman, once she had settled herself back onto the bed. "No one has returned once the Guards have taken them away. Whenever the Guards take someone away, I try to remember their faces, and I've been keeping an eye out for anyone who resembles them, but I have never seen a repeated face."

"They didn't take you away. I was sure they would. I wonder why they didn't?" The black man said, putting a hand on the black-haired woman's knee. She looked up at him, blushed and looked away.

"I know. It's still a terrifying thought." The black-haired lady said to her friends. "What would I do without you Sophie?" She grasped the brown haired woman's hand and squeezed it.

"So, what do we do now?" The one-legged man asked, looking between the two women.

"What do you mean, Jeff?" The brown haired woman, Sophie, asked the one legged man; Jeff.

"I want to get my friend back. If he is indeed still here somewhere, I need to find him," he said angrily.

The women exchanged a look of understanding then looked back at Jeff. "Should we show him Mary?" Sophie asked the other woman.

Mary hesitated then nodded. Taking a deep breath, she walked over to the bunk opposite and rummaged through the bottom drawer. She walked back to the bunk and handed Jeff a small, battered book.

"What's this?" he asked, confused, turning the book in his hands, fingering its peeling spine and flicking through the pages.

I leant forward in my seat in excitement.

"It's a copy of the Bible," Sophie whispered.

"What? Where'd you get it from?" Jeff asked.

"Yes, where did she get it from?" Astinal muttered out loud, leaning back in his chair, folding his arms across his chest and frowning.

"It doesn't matter where I got it from, but this holds proof of what we have been searching for," Sophie replied. "This is supposedly the 'Word of God', but nothing in it points to the afterlife looking like this, does it?" Jeff said nothing, instead staring at the book in his hands, frowning.

"No, I guess it doesn't," Jeff replied. "I haven't read it myself, but from what I know of it, I'm sure it didn't describe the afterlife like this." He turned the book over in his hands again to the front cover, which had an illustration of a cross etched into the leather, and then had faded gold detailing on the spine.

"It makes me question everything else in the book," Sophie said.

"Like what?" Jeff asked, still distracted by the aged book in his hands.

"Does 'God' even exist," Sophie said, making quotation marks in the air over the word God. Both Mary and Jeff stared at her, Mary's mouth hung open, but Jeff's lips were in a tight line.

"How's this going to help me find my friend?" Jeff asked, confused.

"We can use this Bible to meet Him. We should corner one of the Guards and ask him to take us to Him," Sophie said, straightening her back and shifting closer to the other two. "Then we can demand to know where your friend is, and ask any other questions we have."

"How are we going to do that?" Mary asked. "They never stop to talk or even acknowledge anybody's existence. You have already said so yourself, Sophie."

"I'm working on something," Sophie said.

"Can you tell us what?" Jeff asked, leaning forward, a greedy glint in his eye.

"No, I haven't finished yet. When it's done, I will tell you, but in the meantime, just act normally and make sure none of the Guards figure out we are planning something," Sophie cautioned.

"Yeah, I guess we can do that," Mary agreed, looking at Jeff for an agreement. He nodded back, his features stern.

"Oh, Hell," I said, sighing.

"Code Red," I looked over at Astinal, he had his hand to his temple and looked at me with a grave expression on his face. "I will do, Sir," he said and paused, staring at me with angry eyes. "Assemble."

Using the keyboard, I panned out of Mary's view and one by one, the Guards in the Afterlife disappeared, leaving the souls unwatched, but it had to be done; this was protocol. I zoomed back into Mary's view, Jeff still had the Bible in his hand and Sophie stared accusingly at Stuart Willis.

"What are you going to do?" I asked Astinal.

"What needs to be done." Astinal replied, standing up from the chair and facing me.

"What do you need me to do?" I asked, looking up at him.

"Trust me." He shoved his helmet onto his head, tucking an errant curl beneath it.

I scoffed and glanced back at the screens at the trio sitting at the bunk. "Trust you, Astinal?" I asked. "When you don't even trust me?"

"Yes, trust me." He turned away and with a hand on the door turned back. "And meet in the Altar room, we need to discuss next steps," he paused. "I need you by my side. I know you do not understand at the moment, but I will explain soon."

He walked away leaving me alone in the Viewing room. I thought about ignoring his orders and leaving him in the meeting alone — I contributed little anyway — but thought better of it. I sighed and picked up my helmet from the console table and put it on. I stared at the screen for another couple of minutes hoping the trio would say something else which would incriminate them further, but their conversation turned inane, as though they knew they were being watched; impossible.

We needed to act fast to put a stop to this. So, instead of walking to the Altar room, I closed my eyes, held a hand to my temple and transported myself there. The room was already filled with Guards, so I was made to weave my way through the thick crowd to my designated position.

"I am glad you saw sense, Macus," Astinal said when I reached him. He had just been in deep conversation with a tall Guard I vaguely recognised moments before I reached him.

I grunted in response and faced the crowd of Gladiators in front of me; a sea of red plumed helmets and spear points.

"Thank you for gathering at such short notice," Astinal started. "I will try to keep this meeting short so you can get back to your duties." He paused, and I watched as the other Guards shuffled from foot to foot eager to find out what this impromptu meeting was about. I, too, was curious as to how much Astinal would tell them. Would Astinal trust in them, or shun them as he had been doing me?

"There has been another breach. Along with watching over Violet Deneuve, I need you to keep an eye on her sister Mary Deneuve," he paused, looking around the room. "This is a matter of import. We need to keep everyone in check. There cannot be any more unexpected events occurring, otherwise all Hell will break loose. Search anyone who looks suspicious and keep an eye on any groups converging; this is for everyone's safety. Turi will brief you further." A tall Guard held up his spear in acknowledgement.

"Okay, men." Turi's deep voice reverberated through the room, forcing everyone into rapt attention. No one dared fidget or disobey. "We have no time to build a schedule yet, so I want you two, Parks and Waif, to watch Mary for now. Tomorrow I will brief you on a firmer schedule, when I have set it. Move out." The Guards filed out of the room and Turi followed, taking the rear.

"You don't truly believe we are doing this for the soul's safety?" I asked Astinal once the room had emptied.

"Yes, Macus," he said.

"I don't believe you," I said. "I know you are just following orders." Astinal didn't respond.

"So you trust Turi?" I asked, knowing, at that moment, I sounded upset.

"Yes, I trust Turi to get the job done and not let emotions get in the way," Astinal said, turning his cold blue eyes to me.

"What is that supposed to mean?" I asked, taking a step back away from his hate filled eyes.

"I know what you did, Macus. It was against protocol," he replied. "Do you want us to get in trouble?"

"By who Astinal?" I asked. "Who will punish us? Who do you speak to?" I pointed to my temple, gesturing that I knew there were people he talked telepathically to who I had never met before. As his second, I should have met them by now or at least been briefed about their existence.

"That's for me to know," he paused. "As soon as you get your head together and realise that she is not her, the sooner I will trust you."

I shook my head at him, at a loss for words.

"I am sorry Macus, but this is for your own good. She. Is. Not. Her." He said, jabbing his finger in my chest at each word.

I shoved his hand away from me and without further words I de-materialised and re-materialised into my personal chambers. I fought the urge to tear through my room and break everything I could get my hands on. My anger was my only vice, and over the centuries, I had learned to control it; it would be a waste of my training to let go now.

With my fists balled up, I paced the room, taking deep breaths and trying my hardest not to walk over to the vanity. Not to fall into the same comforting routine. I paced for another five minutes, but my heart rate was still sky-high, my breathing laboured and my palms slick to the touch. I needed her. I needed to see her.

Ashamed, I stumbled over to the vanity and picked up the picture frame and clutched it to my chest. I knew the only thing that would make me feel better was to talk to her, touch her, feel her; only then would I know for sure she was her. Being close to her image calmed me. I took the frame away from my chest and gazed at it. She had the same high cheekbones, the same tousled, short black hair, the same sparkling green eyes as the woman I had become obsessed with in the Afterlife. I just hoped that what she had inside her was the same.

"Macus, Macus!" Astinal shouted, running over to me.

"What, Astinal?" I asked, sighing.

"I spoke with her for you," he said, grinning at me.

"You did what?" I asked, sitting up in my bunk and gaping at him.

"I see the way you look at her, so I did something nice for my best friend," he paused. "She's on her way over."

"What?" My pulse quickened. "You didn't have to. I could have made the first move."

"You wouldn't have done anything, and what was I supposed to do, watch you watch her as she sauntered around the place?" he scoffed.

"How do I look?" I ran my hand through my cropped black hair and smoothed down my see-through white t-shirt, hoping it wasn't wrinkled.

"You look as great as you can," he said, clapping my back. "Now go get her."

I craned my neck over Astinal's shoulder. She was striding over me with a heavenly smile on her face and a twinkle in her emerald green eyes.

"Why did you talk to her for me?" I asked him.

"Because I love you man." Astinal grinned at me.

Astinal and I have been through too much together for him not to trust me now. My memory of the first time I met her brought back too many hidden emotions. I had been overwhelmed by his kindness, and the fact that he had my back, but right now I felt shunned from him. I just hope our friendship can withstand this current turmoil.

ELEVEN

THE MEMORIES

"Victor, may I speak with you for a moment?" I asked, walking over to Curtis' bunk, where Curtis, Victor and Nigel were lounging.

"Of course," Victor replied, leaping off the ground. "Shall we take a walk?" He proffered me his arm, and I looped mine through it. "I've been waiting for you to come to me," he said as we walked. Nigel and Curtis stared after us with puzzled expressions, but I did nothing to appease their confusion.

"I think I am being followed," I said, once we were out of earshot of the others, not wanting to worry them with my jumbled thoughts.

"Yes, we are being followed," he agreed.

I hadn't expected him to agree with me so easily, but I breathed a sigh of relief, glad I wasn't going crazy. "I think it's the Guards, have they ever been this watchful?"

"No, I've never seen them act this way; this is new." Victor muttered to himself.

"I've been getting these flashes of images — visions, I guess I would call them — and they always arrive with a headache in my temple." Victor didn't respond, instead allowing me to form my thoughts at my own pace. "Whenever these visions come, I would see darkness and stone," I paused. "They seem to be one in the same, and I would get this overwhelming deep-seated fear whenever they would occur. Red feathers would flash across my vision, similar to the plumes on top of the Guard's helmets, along with spears with bright red blood dripping from their tips. In some of them I am chained to a podium, like the one Curtis described — naked and surrounded by Guards who are whipping me — but in these visions, it's as though I am looking at myself from a bird's-eye view, instead of living them. I think I am remembering something important, but I don't know what. I can't get my thoughts together enough to get a clear picture."

"Strange images have been popping up in my mind too, along with a vicious headache in my own temple," Victor confessed, when I had finished speaking.

"What do you think they mean?" I asked.

"I believe you are right, it means we are remembering, but maybe we aren't supposed to." Victor stopped mid-stride. "Have you told anyone else about these visions?"

"No, you are the only person. I had thought I was going crazy because deep down I knew these visions were real, but I didn't have the memories of places where I had seen them." I gripped onto his arm. It was nice to have him near me, listen to what I had to say and, most importantly, believe me.

"Do you remember our first walk?" Victor asked.

"No," I shook my head. "I honestly can't."

"They must've wiped more of your memory than they did of mine and Nigel's." He scratched his beardless chin. "Because I remember most of it, but not how it ended."

"What are you talking about?" I asked him.

"I remember how it started, what we saw, who we talked to but I don't remember why you were taken ill. I get flashes of Guards and I know they are the essential piece to remembering, but I can't seem to fit them together to recreate what had happened at the end. This leads me to believe that someone wiped more of your memory than mine as you don't even remember the entire day."

"Who do you think wiped them?" I asked, frowning at him.

"The Guards." He said, deadpan.

"The Guards? But they can't do that, can they?" Victor's words were starting to make me nervous.

"I don't know yet, but they must have a host of abilities we do not know. If they can disappear and appear at will, what else can they do?" He raised his eyebrows conspiratorially.

"I do not understand this place — it is governed by a different set of rules that, I guess, we will never understand." I said, sighing.

"It takes some getting used to," Victor agreed. "I usually attribute everything I am not used to to magic. It is the only way I can describe what is going on here, but even that is too vague for me to understand."

"I wish I could find out how this place works." I mused.

"So do I." Victor agreed

"I bet the Guards know. I think they are important," I said. "Have you noticed they are taking so many people away right now." I added, as an afterthought.

"Yes, it's troubling." Victor said, frowning.

"It's getting so bad. I notice at least one a day, but who knows how many takings I don't witness. They are so violent when they do so. Why are they so violent?"

"I don't know." Victor said, sighing defeatedly.

"Where do you think they take them when they go?" I asked, scratching my chin.

"I don't want to know." There was an ominous end to his statement, and a shiver ran down my spine.

We both fell silent. I tried to recall the images which flash through my mind and to find a connection to them, but my recent memory loss had obliterated the connection. If I could just find the missing link, the pieces could fall together.

We had resumed our walk by this point, letting our feet guide us through the maze of bunks. When I had gathered the images and made a coherent picture in my mind — the stone, the darkness, the flashes of spear tips and red plumes of feather, the podium and everything else I had complained of — I refocused on my surroundings. I gave a start as a wall made of the same stone which had been plaguing me for the last two weeks stood before me.

I grasped Victor's arm, waking him from his own reverie. "Look Victor," I gasped, pointing to the wall fifty feet in front of us. I had been so inwardly focused, I didn't see it coming. I looked around and nothing around us had changed, a myriad of people still milled around, the same forced laughter and chatter I had grown accustomed to bounced around, but a change formed in the atmosphere; a palpable heat. Something was amiss.

"This is what we've been seeing. I remember now," I breathed, taking the remaining fifty feet at a jog. I ran a hand over the alive and thrumming Wall. It gave off a wave of warmth several degrees higher than the air here. "Do you remember now?"

"I do," he reached out to the Wall, when he reached it. "We came here and walked the length of it until something stopped us..." he trailed off and closed his eyes, trying to recall the memory of that day.

I ran my hand along the warm Wall, trying to reignite my own memories. We walked alongside it for a time. Every niche turned my stomach, and each dent and fissure, triggered my synapses, but still I couldn't remember what we found in the end. We walked until a breeze hit my face. It carried with it a fresh, spring scent to it, of a meadow filled with wildflowers.

"We stopped here." I said. Keeping my eyes closed, I faced the Wall, placed both palms on it and put my face against the stone. Instead of the warm stone on my face, I felt a cool breeze which told me all was not as it seemed. I fluttered my eyes open and looked straight into the familiar darkness in the stone, and as I did so, a burst of images clouded my vision. Dark, sinister eyes shimmered and swam just out of reach and angry blue eyes glared at me with hatred. "I told you there was something here, but you didn't believe me until you stood right in front of it, like I am doing now."

Victor's arm brushed against mine, as he stood right next to me. "I saw it," he paused. "Then Nigel did. It took longer for him, but once you look into the stone at the right angle, anyone could see it. This is what they wanted us to forget."

"I remember being inside it, but I didn't get very far. I collapsed. That had to have been when I lost my memory. Why would they wipe our memory of this if they didn't have something to hide?" I asked, still staring into the hypnotic darkness.

"We need to find out. There is more going on here we are not aware of. Strange things happen here and we need to find out what, but I fear we have gone about it the wrong way." Victor answered, cryptically.

"What do you mean?" I asked, turning away from the stone and looking at Victor.

"If the Guards have been following and watching us ever since you woke up, we have led them right back to the place they worked so hard to make us forget. I assume we will suffer consequences," he paused. "Come on let's go, we do not want to give them another excuse to hurt us." He grabbed my arm and steered me away from the wall; I tried not to glance back at it, but couldn't help it. When I looked back, only the unassuming stone faced me, the dark imperfection having camouflaged back into it as soon as we had walked away.

"Where have you been?" Nigel asked, when we returned to our bunks. The lights had dimmed to a 'dusk' lighting and Nigel sat alone on the floor next to his bunk. Curtis wasn't with him so I assumed they had gone their separate ways for the day. Nigel sprang up from his seated position, threw his arms around my waist and hugged me, burying his face into my stomach. We had been away for longer than I had realised and the hurt on Nigel's face tugged at my heartstrings, but I knew Victor and I had important things to discuss — things Nigel wouldn't have understood.

"We were refreshing our memory," Victor said, sitting cross-legged on the floor. For an old man, he was nimble. Nigel and I sat as well, facing Victor.

"What do you mean 'refreshing your memory'?" Nigel asked, confused, looking between Victor and I.

"Well, what do you remember of our first walk?" Victor asked him.

"I don't know," Nigel shrugged, playing with the hem of his t-shirt.

"Think," Victor urged.

"Well, I remember we walked around and we saw loads of different people. We saw Mrs Scott, and I got scared 'cause she saw us looking and then we saw the food," he smiled at me. "And then..." Nigel hesitated.

"Yes, go on, what else?" Victor pressed.

"I don't remember anything else, my memory goes fuzzy," Nigel responded, rubbing his eyes. "I think we came back straight after, but then how did Violet get hurt...?"

"Dig deep Nigel. Try to remember," Victor pushed.

Nigel screwed his eyes shut, his face reddening in the effort to bring forth a forgotten memory. "I don't–I can't remember," he said, letting out a breath.

"It's okay Nigel, you don't have to remember just yet, there's time." Victor said, patting Nigel on the back.

"I'm getting a headache. I'm gonna go to my bunk and lie down," Nigel said in a small voice, getting up and walking away from us. His head bowed and he was massaging his temples.

"Why don't we just tell him? Why were you so hard on him?" I asked Victor once Nigel had walked out of earshot. "Wouldn't it be easier to remind him, than to make him remember something he has clearly forgotten. He's not like us."

"He has to remember for himself," Victor replied. "The memory will be clearer if he does it himself."

"We should just tell him," I muttered, crossing my arms over my chest.

"You underestimate him don't you?" Victor said, looking at me out of the corner of his eyes.

"He is really young and a lot of the situations we are dealing with are more of an adult nature. I don't think he's not mature enough to handle it." I said honestly.

"I thought you would say that, but he has to learn things for himself. We can't mollycoddle him. He may look young but he has been through a lot more than either of us have," Victor finished.

"You shouldn't assume you know about my past and my hurdles. I don't make assumptions about you, so I'd prefer it if you didn't do the same," I said, jutting out my chin in defiance.

"I didn't mean to upset you. I was trying to tell you that, even though he may look like a child, we should not treat him as such," Victor responded.

"What makes you so sure?"

"You were not here when he first arrived. You did not see the state he was in, nor have you seen his transformation." I felt guilty. Who was I to think others had had a better life than me? In the grand scheme of things, I had it easy compared to others, and besides that, I chose to come here.

"I'm sorry for assuming," I said, my face reddening in embarrassment.

"There's no need to apologise. Learn from these things, and never judge a book by its cover, Violet. Learn that, especially if you want to meet Him," Victor said.

My head snapped up, I glared at Victor, trying to read his expression, he met my gaze, but his face showed nothing. "How-?" I started.

"You don't need to say anything for me to know your thoughts, Violet," Victor said, interrupting me. "Your actions and reactions let on more than you think and I have taken notice. I also witnessed the journey you have taken since your memories were wiped. You are strong and you are getting stronger every day. I remember when you first arrived, how keen you were to explore — even with your body in that state — and find out more information about this place. I haven't seen such tenacity in someone here since Nigel."

I shook my head, trying to grasp what Victor had just revealed. "I didn't want to tell anyone out right," I admitted. "This is a sensitive matter and I knew I needed to find someone I could trust," I looked into his steely gray eyes. "Can I trust you?"

He nodded his head. "We want the same things Violet," he paused. "But why are you looking?"

I didn't speak for a minute. I hadn't even answered this question myself. "I needed to know why He made my life so miserable when everyone else around me went through life so easily."

"I understand," he said, leaning forward and looking into my eyes. "I want to help you. I have been through too much for me to be dumped here and left to rot. I need my questions answered too."

"What about Nigel, do you think he can handle it?" I asked.

"He is more equipped at handling anything than you seem to think," Victor paused. "Nigel told me what he could remember from his past life and his story is chilling. I bet my life he has experienced more pain than either of us have, and I have fought in two wars."

"I didn't know that about Nigel. I assumed that... I just assumed," I blinked back tears, ashamed I judged someone that I loved so harshly. "I'm sorry."

"As I said, there is no need to apologise," Victor said, laying a comforting hand on my shoulder. "But do you want to find Him together?" Victor asked, raising his eyebrows and cocking his head to one side; a small conspiratorial smile on his lips.

I thought about what we discussed, the Guards, the Wall and our memory loss, and I grinned. I was glad to have found another person here who shared my goal.

"What about Curtis?" I asked. "Shall we bring him in on this?"

"He has a stake in this. We know he desperately wants to find his friend," Victor answered. "Plus, we will need muscle in our group. We can't do much with an old man, a child and a teenager," he finished chuckling to himself.

"Hey," I said. "In the eyes of the law I am an adult."

Victor simply shrugged in response.

"Okay, we will do this together," I nodded in agreement, inwardly thinking I would need all the help I could get anyway.

Victor grinned. "This is what I have always enjoyed doing."

"What's that?" I asked.

"Espionage," he said laughing.

I gave him a questioning look. "What do you mean?"

"Ah, my past." He scratched his chin in thought. "I guess you would need some back story."

I shifted on Nigel's bed, getting comfortable, in preparation of the story ahead.

"As I said, I have fought in two Wars," he started. "World War Two and Vietnam, and both were the most harrowing times of my life, yet I managed to survive them whilst watching my comrades get gunned down and blown to pieces. I was made to participate in a firing squad against a deserter. He had been my best friend." His face grew so morose, I yearned to take away his pain, but I knew my comfort wouldn't be accepted. "You don't have to look so shocked Violet, we all have our past to deal with. This is just my story. Anyway, as I was saying, two wars… in Vietnam I started as a soldier, but quickly grew in ranks to become a sergeant, but I was deemed too useful for the front lines. One day a gray haired man came into my tent, he ordered all my men out and sat me down. He offered me a new role, as a spy. I quickly accepted, thinking this was the only way I would survive the War. For the rest of the war, I was used to gather intelligence on the enemy's army. I was to find dissidents within the enemy forces and persuade them to defect. The missions were dangerous and the consequences, if I were caught, would have been certain death, but I was a master of it."

"So how are you going to use these skills here?" I asked, genuinely curious.

"Well, whilst the Guards spy on us, we will spy on them. We need to know when and who is watching us. Once we've figured that out, we can get back to the tunnel without them knowing, and see what's hidden inside it."

"Brilliant. When should we tell the others?" I asked, excitedly.

"Tomorrow." He said.

I yawned and rubbed my eyes. Victor yawned and stretched beside me. I knew it was nearing the time to sleep. Nigel was making his way back towards us, kicking his feet. Victor and I got up from his bunk and walked over to our own so Nigel could be alone. Victor stopped halfway to his, looked back and said, "We'll talk again in the morning."

He walked back to his bunk and lay on top of it. Nigel crawled under his blanket. Neither of them went straight to sleep. Victor lay on his back, and the dim lighting reflected off his bright eyes, as he stared at the ceiling far above us, deep in thought. Nigel lay unmoving but the absence of his soft snores suggested he was also awake.

I sat up on my bunk for a while. Since getting to the Wall again today, the Guard's dark eyes, which had tormented my thoughts, were now so clear in my mind. He had been at the Wall when I had fallen ill, and I had also seen him this morning staring at me when I woke up. Now that my memory had returned and I had the chance to think about it, I had seen him watching me ever since I had arrived. He always seemed to be nearby.

I suddenly remembered the small package Mrs Scott had given me when we had visited her last. I had chucked it in a drawer and completely forgotten about it until now. I reached over to the bedside table and slid the top drawer open, afraid of making too much noise at this late hour, and rummaged around for the object. I felt it at the back of the drawer, closed my hand around it and drew it out, quietly shutting the drawer afterwards. The lights had dimmed further, but there was still enough light for me to see what I was doing. I carefully opened the gift, wrapped in brown packaging — identical to the paper used to wrap the clothing we had been gifted — silently wondering what lay inside. Something shiny attached to a leather chord, slipped out onto the bed covers. I grabbed it and held it in my hands, turning the stone this way and that so that the dim light glinted in the luminous, green stone. I didn't immediately recognise the stone, but untangled the thin chord and put the necklace on, tucking the pendant underneath my t-shirt.

I turned to the direction the Wall lay, wishing for its comforting warmth, but it stood too far away. I shifted in my bed and closed my eyes. It took me some time to get to sleep, as thoughts of Hell, of the events of today and of those hauntingly dark eyes took over my thoughts.

The next thing I knew, Victor was shaking me awake very early the next morning.

"He remembers." Was all he said before walking away. It was all I needed to hear. I jumped out of my bed, pulled on the white jacket

I had worn daily and strode the three paces to Nigel's bunk. The lights hadn't brightened to their fullest capacity — giving the space an eerie golden glow — and through the half-light, I could see Nigel and Victor sitting on Nigel's bunk, shrouded in shadow, waiting for me. I hastily ran a hand through my short messy hair to neaten it, patting down the ends which persistently stuck up in odd angles no matter how hard I tried to tame them.

"Tell me everything you remember Nigel," I commanded, perching on the edge of his bed, excited to see some progress.

Nigel sat on his bed cocooned in his blanket, his small face peering through the gap. His big brown eyes were wide and excited. He recounted all of his experiences, and he even mentioned that he thought the Guards had been following him too.

"I like to go for walks to see my friends," he began. "But lately the Guards keep on staring at me, and when I catch them, they won't look away. They would keep looking at me like I did something wrong, but I haven't done anything wrong. Sometimes they would come and talk to me and say normal things, like 'How's your day going?', or 'Who are you visiting today?' and 'Where are your friends?', but they would get angry with me when I wouldn't tell them anything about you guys." He looked up at me with pleading eyes, his face gaunt in the half-light. "I didn't tell them anything, I swear."

"It's okay Nigel," I said soothingly. "What else do you remember?"

"I remember how you got ill and I remember the Wall," he said excitedly. "I remember the Guards threatening us and the darkness in the Wall. It looked like a tunnel," he paused. "I also remember why you became ill. What are we going to do, Violet?" He looked deep into my emerald green eyes and I knew, in that moment, I had his trust. I grasped his shoulder and pulled him into a tight hug. He clumsily extricated himself from his blanket and wrapped his arms around me tighter than I expected, squeezing the air out of me.

"We don't know just yet, but we will figure it out," I murmured into his hair.

Nigel lifted his head from my chest and looked up at me. "Did I do okay Violet?" he asked, a worried expression marring his face.

"You did amazing, Nigel," I said.

"What about Curtis?" Nigel mumbled, putting his head back against my chest again.

"What about Curtis?" I asked in return.

"Do you think he will want to know what we have uncovered? He told us about his friend who went missing and he wanted to find out what happened to him," Nigel said. "If I was him, I would want to help us too."

"Why don't you ask him yourself?" Victor said.

We looked up from our embrace and watched Curtis stride over to us with a bemused smile on his face.

"What's going on here then?" he asked lightly, hovering over us. Nigel, Victor and I looked up at him, grinning wildly. I patted the space next to me on Nigel's bed and Curtis sat with us.

"Are you ready for an adventure?" Nigel asked him, crawling into my lap to get comfortable.

"What kind of adventure?" Curtis questioned, raising his eyebrow.

"The adventure that will give you all the answers you are looking for," I replied, cryptically.

Curtis sat with us and we told him all we remembered of when I had fallen ill and our suspicions after I had awoken.

"We believe someone wiped our memories, Violet's more so than mine and Nigel's," Victor began.

"Someone wiped them?" Curtis asked. "How do you know?"

"Well, none of us could remember how I had fallen ill." I explained. "For me, it was as though someone had bored a hole in my brain and everything I had experienced on the first walk had leaked out of it. I remember how I got here, and the obstacles I went through, but a big chunk of time is missing from my time here in Hell. So yesterday, when Victor and I found the Wall again, and that strange tunnel inside it, our old memories came flooding back."

"Also, the Guards have also been following us," Victor added.

"I've noticed that too, but I didn't know what to make of it," Curtis said, scratching his chin.

"I didn't either," I said in agreement. "But for all of us to notice, there must be truth to it."

"But what I don't get is, why did whoever wiped your memories wipe more of Violet's memories, than you two?" Curtis asked, looking from Nigel, to Victor and finally to me.

"I have a theory," Victor chimed in. "I believe they thought Violet was mentally stronger than us — the leader of our group — and with fewer memories it would be harder for her to remember what had happened at the Wall than Nigel or I; but they didn't realise how strong Violet is. Nigel and I only remembered because of her. She helped us remember even the small amount of memory they deemed her to keep."

Curtis nodded solemnly in agreement. "So, what do we do now?"

Victor motioned for us to be quiet. He stared intently over my shoulder, and before I looked, Victor spoke. "I think he wants a word with you Violet," he said pointing to a spot behind me. I spun around. The dark eyed Guard — the one that had occupied my thoughts for weeks now — stood five bunks away, staring right at me. Then he beckoned me over to him.

Nigel moved from my lap to the bed allowing me to get up from the bunk. I took a deep breath and walked over to him, twisting my hands together and running through different dread-filled scenarios in my mind as to why he wanted to talk to me, all of which, for some reason, ended in my beheading. I stopped short two feet away from him.

"You need to come closer." His whispered words pulled me closer to him than any action would have. My legs moved of their own accord, closing the gap between us until we were mere inches apart. His body heat radiated from him. He seemed to run at a higher temperature than I did. A single bead of sweat ran down his tanned skin from the nape of his neck. I followed its tracks until it tangled into his coarse chest hair and disappeared underneath his chest plate. At this proximity, I could smell a faint waft of lavender coming from him. My favourite scent.

We stood facing each other for a moment without speaking, drinking in each other's features and attributes. He was a head and a half taller than me, so I had to crane my neck to look up at his face. His strong square jaw, chiselled cheekbones, and long dark lashes which framed his now familiar coal black eyes spoke of an ancient beauty. His muscles were sculpted to perfection, each well defined, and even though he stood calmly, his biceps bulged and thick veins popped out from beneath his forearms, clearly displaying the powerful strength which he held in check. I almost reached out a hand to touch him, to feel his warm skin beneath my fingers. I desperately wanted to trace his veins, hold him and take away the tension he had built up over the centuries, but I held back. I looked back up to his face and ran my eyes over his full lips and envisioned myself wrapped in his strong arms, one of his hands cupped behind my neck and the other lovingly stroking my cheek. In this fantasy, our lips would meet, tentatively at first, but the tension would build and our kisses would turn passionate in an instant.

He cleared his throat, snapping me out of my glorious fantasy and I wrenched my eyes away from his lips to meet his dark ones. "You need to stop," he whispered, barely moving his lips, but with each word, fear rippled through my body.

"What do you mean?" I asked shakily.

"Don't play dumb Viole. You are better than that," he muttered.

"How d-?" I started.

"It doesn't matter how," he interrupted. "Now, shut up and listen. I am not supposed to be here, but I came to warn you. They are watching, they know and you need to stop," he finished, looking pleadingly into my eyes, as though he was trying to convey a thought he was either unwilling or unable to articulate. His energy swept over my body, drawing me closer to him.

I succumbed to the urge for physical contact, and placed my right hand gingerly on his bicep, but that wasn't enough. I clutched at it, but it was so big, I couldn't wrap my hand around it. He shivered beneath my fingers and his heat coursed up through my arm and slowly warmed my whole body. I looked up to his face but his eyes were glued to my hand on his skin. He finally looked back at me and in those coal black eyes I sensed a love they held; a love for me.

"How do you know my name?" I asked.

He looked down at me and took the hand I held to his arm into his own; he did not respond to my question, but simply held my hand in his.

"Why do I keep seeing you everywhere?" I was becoming frustrated. "Why do your eyes follow me and why do I think this is not our first meeting?" I took half a step closer to him, closing the space between us further still.

"Because it is not our first meeting. We have met before," he answered. "But it was long ago, in a time we have both forgotten, but that is not what I came to talk about. You need to let this go."

I tried to take my hand out of his, but his grip tightened, desperate to keep a hold of me. I sighed.

"Why are the Guards so aggressive?" I asked. "Why do they take us away and where do they take us?" He didn't respond to my questions.

"If you will not answer my questions then it's best if you go," I said. Reaching my other hand up, I gently extricate myself from his vice–like grip breaking the physical connection between us. I rubbed my hand where the ache of his grip still lingered and finally tore my eyes away from his.

"I am sorry, I didn't mean to hurt you," he said, reaching out to hold my hand again, but I flinched away from him, afraid of the pain he could inflict upon me.

"Thanks for the warning," I muttered, backing away from him. "But I'm going back to my friends." I took one last glance up at his face but he had already shut down. His eyes had turned impassive, the set of his jaw had turned hard and his posture suggested that he had put a barrier up between us. If I wanted to go back to him, I wouldn't have been able to. As I walked away, I put my fingers to my lips and tasted the saltiness of his skin on them and closed my eyes inhaling his somehow familiar scent. I looked back when I reached the bunk, but he had already disappeared.

"What did he want?" Victor asked when I had settled back onto Nigel's bunk.

"Yeah, what did he want?" Curtis asked, glowering darkly at the spot where the dark eyed Guard had just stood.

"He came to warn us," I said, frowning at Curtis' negative response. "He said, 'they are watching and they know what we are doing'."

"The Guards are watching us, they haven't made it hard for us to notice," Curtis scoffed, still glowering off into the distance.

"Yeah," Nigel agreed, climbing into my lap again.

"They don't know anything, I bet they're just trying to scare us," Curtis said. "I say we carry on. I need to know what happened to David." He slammed his fist onto the bed, and his face was contorted in anger and grief over the loss of his best friend.

"Calm down Curtis." Victor chided. "We will find the answers we are looking for, but we need to be careful and take his warning seriously. That guard wouldn't have spoken to Violet if he didn't think she was in danger. This is out of character for them. We have to take this warning seriously."

"How do you know what the guards think, or is this just another one of your theories?" Curtis jeered at Victor.

"Please Curtis, no matter what happens now, we are all in this together," I said. "We can't turn on each other when we're working towards the same goal."

"Sorry Violet," Curtis said, finally looking at me. "I am just trying to wrap my head around the fact that our progress seems to have halted just because of a Guard's warning. I need to know what happened to David. I need to know if I can find him again." I smiled gently at him and he seemed to calm down, looking at me with sorrowful eyes.

"Let's try to find out as much as we can about this place, but now we will have to be more discreet," Victor said. "Be careful about where we speak and make sure no Guards are around us when we do so."

"Okay," Curtis conceded; I squeezed his hand, glad he had calmed down and I saw a small smile tug at the corner of his lips.

I looked around, making sure no Guards were in sight. "Curtis, do you remember anything that happened the day you followed David? Think hard, you must've some memory of that night left."

Curtis stared off into space, withdrawing into himself — his eyes glazed over and held a far away look — to search for those forgotten memories. His furrowed brow deepened the longer he thought. He put his head in his hands and groaned. "I remember following him," Curtis intoned. "He was walking fast between the bunks, as though he had taken that specific route many times before and knew it off by heart. I remember him stopping to talk to Mrs Scott, they spoke for a couple of minutes and then he hurried off. I didn't have time to speak to her, I waved, but she didn't seem to see me. Anyway, David walked a long way, he didn't stop again, but kept on walking for around half an hour. I tried to stay a good distance away so he wouldn't suspect me of following him."

"Did you see anyone acting suspiciously?" Victor asked.

"No," he said. "But the Guards watched us, much like they watch us now. I didn't think anything of it back then." Curtis answered, as though he was in a trance.

"Okay, so you saw Guards. What happened next?" Victor urged.

"The memory becomes foggy. I am not too sure..." Curtis hesitated.

"Did you see a wall?" Nigel asked, trying to keep Curtis focused on his train of thought.

Curtis put his head in his hands, rubbed his eyes in his palms, then rubbed his temples and groaned. "I think so..." he mumbled.

"You have to be sure, Curtis," Victor pressed.

He looked up, his eyes still closed, but then his face cleared, the strain of recollecting lifted from his tense features and he smiled an ethereal smile. "Yes, I remember. I caught up to him at a wall. It was such an unusual wall, it radiated heat and thrummed with life. He jogged up to it and pressed his face against it as though he was looking through it."

Nigel and I glanced at each other and shared a smile of relief. Curtis was remembering and his grin widened. "He talked into it, as though there was someone in the stone. He stayed at the Wall for half an hour before making his way back to his bunk. On the way back, he stopped and sat with Mrs Scott again and they talked for a long time. I left them to it, as I couldn't hear what they were saying, and he didn't come back for another few hours. I believe they had been talking the whole time, but I can't be sure. I have gone to see Mrs Scott since then to ask what they talked about, but she refuses to tell me. She also won't tell me if he went elsewhere before he came back to the bunk. She repeatedly tells me I have to wait until I am ready."

"We're planning on heading back to the Wall to find out what's inside the tunnel David was talking to, but it will take a while to plan," I told Curtis.

"We want to find out where it leads. The Guards wouldn't have stopped us going through it, if it didn't hold answers," Victor added.

"We need all the help we can get. Will you help us Curtis?" I asked him, grasping his arm and looking desperately into his eyes.

Curtis nodded to each of us but his eyes lingered on mine. "I will be glad to."

"But first, we need to visit Mrs Scott," Victor said smiling. "Well done." He added, clapping Curtis on his back.

I took my hand off Curtis' arm and put my fingers to my lips again. I could still smell the faint lavender scent of the dark-eyed Guard and smiled. I smiled wider when I remembered that it was the arm which I had lost all movement in when I had first gotten here and grinned thinking of the progress I had made since then. Looking around at the three people around me and my heart burst with love. I was so lucky to have found them, and even luckier that they were willing to help me.

TWELVE

MRS SCOTT'S STORY

I strode into the Altar room tearing off my helmet and threw it across the room. It crashed into the wall and the echo of the collision rented through the air. "It is her!" I shouted, adding my voice to the din.

"Macus, calm down," Astinal yelled, striding over and putting a hand on my shoulder. He guided me to a chair which had materialised in the middle of the room. "Sit and tell me what's the matter."

"I spoke with her. I know I shouldn't have Astinal, but I needed to speak to her, touch her. She is her. I know it, Astinal." I licked my lips. "I needed to tell her she was in danger, but she wouldn't heed my warnings. She was too busy asking unnecessary questions." I pounded my fist against my thigh, my whole body shaking; the heat from her hand was still seared on my skin.

Astinal crouched next to me, holding my fists in his huge hands. "Macus, I don't understand. You will have to calm down," he said. "They can hear you," he added in a harsh whisper.

I took a deep calming breath and whispered. "I spoke to her today, Astinal."

"But, you shouldn't have, how could you be so stupid?" Finally grasping what I meant, it was now his turn to be angry.

"I am sorry, but I couldn't just sit idly by. I needed to warn her — she was being reckless and stupid. How could she do this to me again?" I cried.

"Are you certain it is her?" Astinal let go of my hands.

"I have never been as certain of anything as this in my life. I spoke to her. I touched her. I know it," I told him, trying to convey my sincerity.

He took a deep breath. "Well, we will have to do everything in our power to stop her from making the same mistake. What do you have in mind, Macus?" Astinal asked, his face still a hard line. I smiled at him, knowing his trust in me had returned, even if he seemed reluctant to help me.

"I am not too sure yet, but when I have a plan I will tell you," I replied. "But I need to know one thing Astinal?"

He only grunted in response.

"Do you trust me?" For some reason, in these past few weeks his trust in me had waned, and now more than ever, I needed his full support.

"Events are happening that you cannot know about yet," he started. "Even if you have already gleaned most of the details."

I looked at him confused. "I don't understand."

"I cannot, in good conscience, tell you everything yet, but I will. I promise." He finished.

I nodded, still not satisfied with his response, but knowing he was being honest. "Right, I will tell you when I know how we can help her." I said, deciding to drop the subject.

"Good. I eagerly anticipate the day we save her." The corners of his mouth lifted, but immediately returned to a frown.

"And you will be by my side?" I asked.

"Always, brother," he replied. "Now, I was about to call you Macus. I summoned Stuart Willis in to give us an update on his task. Are you ready to get back to work?"

"Yes," I replied nodding, heaving myself off the chair. I heard the rattle of chains under the armrests and shuddered at the sound. I strode over and picked up my discarded helmet, brushed the dust and debris off it and pushed it onto my head to try to hide my reddened face and tear-filled eyes. The chair had disappeared when I came back to Astinal's side. He stood behind the Altar facing the door. We waited in silence for a minute, then a knock came. The door opened without waiting for an answering call, and through the opening Turi walked in.

"Stuart Willis, Sir," he announced, banging the butt of his spear once on the floor. Stuart Willis shuffled in. His awful stench preceding him, his back was bent over double, shoulders hunched and head hung low. He didn't look up at either Astinal or myself, instead focusing his gaze on the earthen floor.

"Turi, you may leave us." Astinal dismissed the Guard, and the door snapped shut behind him.

Astinal did not speak, filling the room with a palpable tension. Stuart shuffled from foot to foot and rubbed his throat staring at the floor; still refusing to meet our eyes. Finally, after five minutes of tense silence, he glanced up, looked at Astinal and then at me — obviously looking for a reason for the uncomfortable delay — before staring back down at the floor.

"Erm..." Stuart started, tearing his hands away from his throat and wringing them together.

"What have you found for us?" Astinal interrupted.

"Well, erm, well-," Stuart stuttered.

"Spit it out, boy," Astinal shouted.

"Well, they, I mean to say, the black-haired woman and her friends, well, they just hang out together, y'know." Stuart muttered, shrugging.

"What do you mean 'just hang out'?" Astinal spat out. "Explain yourself."

"Sorry ma–Sir," Stuart squeaked out. I rolled my eyes at the pitiful show Stuart was giving us. "They ain't done nothin' out of the ordinary. I watch 'em all day and they talk and laugh but they ain't done nothin' suspicious, but I'd like to add, you ain't given me any par-parameters."

"Parameters? Parameters?" Astinal yelled, gripping the altar in a white knuckled grip. "I need not give you parameters. I only need to tell you to do something and the reward should be more than enough of an incentive for you to get the job done."

"But I don't know what I'm searchin' for," Stuart yelled.

"You do not speak to me in that tone," Astinal roared back.

Stuart shrank back. "I am sorry, Sir," he apologised. "I didn't mean to... I ain't found any evidence of anything other than friendship, Sir." He finished, looking downcast.

"You may leave," Astinal dismissed him, tsking as he turned away from him.

"What about my payment?" Stuart asked, taking a hesitant step forward.

"Payment? Payment? You expect me to pay you when you haven't even completed the job?" Astinal spun around and strode around the altar towards Stuart, his face contorted into a look of pure rage as flecks of spittle flew from his mouth. Stuart took one look at Astinal, spun around and ran, but the door swung open just as Stuart reached it and he ran straight into it collapsing onto the floor on his arse, scrambling to his feet as Turi walked in.

"Take him." Astinal commanded. Turi and another guard — drawn in by the sounds of raised voices — grabbed Stuart by the upper arms and dragged him out. The door snapped shut behind them, but I could still hear Stuart's muffled yells as they dragged him down the clinically white hallway.

"What a waste of time," Astinal muttered under his breath.

"I agree, he is an utter waste of space," I said.

"I thought the incentive would be enough to have him on our side," Astinal muttered.

"Shall we dispose of him?" I asked.

"I don't know," Astinal replied.

"Has he compromised us?" I asked.

"No, I know he is too stupid to do anything against us," he paused. "But in any case, keep an eye on him. A change is in the air and we will need every man we can get on our side, even if it is scum like Stuart Willis."

"I will leave you now, Astinal," I said, taking my leave.

"We will speak soon, Macus. Take care," Astinal said to my retreating back.

Unsure of how to go on, and having no obligations for a few hours, I made my way to my personal chambers. I had a tendency to walk through the empty white corridors every time I needed to think. The clinically empty atmosphere helped me clear my mind, and today was no different. I didn't trust Stuart Willis, and I just hoped he wouldn't betray us.

My chamber door opened of its own accord when I was five feet from it, as though it knew I was approaching it. I strode through the threshold without breaking stride, and closed and locked the door behind me; not wanting anyone to disturb me. But, now I was in the place I yearned to be, I found that it was too claustrophobic. The sweet smell of birch smoke, which I had burnt last night, hung heavy in the too hot air.

Not knowing what to do with myself or where else I would go, I made my way over to my night stand across the room. I knew what it held and I would just be torturing myself, but after my recent meeting with Violet, I had to see her again; even if it was a cheap imitation.

I picked up the gilded silver picture frame and held it to me. It had been years since I had thought of her, and now in the last two weeks, I couldn't stop thinking of her. The image I held in front of me was a faded black-and-white photo which looked remarkably like Violet. It had been taken long before anyone had invented the camera. I stared at the image in awe of the beauty radiating in the woman's eyes. The resemblance between the woman in the image and to the woman in the Afterlife was uncanny, and now there were three of them.

"Did you come back to me?" I asked the still image.

She didn't respond, and I didn't expect her to. "I have waited for you to come back for centuries." I continued, I needed to speak to her, and seeing as she ignored my warnings earlier, this seemed to be the only way to do so.

"Today I felt it - when we touched - the electricity which coursed through me, which still courses through me, was a testament to the truth," I paused and licked my lips, nervous to say the words to her. "You are her, Isobel. You came back and I am so happy. Now we can finally be together again."

"Macus, the afternoon meeting will begin in five minutes. Meet me at the altar room." Astinal's voice rang in my head and I jumped at the sound. I hadn't been aware of how much time had passed and now I was being summoned to return to my duties. I ignored his summons and stayed in my room to brood. I wouldn't be good company at the moment anyway. Astinal didn't summon me again and I was glad for it.

I undressed, dropping my clothing where I stood and crawled into bed. I lay the picture frame next to me and tried to clear my mind. It was some time later that I fell asleep, with thoughts of Violet, Isobel and our intertwined lives penetrating into my dreams.

Over the next four days, Curtis, Nigel, Victor and I spent every minute of every day — which we didn't spend sleeping — together, perfecting the plan to reach the tunnel in the Wall again. I felt deeply that I needed to know what lay beyond it. It had to be a key to finding out how this place works. The Guard's wouldn't have tried to stop us going through if it wasn't an important place here. We devised a timetable to pin down which Guards watched us at what time. The first Guard to watch us had dark eyes. By now I recognised him by the set of his shoulders and his gait. He was the Guard who had come to warn me. A shorter Guard with piercing blue eyes, that I could see from my bunk, then relieved him after a couple of hours. He had only started to watch us after the dark-eyed Guard had come to speak to me the other day; which I thought was suspect. I wondered what he wanted with me, and why he started watching me *after* the conversation with the dark eyed Guard.

When I caught him watching us for the first time, it triggered a memory of the Wall; a memory which hadn't resurfaced beforehand.

I remembered he had been with the dark-eyed Guard at the Wall on our first walk. He had been the one who threatened us with his spear. Whilst watching us, the blue eyed Guard would never keep a low profile or pretend to be doing something else, unlike the other Guards. Instead, he kept his gaze trained on us with a deep frown on his face, as though everything we did pissed him off.

"I can't believe that blue eyed Guard isn't discreet in his watches," I scoffed from my bed.

"I know," Victor agreed, hearing me. He got up from his bunk and made his way over to me, keeping a watchful eye on the blue-eyed Guard as he did so. He sat next to me and made himself comfortable. Neither of us spoke, preferring to remain silent as we watched the Guards, as they watched us.

Two hours later, a taller Guard relieved him. This Guard walked around us in a circle around a 100-metre radius. He didn't pay too much attention to us but I knew he would always keep us in his line of sight. Several more Guards watched us throughout the day, but I could never make out any identifying details in their faces, having to, instead, rely on the time of day to know which of the Guard's were watching. The daily timetable and rotation didn't change, making it as easy for us to keep track of them and refine our plan, as it was for them to keep track of us.

"One of the Guards is watching you guys again." A dark-haired woman whispered to Victor and I. I recognised her and I knew she lived at least a five-minute walk away from us. How would she know that a Guard was watching us.

"Really?" I asked, trying to be casual. "I hadn't noticed, thanks for telling us." I glanced at Victor but his face was impassive, giving nothing away to the strange lady.

"I'm afraid that they will take you away," she said. "Like the others." She added the last bit in a scared whisper.

"Why would they do that?" I asked. "We've done nothing wrong."

The lady shrugged, looking a little bewildered, and walked away from us.

Several times a day, visitors came over to our bunks to inform us of the Guard's strange behaviour. Each time, we lied and pretended not to have noticed, so as to not raise suspicion amongst the others. As often as people came to warn us, others kept a wide berth, not wanting the Guards to turn their attention onto themselves.

Nigel and Curtis made their way over. They had just come back from a walk and they glanced at the dark-haired lady as she walked back to her bunk.

"Another warning?" Curtis asked, settling on my bed and putting a warm hand on my knee.

"Yes," I replied, taking his hand in mine and squeezing it. "More people come to us daily, but I'm afraid to trust them. I don't know them as well as I know you guys." Curtis, Nigel and Victor each looked at me and smiled. Curtis took his hand from mine, scratched his nose, and then rested his hand on his own thigh. A wave of sadness washed over me when he didn't hold my hand again. I had grown used to his touch over the last few days, but deep down secretly wished it was the dark-eyed Guard's touch instead. I still remembered how warm he was, and even though his scent had dissipated, wafts of phantom lavender still haunted me.

"So now we know who watches us and when, when can we go back to the Wall?" I asked the others, trying to get my mind away from thoughts of the dark-eyed Guard.

"We need to go as soon as possible," Curtis said.

"We need to see Mrs Scott first before we make a move," Victor chimed in, in a calming voice. "We need to hear her account of what happened when David went to see her, the day he disappeared. We need all the information we can gather before we do anything." Victor finished.

"Okay, but we need to do this right," Curtis said. "If Mrs Scott wouldn't tell me what David talked to her about, then we don't stand a chance of getting the information out of her with all of us crowding around and berating her." He paused. "You should go on your own, Violet — Mrs Scott would respond better to you alone."

Both of the men looked at me, waiting for my response.

"She seems interested in you," Nigel said. "We just came from her bunk and she asked after you."

I sighed, knowing I wouldn't be able to get out of this one. "Fine. I will go." I said, defeated. "But if you expect me to remember everything she says verbatim, then you have another thing coming."

"Your memory has been satisfactory so far, and I am sure you will remember the important parts," Victor said, helping me off my bunk and steering me toward Mrs Scott's.

"Don't be too long," Curtis called after me, as I shuffled away.

I took my time walking to Mrs Scott's bunk, nervous at the reception I would receive and unsure of whether she would talk with me at all. I didn't have the same faith as the others, and if she didn't, I would have to go back to the others having failed on my quest for information. What should I say to her? How should I broach the subject of David, the Wall, and everything else they had sent me to find out?

Several faces jumped out at me as I meandered my way to her. Some of them I recognised — Smith and Günter — but most of the surrounding people were strangers. I was used to knowing everyone in my vicinity, having grown up in a small town, and it was hard not being friendly towards people here. I hoped the atmosphere would change, but I cannot control others' emotions.

The route to Mrs Scott's bunk came as instinctual as though I was walking to school. It made me pause and wonder how I knew the route, but this was not the time to ponder it as I had just reached her bunk. Her wizened body sat in her old wooden rocking chair. Her eyes were shut. I was afraid she was sleeping. I was unsure of whether to wake her, but I tiptoed over to her anyway.

"I have been waiting for you, my dear," Mrs Scott croaked out, her eyes remaining closed. "Come, please take a seat." She gestured to her bunk.

I was taken aback and wondered how she knew I was there, but shuffled over to her bunk and perched at the edge of it, as I didn't want to disturb her pristine bed. I smelt her fresh flowery scent and smiled. A nondescript man came over carrying a familiar wooden cup full of steaming liquid.

"Here, Guest of Mrs Scott, please take this drink and make yourself comfortable," he said in a meek voice. He pushed the cup into my hand and I had little choice but to take it.

"What's in it?" I asked him, sniffing it. The complex scent of a mixture of different herbs assaulted my nose, but too many of them were vying for my attention for me to note them individually.

"It's just a calming tea — nothing poisonous." He smiled at me, revealing blackened and rotting teeth. I looked away from him, suppressed a revolted shudder and took a small sip of the tea, as he hovered over me watching intently. At first, the tea tasted bitter, but the aftertaste had a sweetness to it which made me want more. I took a longer swallow next time, closed my eyes and savoured the flavours. I picked out the strong mint, subtler dandelion and aniseed flavour, but there were many others I couldn't place.

"The tea's good isn't it?" Mrs Scott asked, snapping me out of my reverie.

"Mmm, yes it is," I agreed, glancing over at her. She had sat up in her rocking chair, her head resting on her steepled hands, and was staring at me.

"Why are you here, Violet?" She asked, sitting back in her chair but keeping her eyes trained on mine.

"I guess I'm looking for answers," I said.

"What are your questions?" She asked, accepting an identical wooden mug full of hot tea from the same man who had given me mine.

I took another sip of the tea to gather my thoughts and buy myself an extra couple of second's thinking time. "Well," I started. "I'm not too sure if you've heard, but my friends, Victor, Nigel, Curtis and I, have noticed that the Guards have been following and watching us over the past two weeks?"

"I heard about that and have seen it with my very eyes." She motioned, with an empty hand, for me to go on.

"And we've experienced different levels of memory loss all stemming from similar experiences." I paused, taking another sip of tea. "I didn't know that I had lost my memory at first, so it took me a while to realise that it had been modified. Flashes of images would come to mind which I didn't remember ever witnessing. A headache brewed whenever they appeared, and, at the same time, a weird sense of foreboding would come over me. I confided in Victor and he admitted that he experienced a similar memory loss. Slowly, Nigel, Victor, Curtis and I regained our memory, and we realised it was because we all went to the Wall." I took another sip of tea when I had finished.

"Yes, Curtis has mentioned that. Where is he? I would have expected him to come with you, or did he think I would talk to you more candidly without him here?" She smiled and continued without waiting for an answer. "Very well, I will answer your questions."

"Curtis told us you were good friends with David, the man who had occupied the bunk next to his. He said David spoke to you after coming back from the Wall, right before the Guards took him away. I was wondering if you could tell me what you talked about?" I looked at the dregs of tea leaves — coated by a single sip of tea — left in the cup instead of looking at Mrs Scott. I thought that if I looked right at her, she would change her mind and not tell me a thing.

Mrs Scott didn't speak for a moment, and thinking I had been right, I put down my cup on the bedside table and geared myself up to leave.

"David was a lovely but foolish man," she finally said. "When I first met him, two years after he came here, he had it in his head he wasn't dead and he could escape and go on living the life he had lived down there. I was the only person who knew he thought this way, everyone else thought he was just in denial, much like most people here. But, a month after our first meeting, I noticed he would disappear for hours at a time. I sent one of my loyal friends to see what he got up to. He came back and told me David was sitting at, what you call, 'The Wall', talking to himself. My friend didn't know who he spoke to, or, if he indeed spoke to anyone at all. I was too weak to make the journey myself, so I called David over to my bunk after one of his trips to question him. He was unwilling to share his experiences, and knowing I would have to gain his trust, I told him a story from the old times."

"What was the story?" I asked.

"That's for another time, dear," Mrs Scott smiled. "He trusted me more after hearing it, and he finally told me what he saw inside the Wall."

"And, what did he see, Mrs Scott?" I asked her, sitting up a little straighter on her bed.

"Patience my dear," Mrs Scott cautioned. She drained the rest of her tea and set the cup aside on her bedside table. "He said he saw a dark space inside the Wall, but I am sure you know of that, don't you, dear. He also told me he heard voices sometimes and he could communicate with them. The voices would change over time, and sometimes he spoke only to himself, listening to the echoes of his own voice ringing back to him." She paused. "He said that sometimes the voices on the other side would describe where they were, and their surroundings sounded eerily similar to where we are now." She gestured around the room. "Every time he went to the Wall, he came and told me what he saw or who he thought he was speaking to. The last time I spoke to him, he told me he had walked through the Wall."

"Where did it lead him?" I breathed, trying to suppress my impatience for answers. She leaned forward and narrowed her eyes. "Here my dear," she answered. "He believed he had walked through to the other side of the Wall, to the other side of Hell, but I believed he emerged from within the wall to find himself back where he began."

"So, either way, he ended back here, in Hell?" I asked. "But how? I was so sure it would lead to another place. Surely it cannot just lead back here?"

"That is what he told me and that is what I will believe until I can see for myself." She finished, leaning back again in her rocking chair.

I thought about what she had said, as she sat in her chair, rocking gently back and forth, and drained the last of my, now cold, tea. I hoped its healing qualities would give me some insight into the story because I felt more confused than I did before I came to talk to her.

So David had gone through the Wall and he had emerged back here. Maybe the darkness doubled back on itself in the Wall, or perhaps it played with your mind and led nowhere. Maybe it wasn't even real. But how could that be when the Guards were so adamant about stopping us from entering it in the first place. They clearly didn't want us to see what lay inside the tunnel.

"What I don't understand is how?" I pondered out loud.

"How what?" Mrs Scott asked, responding to my musings.

"How did he get through the Wall without someone stopping him?" I asked. "Before I had taken two steps inside the tunnel, two Guards had appeared and threatened us with their spears. How could David have walked through without anyone stopping him?"

"He had said that after he came back through the Wall, two Guards were waiting for him. He told them a vague story of what he was doing there. I can't remember exactly what he said now, but that is unimportant. He also told me that the Guards believed him but apparently not for long." She paused, then went on. "I noticed a Guard nearby watching us as we talked that day. He had put a hand to his temple and said something, but he was too far away for me to make out his words. He then disappeared."

"So the Guards knew he went into the Wall and I bet that's why he became ill, but why did they wait so long after catching him at the Wall to take action?" I asked, still confused. "How do they make someone ill without touching them or giving them anything? When it happened to me, it felt instantaneous and neither of the Guards were touching me at the time."

"I do not know the answer to that question." Mrs Scott replied morosely.

"What else did the two of you talk about that night?" I asked her.

"Nothing and everything, but that conversation has nothing to do with your current predicament," she said, giving only a vague answer to my question. "This place holds secrets, most of which I am not aware of. It has its own rules and I have had first hand experience that those who govern here are free to change those rules whenever they please. You will never fully understand this place. I have been here for as long as I can remember and I still do not know all of its hidden intricacies. I have also witnessed it change and evolve. I have witnessed dramatic events that have altered its shape and integrity, but, still, I do not know how the magic works here."

"How long have you been here?" I asked, folding my hands in my lap.

"I have been here far longer than human-kind has ever been on Earth. I have been here far longer than your Scriptures have even hinted at," she said. She raised a hand to her face and rubbed an eye, and in the movement I glimpsed the red mark on her palm. I kept my gaze trained on the back of her hand, hoping that she would move it again so I could get a better look at the imperfection. My palm tingled the longer I stared at it and I started to massage it.

"What is that?" I finally asked, pointing to her right hand.

"Does it hurt you?" She asked in response.

I carried on massaging my palm and she mirrored my movement.

"It just aches. Why do you ask?" I asked.

She didn't respond.

"Does it bother you too?" I pressed. She frowned at me from her rocking chair and not wanting to anger her, I remained silent. After a minute or so, her face softened.

"If you want to see what is within the darkness, you will need a solid plan," she said, changing the subject matter completely. "I hope you will get through, but I fear you may be making another mistake." I assumed she was referring to the first time I had found the darkness in the stone wall and returned with amnesia, so I thought little of her concern. "I cannot be of much help, I'm afraid. I can neither stop you, nor help you. You are alone in your quest. All I can say is keep drinking that tea. Whenever it is offered to you, never reject it."

The same man who had given me the tea walked towards me along with three other men who I hadn't noticed before. They flanked me. One of them picked up my cup from the bedside table and put it away. I knew it was my time to leave. "Thank you for your time, Mrs Scott," I said sincerely. "But I am not making the same mistake. I am not alone in this. Victor, Nigel and Curtis are here to help me, and we have a solid plan. Things will go better this time around, now that we are more prepared. Goodbye."

Not wanting to overstay my welcome, I walked away from Mrs Scott and her friends. I ran the conversation through my mind, so I would remember even the tiniest detail. I didn't want to forget anything important. I frowned though, worrying that I had failed my mission, as I didn't get Mrs Scott to tell me what specifically she had talked about with David on the day he fell ill. I hoped Curtis wouldn't be too disappointed.

It took less time to get back to our bunks than it had taken to get to Mrs Scott's. I wound my way between the bunks at a jog, and soon spotted the three of them sitting, waiting for me on Nigel's bunk. I jogged right up to them, breathing hard from my exertion. Curtis stood up to make room for me. I sat between him and Nigel and they both shifted as close to me as possible, once I had made myself comfortable. Each of them looked at me expectantly.

"So...?" Victor asked impatiently, before I had even had a chance to catch my breath.

I took a deep breath and launched into the account of the conversation between Mrs Scott and myself. I took my time, trying to recount every word we exchanged, and not wanting to leave any detail out. But when I finished, Curtis looked ashen-faced.

"I knew he was up to something, but I couldn't figure out what," he muttered. "She didn't tell you what they talked about the day he fell ill?"

"No, I'm so sorry Curtis," I said, I grasped his hand as a tear fell down my face. "I asked, but she always skirted my question. I'm sorry I failed. I'm sorry I didn't get as much information as we wanted. I tried, I promise." I choked out. Curtis snatched his hand out of my grip and looked down at his feet, avoiding my gaze.

"You didn't fail, Violet," Victor interjected, noticing the change in atmosphere between Curtis and I. "You've found out some insightful information; even if it was not everything we would have liked to have known. And," he continued, "whilst you were gone, we discovered a break in the Guard's schedule."

"Did you?" I asked, with renewed hope, wiping away the tears from my cheeks. "What did you find out?"

"We found a sizable time gap between the fourth and fifth Guard change," Victor whispered, raising his eyebrows in a comical way.

"That's great news," I gasped, smiling at Victor.

"When?" Curtis asked, simply. His face was deadpan, and he was still avoiding my eyes.

"In the next two days, but we have to be sure," Victor answered.

Curtis nodded and stood up. "Fetch me when you need me. In the meantime, I'll be at my bunk." He turned and walked away.

We watched him, his back stiff and his hands stuffed deep into his trouser pockets. Nigel had laid his head in my lap during the recount of my talk with Mrs Scott. I looked down at him and saw that he was asleep.

"We better keep an eye on him," Victor muttered, not taking his eyes off Curtis' retreating back. He didn't look away from him until Curtis had lay down on his bunk and draped his arm over his eyes, shutting out the world.

"I'm worried about him." I said. "I desperately wanted to get the answers to his questions. Now I fear he blames me for not having them, but I tried Victor."

"He just needs time. He will soon understand that you are not to blame, and that you tried. The truth is often kinder than where our imagination leads us. I feel sorry for him," Victor said. "He still doesn't have closure. There must be some truly awful thoughts going through his mind at the moment."

"I wish I could help him," I said longingly.

"There is nothing we can do for him. As I said, we will need to give him time to calm down before we approach him."

"What is the plan, Victor?" I asked, steering the conversation back to more pressing matters. Victor turned to me and smiled conspiratorially. We stayed up for most of the night talking over important details. We mainly went through the Guard's schedule, what Mrs Scott told me and what we thought we would find on the other side of the tunnel — until Nigel stirred.

"We better get to bed. We will need to rise early if we are to confirm the time-gap." Victor said, yawning. He picked Nigel up, settled him down on his bunk and made his way to his own. "Goodnight." He called gently from his bunk.

"Goodnight," I half-whispered back.

The lights had dimmed hours ago and an eerie darkness shrouded the place. Strange shapes in the shadows rippled and eddied of their own accord, creating menacing creatures out of nothing. Troubled, I stretched out on my bunk, very glad to move freely, and only slightly annoyed at the pins and needles spreading up both of my legs. I massaged my calves to get the blood flowing, but was stopped short by a strange thought. If I was dead, why was blood flowing through me? Why did I get pins and needles? Why did I breathe and talk? I was surprised that these thoughts hadn't crossed my mind before now. I was also surprised that everything that was happening to me here all seemed fitting, as though there was no other way for anyone to live in the afterlife. I had been reborn again to live my second life. A second chance had been handed to me and I would not fuck this up. I will succeed in my quest.

Thoughts of the strangeness of this place plagued me all night long, along with the Wall and darkness within it. Greaves and spears, and the coal black eyes, which I realised had tormented me since before I had died, occupied my thoughts too. But by the time I had woken up the next morning, only thoughts of the time-gap occupied my mind. All thoughts of the visions that had been plaguing me disappeared as though they never existed in the first place.

THIRTEEN

REVELATIONS

Jeff became a constant part of my life. He had slipped right into my daily routine as though he had always been around — even though it had only been less than a week since we met — but I didn't mind. The mysterious notebook had preoccupied Sophie's mind for a while now, and she didn't have much time for me. So I welcomed his company whenever the notebook distracted her.

"Where's Jeff?" I asked Sophie.

"I haven't seen him this morning," she muttered back.

"Hmm, I'm going to look for him," I said, standing from my meditative position on my bunk.

She didn't respond, but remained seated on her bed, her eyes closed and an air of serenity draped over her. I frowned at her, wondering how she could remain so calm when she was faced with such an uncomfortable situation. I glanced at Jeff's bunk and spotted him in his usual position — perched on the edge of his bed, rocking back and forth, and pawing at the empty air where his right calf should have been — muttering to himself. Now that he had introduced himself, and we had become friends, I felt comfortable enough going over to him and finally finding out what occupied his mind whenever he acted this way.

I glanced once more at Sophie, but she had apparently forgotten about me. I was about to ask her if she thought it was a good idea to disturb Jeff, but talked myself out of it, confident that our newfound friendship would mean that he would confide in me how he was feeling in these intense moments. I strode towards him, a cloud of apprehension building around me at every step. I tried to shake off the unease, but it strengthened as I neared his bunk. I felt eyes boring into me, and subtle head shakes, as though his neighbours were warning me to stay away from him. Ignoring my overactive imagination, I steeled myself and walked right up to him, my shadow casting itself over him in an ominous way.

He didn't acknowledge me straight away, and I was afraid he didn't hear my approach or sense me standing right in front of him, as his eyes were squeezed tightly shut. I reached out a hand to tap his shoulder but his voice stopped me short.

"What do you want, Mary?" His tone was unlike anything I had heard from him before. I was used to his jovial demeanour, so his dark tone shocked me. I didn't have a response. I stood frozen, my hand hovering over his shoulder, and my mouth hanging open in shock. How could he speak to me like that, I asked myself.

"I said, 'what do you want Mary?'" His tone was still dark. He then lifted a hand and rubbed his face in exasperation.

"I came to see if I could help you with anything," I said in a small voice, bringing my hand back to my side.

"Does it look like there is anything you can do?" He asked sarcastically, chuckling humourlessly.

When I didn't respond he lifted his face and glared up at me. I took a step back away from him, truly terrified by his expression. I glanced around me, trying to catch his neighbour's eyes, but they all looked resolutely away.

"Sorry, Jeff I thought that now we were friends–,"

"You thought that what? Now that we are friends, you could come and disturb me?" He stood up from his bed, his face transformed into a mask of pure rage.

I took another step away from him, my eyes wide with fear.

"Scared are you?" He asked, leering at me.

His hand shot out and gripped my upper arm. I tried to yank it out of his grip but he was too strong. He pulled me closer to him so that our noses almost touched.

"I did not ask you to come here and bother me, whore." I said through gritted teeth.

"I'm sorry, Jeff," I whimpered. "Please let go. You are hurting me."

"Do not disturb me when I am having my alone time again." He said, menacingly.

I nodded vigorously at him, trying to pry his hand off my arm at the same time. He clutched at my other arm with his other hand and glared at me for half a minute and then shoved me away from him. I gasped and clutched at my arms, massaging the spot where his fingers had dug into my flesh; I knew bruises would appear there the next day. I looked around again at his neighbours. Some gave me sympathetic looks, which I appreciated, but most of them avoided my eyes, scared to get in between an altercation like this if they didn't need to. As I backed away from Jeff, a bald man stood up from his bunk.

"Please don't judge him when he acts this way," he muttered.

"I–I," I stuttered.

"Give him another chance. He has been happier since he met you, and his 'episodes' are much less aggressive. He just needs his time alone, that's all." He nodded at me, walked back to his bunk and lay down.

"What's wrong Mary?" Sophie asked me when I reached our bunks. "Did you find Jeff?"

I told her what had happened between Jeff and I.

"Are you sure you want to be friends with someone like that?" She asked when I had finished the story.

"I am going to give him a chance to explain himself, and then I will see." I said, holding back tears.

It took Jeff a couple of hours to become himself again and when he made his way over to me, his head bowed and an apologetic look on his face, I knew I couldn't stay mad at him.

"I am so sorry, Mary," he said, kneeling in front of me and taking my hands in his.

I hesitated for a minute, trying to gather my thoughts and figure out how we could continue in this friendship.

"It's okay, Jeff. I shouldn't have come to you when you were in that state. I should've known better." I shook my head at my own stupidity.

"I cannot lose you as a friend." He said, squeezing my hands in his. "Thanks to you, I was able to come over and apologise in a matter of hours, instead of the days it would have taken me before I met you. Without you, I cannot function. Without you my world becomes dark and I cannot escape my waking nightmares. I need you to balance me out again. I am so sorry." He repeated. He rested his head on our entwined hands, his shoulders shaking.

"I promise not to bother you during your alone times, if you promise to never speak to me like that again, Jeff." I said compromising.

Jeff nodded vigorously, but didn't raise his head. His shoulders stopped shaking, but we remained seated together, offering each other the little comfort we could give in this oppressed place.

I am ashamed to say that it took me a while to trust Jeff again after that incident. The anger in his eyes had been terrifying, and I still walked on eggshells around him for days after, which annoyed Sophie to no end.

"Just go and speak to him and tell him how you feel," she said, two days after Jeff's episode. "I know you still feel a little sensitive, so just be an adult and talk to him."

Jeff had just slunk away, his face dejected, when I had flinched away from his touch. He only wanted to pat my arm, but the physical and emotional remnants of our argument still lingered and I was afraid he would hurt me – even accidentally.

"He's gone now, Sophie. I will have to speak to him another time," I said, glancing at his empty bunk and feeling the knot in my stomach tighten. "And how can I explain to him that he frightened me so much that I don't think I want him around anymore?"

"You have to be honest with yourself. I see the way you two acted together before this whole fiasco happened and your friendship was blossoming beautifully." She said.

"I know, but what if he hurts me again?" I asked, a pained look on my face.

"There is no way to know that. You can only trust in his remorse, and hope he doesn't lose his cool again, and you can avoid him when he is in one of his moods. Problem solved." She said, spreading her hands in the air, as though everything was final and would go back to normal after we had had our conversation.

I didn't respond, instead I scowled at her. Deep down, I knew she was right. I thought back to the apologetic looks Jeff had been shooting me for the last two days and knew that he wanted our friendship to go back to how it was. "I know Sophie–." I didn't get a chance to finish my sentence, as Jeff came running over interrupting our conversation. Rivulets of sweat coated his body.

"You have to come with me, Mary," he said, once he reached me. He held his hand out to me and I hesitated. "Come with me please? I need to know that I am not going crazy." Without a second thought, I put my hand in his, and he squeezed his over mine.

"Thank you," he breathed.

He pulled me up from my bunk and led me away quickly. I had no choice but to keep up with his fast pace.

"I'll be back," I called over my shoulder to Sophie as an afterthought. I didn't hear if she responded, but I didn't care. I was just glad Jeff and I would get to spend some time together. "Where are you taking me?"

"I have found Joe, he's here." He said, simply.

"What?" I asked him, hoping he would give me some insight to what was going on.

He didn't answer me. Instead, he kept a tight grip on my hand and dragged me between the bunks, hellbent on reaching our final destination. We suddenly stopped and crouched down at an empty bunk. I looked around us, and recognised nothing.

"Jeff, where are we?" I asked, panic creeping into the edges of my consciousness.

"There he is," he said, ignoring my question.

"Joe? Where?" I asked, looking frantically around.

"There." He pointed to a man sitting three bunks away. He had a buzz-cut hair style, like the one you receive in the Army when you first enlisted and he wore his white t-shirt in a vest, much like Jeff's. His muscles were well defined and his skin had a slight tan as though he had spent his last few years alive in the sun. "I recognised him from his t-shirt."

"Are you sure that's Joe?" I asked, squinting at the vested man, trying to get a better look at him.

"Positive. We had both cut ours into vests, because that was what we were used to when we were alive." Jeff nodded to himself.

"So, what's the plan?" I asked, shifting into a more comfortable position.

"I haven't thought that far ahead," he admitted, looking at me out of the corner of his eyes with an odd look on his face.

I sighed and pinched the bridge of my nose in exasperation, knowing I would have to come up with a plan.

"I'm sorry Mary, I just needed to know if it was him." I suddenly stood up. "Where are you going?" He hissed.

"I'm going over to him to ask him if his name is Joe," I said, I took two steps away, but turned back. "What was his last name?"

"Brisket." Jeff remained crouched behind the bunk, trying to keep himself from his friend's view. I rolled my eyes and marched over to the muscled man.

"Are you Joe Brisket?" I asked, once I reached him.

"Who's asking?" He turned away from his three companions — each sporting the same buzz-cut and muscular physique — and glared at me suspiciously.

"I know a friend of yours," I said cryptically, glancing back to where Jeff was still crouched behind the bunk. "Do you know that man over there?" I jerked my head in Jeff's direction.

Joe took his time scrutinising Jeff, but then looked up at me with a blank expression. "No." He turned away from me back to his friends.

"But you are Joe Brisket, right?" I asked.

"I don't know who you are talking about." He said, not turning to me, as though the conversation was already over.

Jeff appeared at my side, his hands shoved deep into his white trouser pockets. "Joe?" He asked in a quiet voice.

Joe jerked his head up and glared straight at Jeff with a cold look on his face. "I am not who you think I am."

"Joe, please, it's me Jeff," Jeff paused and licked his lips. "You used to live next to me."

"I don't know who you are." Joe stood up and took a hasty step back, a look of panic flashing across his face. "Please, just leave." He added through gritted teeth and glanced around.

I followed his eye line and saw a group of Guards pointing at us.

"Look," I tugged at Jeff's t-shirt and pointed in the Guard's direction. "We had better go."

Jeff seemed reluctant to leave Joe, frowning at him and ignoring my persistent tugging. "I just needed to know you were okay."

I looked around at Joe's neighbours and they were shooting us subtle glares, wanting to both make eye contact to show their anger and avoid it to evade any unnecessary confrontations. I glanced again at the crowd of Guards, they were walking towards us; their spear butts banging on the floor at every other step.

"Come on Jeff, we have to go," I said. "Now." I added, when he didn't immediately move.

I tugged at his arm and led him away. He followed slowly, dragging his feet with his head bowed dejectedly.

"At least you know he's still around, Jeff," I said, patting his arm.

"But he is different now. I know he knew me, he just didn't want to admit it. I wonder why." He said, stroking his chin.

"I don't know, but we have to get away from here now." I chanced a glance back to where Joe stood and saw a group of Guards surrounding him. Not wanting to know the outcome of the confrontation, I turned to face where we were heading, hoping Jeff would be able to guide us back even in his devastated state.

When I caught sight of my bunk, I breathed a sigh of relief. I had been completely lost and when I saw familiar surroundings, I was ecstatic.

"I am going to my own bunk," Jeff said, still looking upset.

"Okay, I will see you soon," I said in farewell. "Don't let this bother you too much." I added, as an afterthought.

"I will try." He said, sighing morosely.

I walked to my bunk and lay down next to Sophie, who was sitting on it.

"I have a theory about the Guards," Sophie whispered, when I had made myself comfortable.

"Shoot," I replied lazily, running my long black hair through my fingers and examining the damaged ends. I had grown tired of talking about the Guards. I wanted nothing more than to be with my new friends in peace.

"They have become more blatant in their observations," she continued.

"Mmm?" I murmured, not really caring.

"Maybe they are onto us?" She suggested,

"What do you mean, 'onto us'?" I rose from the bed, rested on my elbows, and frowned at her. Her words had finally caught my attention.

"I mean, maybe they suspect we are planning to rebel," she paused. "And they are aware we suspect something is not right about this place."

"But how would they have found out?" I asked lying back down and becoming distracted with my split ends once more.

"Beats me," she replied. "But the Guards gather in groups now and follow us whenever we leave our bunks. It's as though they are waiting for the right time to stop us from rebelling."

"Rebelling? We don't even know what we are going to do." I said, scoffing at the absurdity of what she had just said. "What *are* we going to do, Sophie?"

"I haven't made a proper plan yet, but I am working on it." She muttered, looking out into the distance at a group of Guards who were standing in a circle watching us watch them.

"Why won't you tell Jeff and I what you write in that notebook? We deserve to know the details. We are in this together after all."

"The less you know the better," She said, placing a protective hand on her notebook.

"The less we know the better," I mimicked quietly to myself. "I am getting sick and tired of this Sophie. If you don't tell us something soon, then I will take matters into my own hands. Someone sent me here for a reason and I have done nothing about it, I have just sat with you and played spy."

"Be quiet, Mary," Sophie hissed at me. "Do you want them to know exactly what we are planning? We whisper and are secretive because what we are doing is wrong. If you keep on shouting about our plans for everyone to hear, we won't be able to carry them out."

I rolled my eyes and looked away from her. I was angry at her for not revealing her plans, and angry at myself for not being confident enough to take on the leadership role; simply allowing Sophie to call all the shots. I had never been the leader. Even in life, I had always followed.

"I have a vague plan. I wanted to wait until I had it sorted out in my head before I approached the two of you with it, but if you are going to be this way..." Sophie said thickly, wiping her eyes.

"If you share your plan, you can gain a different perspective. It might help you put those difficult pieces, which you cannot grasp, together." I put an arm around her and pulled her close for a quick hug. She accepted the affectionate touch, smiling weakly, then pulled away, wiping her eyes vigorously. She bent to retrieve her notebook out of her bottom drawer of her bedside table and flipped through the pages.

"Okay," she started, still sniffling. "What you said the other day has been grating on me."

"What did I say?" I asked, sitting up and facing her on my bunk.

"You asked me where the souls go when they get taken away," she replied. "What if they get taken to Him?"

"Do you think so? That seems a bit far-fetched, but it would be so handy if that happened." I said, leaning closer to her. "Then how will we get taken to Him? The reasons behind the Guards taking away people seem so random."

"Well, there is the obvious," she said, nonchalantly.

"You keep on saying that, yet I still don't know the obvious," I replied, trying to keep the exasperation out of my voice, as I had already upset her once today.

"We could eat the foo–" she began

"Ew." I cut her off before she had the chance to finish her last word, knowing exactly what she was going to say and hating the idea as the image of the rotting food sprang to mind.

"I am not saying it's a good idea," she said, looking back at her lap at my admonishment.

"We will have to make a scene," I suggested instead. "Something big enough to permit us to get taken away."

"Well, it's not the best plan, but I guess it's all we've got." Sophie said.

I grabbed the notebook from her hand and looked through the scribble-filled pages, struggling to decipher most of her handwriting. As I flipped through the pages, I noticed she had circled and underlined certain phrases.

"What's this?" I asked, pointing to a bold and circled statement: 'What if there are other spaces?' it read.

"Oh," Sophie said, when she realised what I pointed to. "That's just some of my musings. I want to find answers, but I don't know where I can find them."

"So you think there are other spaces apart from this one?" I asked. "Yeah, me too. How can they fit the billions of people who have died over the millennia into this one space. There has to be more of these?"

"We need to expose all the lies the Bible has fed us and find out what's really going on here," she said while vigorously rubbing her stomach.

"Maybe Jeff's neighbours will remember something from when his bunkmate, Joe, was taken away. Maybe they could accurately recount what had happened." After a moment, Sophie said, excitedly. "Why don't we just ask Jeff? He may remember what happened that day, if we ask him in the right way. Is he still at his bunk?"

"We can't ask him now, you know how he gets. I don't want to be on the receiving end of another one of his episodes. We should leave him and ask him when he's himself again." I flipped through another couple of pages but something made me stop. "What's this?" I asked, pointing to a complicated looking diagram on one page.

"This is their schedule," she replied.

"Who's schedule?" I asked.

"The Guards', obviously. I've noticed a pattern in when they rotate their watches and how long each one lasts. This shows who they are, where they are, how many watch us and who takes over their watch," Sophie whispered proudly.

"What are these symbols?" I pointed at some patterns at the top of the page.

"Oh, they're codes. They represent the patterns each Guard has on their helmet." She replied, smiling up at me. "That's how I know who's who."

"That's so cool," I breathed "Can you explain it to me?" She had told me she had loved to do puzzles when she was alive and I liked that she had found something equally as challenging to do here. I hoped it proved useful in our quest to discover the inner workings of this place.

She rubbed her stomach again, deep in thought, before starting. "The first Guard appears when the lights brighten in the morning.

He's represented by this triangle. He's tall and always alone. The second Guard comes around two hours later. This circle with a dot in the middle, represents him. They usually talk for around five minutes — most likely giving a short debrief about the three of us — then the first Guard leaves. An hour later, a third Guard comes and stays with the second Guard until the lights get to their brightest, which I assume is midday. He has three wavy lines on his helmet." She paused.

"What happens next?" I asked, intrigued.

"This is where it gets interesting," she continued. "Something calls the Guards away, as even the ones standing farther away, not watching us, disappear. They all put a hand to their temples, nod, and then disappear. That must be how they communicate with each other." She frowned

"By putting their fingers to their temples? Like Charles Xavier in X–men?" I asked, laughing. She frowned at me, not understanding my reference. "Never mind," I muttered.

"We have a minute before two different Guards come," Sophie continued. "These Guards stay for two hours before one Guard comes and relieves them."

"How do you know this?" I asked, impressed.

"It's easy to figure out their pattern if you watch them closely enough, and because they don't change their routine from day to day, it makes it easier still. Now, as I was saying, the single Guard who comes in at, what I assume to be, two o'clock stays for another two hours and then all the Guards disappear again at four." Sophie stopped and looked at me.

"They put their fingers to their temples and leave? All of them?" I asked.

"Yes, they leave, but this time they stay away for longer before coming back to watch us. That's our window to..." She trailed off looking at her notebook as though it held all the answers.

"To blow this place wide open?" I suggested.

"Yes," she paused. "But how?"

"We could actually blow it up," I said, shrugging.

"We can't blow anything up," Sophie said, frowning.

"Well, what can we do?" I asked, lifting my hands up in exasperation.

"Let's think about it, put our heads together and come up with a plan," Sophie said. "I guess talking about it out loud helped put my thoughts in order." She grinned at me, and I grinned back at her.

"We can ask Jeff, he'll know what to do," I said. We both looked over to Jeff's bunk, but he lay beneath his covers, hidden from sight.

"Tomorrow though?" Sophie suggested.

I nodded in agreement. "So is that settled? Jeff will help form a plan, I will get taken away, and then find out who this God-person is."

"Why do *you* get to get taken away?? Why can't I? I want to meet Him too," Sophie complained.

"I don't want you to get hurt. If the plan we come up with goes wrong in any way-"

"Which it is bound to do," Sophie interjected. "We are not exactly spy masterminds." "Exactly, so if it goes wrong, it will be on my head. You have been through enough already. I don't want you to suffer any more," I muttered, choosing to ignore her last statement and looking away from her.

Neither of us spoke to each other again that night. I yawned, and went to my bunk after a couple of awkward minutes, but didn't fall asleep until much later. My mind raced as I mentally digested the information Sophie had given to me tonight. I was glad she had confided in me. This had been my only goal in life, and I was eager for a plan to form.

The lights finally dimmed to their darkest and my last thought before my brain shut down to sleep was to make sure we told Jeff the plan as soon as he was himself again.

Unlike most of his other episodes, it took Jeff a further two days, after the enlightening talk with Sophie, for him to approach us again, but it was under strange circumstances. With nothing new to talk about, Sophie and I had been spending more time apart, each getting sick of the same conversation and nothing coming from it. It was driving us crazy.

I took to wandering the makeshift walkways, searching for my long lost twin. I was adamant that she was in here with me somewhere, I just had to find her. My pace quickened as I neared a familiar head of short black hair, but frowned when I reached her, hand outstretched. A nugget of uncertainty broke through my surety. I remembered the last time I had run headlong to a short black haired woman, and the reception I had received; but this could be her. A middle aged man, with cropped salt and pepper hair sat in front of her. He pointed at me with a warning look and she spun around, a mask of fury on her face.

"Who are you?" She screamed.

I was taken aback. I had no idea how to react. She wasn't her. How could I have been wrong again? My throat closed, and no sound escaped, no matter how hard I tried to explain myself. She leapt up from her bunk, anger radiating through her, and advanced towards me. My body froze on the spot.

"Got nothing to say, eh?" She leered at me, her eyes twitching in anger.

When I didn't respond, she lunged at my throat and closed her hands around it, cutting off my air supply. I clawed at her hands, trying to pry them away, but she was too strong. She manhandled me to the floor, slamming my back against the ground and knocking the remaining breath out of me.

My hands scrabbled at her upper body, trying to push her off me, but the damage was already done. She was sapping the strength from me. My hands simply batted at her body but had no effect in stopping her from strangling me. A troop of Guards hurried over, shouting unintelligible phrases, as my visions blurred. I hoped they ran to save me and not take me away, it was too soon. We hadn't solidified the plan, and I would need to tell Sophie where I was going but everything went black.

I took a deep breath, fluttered my eyes open, and stared into Jeff's face. He was gently slapping my cheek.

"Ugh, I'm up Jeff," I protested, covering my face with my arms and sitting up.

"We have to go," he hissed. His tone alerted me to a significant danger. My senses woke, and I sat up. The commotion next to me made my heart race. Four Guards held my attacker against the floor, but she was giving a good fight. They struggled to keep her calm as her legs and arms flailed wildly. A fist caught a Guard in the face, breaking his nose, and blood spurted everywhere. I was temporarily forgotten, as all eyes were on the struggling woman. I didn't want to stick around to see how long it took for them to turn their attention to me or to see what they would do to me once they noticed me again.

"Mary, we have to leave." Jeff's voice broke through my shock. I tore my eyes away from the commotion and looked fearfully into Jeff's golden ones.

"We need to go," I agreed, nodding.

"That is what I have been trying to make you understand." He shook his head at me, but held out his hand to help me up off the ground.

A Guard glanced in our direction and made a move to stop us, but was distracted by a cry from the salt and pepper haired man and turned away from us. I breathed a sigh of relief, gripped Jeff's upper arm and steered him away whilst rubbing my throat. I glanced back at the commotion and saw that the woman's head was covered in blood and she lay unmoving on the ground. Twenty Guards now surrounded her. One held her down with a foot to her neck, and the others herded the onlookers back to their bunks, trying to regain some semblance of calm.

Jeff and I hurried back to Sophie's bunk, eager to distance ourselves from any scrutiny from the Guards.

"Where have you been?" Sophie asked when we reached her.

"You don't want to know," Jeff muttered, sharing a fearful glance with me before settling himself on Sophie's bunk.

"Were you looking for your sister again?" She asked, shooting me an exasperated look.

I said nothing and sat on her bed, looking down at my hands. Jeff patted my arm, and I looked up at him with tear-filled eyes. I hadn't noticed before, but he had dark shadows beneath his eyes showing his exhaustion, but he still grinned from ear to ear.

"Sorry about the hold up ladies. What have I missed?" He drawled as he found a comfortable position on the bed and kissed me on my cheek; expertly changing the subject. I smiled shyly to myself, glad he understood I didn't want to talk about the fiasco I had just caused.

"Nothing much," I replied, lightly touching one of his scarred, yet muscly, arms, and leaning into his muscular body. I was so glad to have him near me again. "Sophie showed me what was in her notebook." I said, grinning at him and taking one of his large calloused hands in mine and intertwining our fingers together.

Jeff glanced at Sophie with a mock incredulous expression on his face. "Really?" He asked sarcastically. "I wanted to witness that moment. Mary, and I have been wondering what you had been scribbling about."

"She noticed a pattern in the Guard's watches. She knows who watched us and when, and she found a window where they were all gone for ten minutes. We decided that's the perfect time to..." I paused, unsure of how to finish my thought. "Cause some sort of a commotion, so we can get taken away, like that lady did just then." I finished quickly, not meeting Jeff's or Sophie's eyes, knowing that I had caused something bad to happen and feeling immensely guilty about it.

"Yes, we did," Sophie said. "Great progress right?"

"What are we going to do in that ten minute window then?" Jeff asked, looking between Sophie and myself.

"We hoped you had ideas." I replied, sheepishly.

"Well, what did you guys come up with?" Jeff asked, stroking his thumb across my knuckles.

"What about setting off a bomb?" I asked, quickly. "Sophie knows how to get things, things that aren't given out freely; take the tea and the blanket for example. Do you think you could help us make it?"

His face paled. He looked like he had dived deep into one of his episodes. "Jeff?" I asked. "What's wrong?"

"I cannot help you with that plan," he said in a small voice. "We will need to think of something else.

"Why not?" Sophie asked. "It's the only plan we've got for now."

He took a long time to speak, and when he finally did, his voice was even smaller than before. "The last thing I remember before I woke in the darkness and made my way here was an explosion." He looked down at his leg. "The blast..."

"Oh," I breathed, realising what I had just done.. "Oh no, Jeff. Jeff, I'm so sorry." Tears filled my eyes.

"It doesn't matter, Mary," he said, taking my hand in his and squeezing it. "You didn't know. I never told you."

"We don't have to use that plan. We can speak to that 'Stu' guy and find out why he's following us," Sophie said. "It may give us an insight as to why the Guards are following us too. If both him and the Guards are watching us, something must connect them together."

"Okay, that sounds like a good plan." Jeff said, finally looking up at me and smiling weakly. "When can we corner him?"

"Later today, we have that window where we can question him, we will do it then," I suggested.

"Okay," he said, getting up. "I will come back later." He walked away, his shoulders slumped. I put my head in my hands and groaned.

"He didn't tell us, Mary," Sophie said. "This isn't your fault."

"We should have known," I said. "Just look at his leg."

"Hindsight's a bitch," she said. "We will meet later." I got up and left her too it, too embarrassed and guilty to speak.

The morning ticked slowly by. I took this time to do my morning yoga but I found that it didn't clear my mind as much as it had done in the past. Thoughts of our plan were too strong to allow my mind to fully empty. Jeff, Sophie and I didn't speak to each other. We were each at our own bunks, waiting for the ten-minute window when we could corner Stu Willis and question him. I had grown to hate him since we had first spotted him spying on us. Why did he think he could spy on us? Who did he think he was?

The time to strike neared and Stu and his audacity were the only thoughts in my mind. Ten minutes to wait. My blood hit boiling point. At five minutes, I was seething and my nails were imprinting half-moons into my palms as I clenched my fists in anger. Two minutes. I glanced at Sophie. She was sitting on the edge of her bunk, rubbing her stomach vigorously with a deep frown on her face. Jeff lay down flat on his back on his own bunk. He looked calm but I could see his tense muscles and the vein in his temple pulsing. I, myself, sat cross-legged on the floor, eyes shut to the world. I tried to fake a serene air around me, but on the inside, my mind ran a mile a minute, going through the questions I would ask him and imagining what I would do when I finally got my hands on him.

It was as though we were all connected mentally. My eyes snapped open and I jumped up at the same time as Sophie slowly stood from her bed. I glanced around me and smiled when I could see Guards in sight. Sophie and I glanced at each other, then over at Jeff, who was already striding towards Stu's bunk. I strode ahead in the same direction as Jeff's; eating up the space between Stu and myself with long, eager strides. I overtook Jeff, who was right behind me, a mean scowl on his face. If we hadn't been friends, I would have been afraid of him. Sophie hurried a couple paces behind, struggling to keep up under the baby's weight inside her, but she also had a deep frown on her face, making her look threatening even in her state.

Stu had not been paying attention to his surroundings. He leant against the foot of a bunk, with his back to us. All of his attention was on a small red ball he had somehow come across, so he didn't hear our approach. When we reached him, I grabbed him by his filthy, stained shirt and hauled him up to his feet. He squealed and struggled to release himself from my grip; his eyes widening with shock.

"Gerroff!" He shouted, struggling harder still.

"Why are you following us?" I asked through clenched teeth, vigorously shaking him back and forth.

"I don't know what you're talking about," Stu sputtered, trying to pry my hands away from his shirt. "I ain't done nothin'."

"You know exactly what we are talking about, now spill," Jeff growled. I glanced at him a little fearful of his tone but knew he wouldn't hurt me. I wasn't so sure about Stu Willis, though.

Sophie finally caught up with us. She skirted around the bunk so she stood behind Stu. "Guys this is not the right way," she cautioned, looking around us all the while. "There are too many eyes around. Let's go to his bunk."

"Lead the way, Stuart Willis," Jeff hissed.

I let go of his shirt and he crumpled to the floor. He looked up into Jeff's eyes and blanched. Jeff took a step towards him and Stu shuffled away in a crab-like walk before standing up and scrambling over to his bunk; the three of us following closely behind him. The scent of his bunk preceded us and when we reached it, I put an arm over my mouth and nose to block the offensive smell. Sophie gagged at the awful stench and Jeff wrinkled his nose in pure disgust.

"We should have just questioned him at the other bunk, sorry guys," Sophie choked out. I looked at Stu and was surprised to see him sitting on his bed, apparently unfazed by the stench. I had to admit the scene looked odd, but everyone here was so used to keeping to themselves, they didn't look even remotely curious as to what we were doing. We stood around Stu in silence, waiting for him to speak, but he seemed adamant not to break the silence first. I could see Jeff's face redden as he slowly became angrier. I knew he would explode at any moment.

"Speak." Jeff finally spat out.

Stu flinched but still he refused to say anything. He folded his arms in a nonchalant way, but the sweat beading at his brow told a different story.

"Are you deaf? He told you to speak," Sophie said, placing a threatening hand on his shoulder, but Stu looked resolutely away from us, his whole body quivering.

"I don't have time for this," Jeff muttered to us, he turned back to Stu. "We don't want to stay near this filthy bunk all day." He was losing control. Sophie, and I glanced at each other with the same apprehensive look in our eyes. I was afraid that if he got too out of control, neither of us could restrain him.

Stu glanced at Jeff but looked quickly away, his eyes wide with fear, yet still adamantly refusing to answer our questions.

Jeff grabbed Stu by the chin and forced him to look into his eyes. Stu struggled to escape Jeff's grip, but Jeff, like me, was too strong. Jeff leant closer to Stu's ear and whispered something. The blood drained from Stu's face, and he turned as white as a sheet at Jeff's words. Stu's whole body shook, and still Jeff whispered in his ear. Finally Jeff stepped away, let go of Stu's t-shirt and folded his huge arms across his chest.

"What did you say to him?" I asked Jeff out of the corner of my mouth.

"Nothing much, just threatened him a little," Jeff replied, frowning down at Stu from his great height.

"O–o–okay, okay," Stu sputtered. "I'll tell you." He glanced at Jeff but, again, looked away, swallowing hard. "They came to my bunk–"

"Who came to your bunk?" Sophie interrupted.

"Some Guards. I dunno what they looked like, I swear," he added, cringing back from the glare Jeff had given him. "They came and woke me up. I was sleeping, see. They asked me to do 'em a favour. They pointed to you," he gestured at me. "And said they'd give me what I wanted if I followed you for a bit and tell them what you all did."

"What did they say they would give you?" I asked, frowning.

"They didn't say," Stu said.

"Liar," Jeff growled, taking a step towards him and clenching his fists.

"Okay, they told me," Stu whimpered. He licked his dry and cracking lips. "They said they'd get me drugs."

"What kind of drugs?" I asked, intrigued by the Guard's promises..

"They didn't say which kind," Stu said petulantly, picking at the frayed end of his blanket.

"When did they say they would give it to you?" Sophie asked.

"They said I'd get them when I finished the job, but that was weeks ago," Stu whined. "Anything else?" Jeff sneered at Stu.

"No, nothing. I swear that was it... well, they asked for a debrief about a week ago and I told 'em you guys just hung out. That you ain't done nothing wrong. I tried to cover–."

"We don't need your help," Jeff said. "And remember, if we see you skulking around again..." Jeff trailed off.

Stuart gulped, leaning away from Jeff's murderous stare.

"Come on ladies, let's go. We don't need to be around this vermin any longer," Jeff took hold of my arm and steered me away from Stu. When we had walked five or six feet away from Stu's bunk, I felt like I could breathe again. My body thanked me for the fresh air as I drank deep lungfuls of it.

"What do we do now?" Sophie asked when we sat back at her bunk.

"Now we make a plan to meet these Guards who bequeathed such an important mission to Stu," Jeff joked.

"But how?" I asked.

Jeff shrugged and said. "We go up to them and ask them why they are following us."

FOURTEEN

VICTOR'S CAPTURE

"We should do it today," I moaned to Victor, Nigel and Curtis. We were sitting at our usual spot, at my bunk. "I can't wait any longer."

"Today?" Victor asked, licking his lips nervously.

"When else will we do it, Victor?" I asked him, scoffing. "We can't keep on putting it off. We need to strike. I need to know what's inside the tunnel and what the Guards are so adamant about keeping away from us." I said, leaping off my bunk and pacing back and forth in front of them.

"Violet, calm down, you're drawing attention to us," Curtis hissed at me, yanking my arm and pulling me back down onto the bunk.

"Okay," Victor said, shutting his eyes and frowning in deep thought. "We will do it today. As Violet said, we have no reason to wait." He opened his eyes and looked at Curtis and Nigel who nodded in agreement.

We had woken early, gathering before the first guard's watch and even before the lights had brightened a little. I had grown restless as the morning progressed, eager to be doing something — anything — other than just sitting around.

"When?" I asked impatiently.

"The gap in the Guard's watches is later on in the day. I will tell you when," Victor replied.

162

I looked at Curtis, Nigel, and back to Victor and nodded.

Curtis and Nigel both nodded in agreement, and that was that. The plan will come to fruition today. Victor didn't tell us when we could go to the Wall at that time and I grew insufferably restless waiting for the moment to arrive; so much so I drove Victor and Curtis back to their own bunks, as they kept on sighing irritably at my impatience. Only Nigel stayed with me to keep me company, but after a while I wished he had left with the others, as I wanted to be alone with my own thoughts rather than being forced to socialise. Nigel left without saying a word once he noticed I hadn't spoken and had been sitting cross-legged on my bunk staring at the same spot for ten minutes. Once he left, I moved from my bed to the floor, closed my eyes and tried to meditate, like Father had taught me to do, but it was difficult to clear my mind. Too many thoughts were jumbled around in my head.

"Victor says it's time Violet," Curtis whispered into my ear a while later. I opened my eyes and looked up into his green ones. "We don't have to do this," he said, helping me up from the floor, guiding me to my bed and sitting with me. "We can always just stay here and-"

"And do what, rot here like everyone else?" I hissed at him, gesturing around the room at the people who sat around us; each of them were staring vacantly into space. I shoved him off my bed and stood. "I didn't come here to rot. I came here to find out what's really happening here. I didn't die early, check out in the prime of my life, to just sit here and do nothing, Curtis." I turned to storm off, but only took three steps before Curtis grabbed my arm and yanked me back. His hands travelled to my waist, and I didn't shrug them off. Instead, I leant my head on his shoulder for a minute, trying to regain my composure so I could speak rationally to him.

I looked over his shoulder and noticed a Guard staring at us. My anger rose as I remembered how they had wiped my memories and those of my friends, and especially how they treated the people here; but in the same instance my anger dampened when the particular Guard with dark eyes floated in my vision. My stomach flipped as

I remembered our meeting. His gaze still burned into my mind and the rough texture of his hands somehow still lingered on mine.

"Don't try to stop me, Curtis," I said, finally tearing my gaze away from the unfamiliar Guard and looking up into his familiar green eyes, but they did not comfort me as they usually did.

"I'm sorry," he shrugged. "But you're making a mistake." He let his hands fall from my waist to his side.

Before I could bite back, Victor and Nigel appeared next to us. "Don't look now, but Mrs Scott is on her way over with her entourage," Victor said, gesturing behind me.

I spun around. Mrs Scott, her back bent, frail and ancient, was hobbling over with a hand-carved walking stick, flanked by two of her helpers. I stiffened, knowing she rarely left her bunk and whatever had brought her out must be serious.

She drew level with me, looked up at me, but she didn't speak for a moment. "You are making a mistake," she croaked out, frowning up at me from her meagre height. "I have seen all this happen before and I do not want it to happen again."

"What have you seen happen before?" I asked.

"I did not tell you all you needed to know the last time we spoke. I should have listened to my instincts and told you more, but we can never know if that would have changed the course of events." She paused and took a step closer. "You cannot make the same mistake again. It will bring you more pain than you have ever imagined. So stop this nonsense and let it be."

"I can't do that," I whispered fiercely. "I came here for a reason and nothing you can say or do will stop me from finding out what happens here."

"What are your reasons girl?" Mrs Scott asked.

"I-I-," I faltered. I hadn't said the words aloud in years, and they stuck in my throat. I looked at everyone surrounding me and shivered. "My Father persuaded me."

A chorus of gasps erupted around me, but Mrs Scott simply nodded her head, deep in thought.

"You will only find more misery and pain. I assure you, you will wish you had let it be, and stayed here because what is inside — what we can't see — is worse than you can ever imagine," Mrs Scott said solemnly, after a minute of tense silence.

"You should listen to her Violet?" Curtis suggested concern etched in the tone of his voice. "Yeah, Mrs Scott knows everything, she may be right Violet, but I'll be by your side anyway," Nigel said. He walked to my side, put his small hand in mine and squeezed it. "Listen to your friends and don't be so hot–headed. I know how this ends. I have already seen how it ends, and it is not pretty for anyone involved." Mrs Scott cautioned.

"What do you think, Victor?" I asked, regarding Mrs Scott's negative comments.

"I think you will do as you please so there is no point in me cautioning you against, or advocating for the plan to go forward. I know I will not be the one to change your mind if you have already made your decision." I nodded, taking in all that Victor had just said.

Mrs Scott ushered me to sit down onto my bunk, and one of her entourage came forward holding her rocking chair. He placed it near me, and with the help of her two main men, she sat herself in the chair. I sighed at the delay in the plan, knowing we only had a small window in which to act. Another of her entourage came up with two cups of tea, handing one to me and the other to Mrs Scott.

"I do not want one, thanks," I said, waving away the cup.

"What did I tell you about accepting a cup of tea whenever offered, Violet?" Mrs Scott asked.

"Why?" I asked, my anger rising. "What does it do? I don't even like tea."

"This tea holds more than you know," she started. "The leaves in this tea keep us sane. This is the only thing that is keeping you driven in your course. If you want to go on with your plan, I suggest you drink it."

I sighed and rolled my eyes, letting Mrs Scott know what I thought of her tea, but took a small sip anyway.

"I know time is of the essence, so I will be brief." Mrs Scott sighed, changing the subject back to more important matters. "Have you heard the story of the woman who tried to rebel?" she asked me.

"Yeah, Curtis mentioned it," I said, through gritted teeth, not understanding why this story was so important.

"Well, it is time I told you who it was. Since you don't seem like you will change your mind." Mrs Scott blew at the steam which rose from the hot liquid. She took a sip and savoured the flavours on her tongue before swallowing and continuing. "The woman was my partner. Who stood by my side for three hundred years. Who I watched die a slow and horrible second death, was you, Violet."

"Me?" I asked, I finally gave in and took another sip of the tea in my hands. Somehow, with this sip, the liquid coursed through me, giving me a renewed confidence. "How can it have been me when I am sitting right here? I can assure you I haven't been alive for hundreds of years."

"The woman was your age, twenty-one." Mrs Scott continued, ignoring my comment. "She was your height, had your hair colour and length. She had your ideas, drive and passion and she also looked remarkably like you. She believed something more was going on here, but all she received was a miserable and humiliatingly long and painful final death." Mrs Scott took another sip of her tea.

"Violet, I don't want you to die like that," Nigel squealed, clutching at my arm painfully. "I don't want to see you in pain. Please don't do this."

"Yes, I have to agree with Nigel on this one Violet," Victor chimed in. "This is a bad idea, and now I'd feel awful advocating it."

"I, too, agree with the others Violet. I'm sorry." Curtis added. "I have grown to care for you since we have become friends, and I am unsure of the odds on this one."

"I see you are wearing my gift," she said, pointing to the bulge beneath my t-shirt.

I took it out and examined it. "What kind of stone is it?"

"It's an Emerald dear," she said. "Do you know why I gifted it to you?"

I shook my head.

"It belonged to her, and now it belongs to you. She used to wear it and gave it to me for safe keeping so I could return it to her when she came back to me."

"Are you going to believe this old lady with her crazy stories she had probably just made up to scare me? I'm going through with the plan, with or without you guys." I looked up and glanced at the surrounding guards. As though right on cue, they held their fingers to their temples and disappeared one at a time at first, and then they were all gone. The time had come. I drained the cup and passed it back to one of Mrs Scott's henchmen.

"Are you coming with me?" I asked Victor, Nigel and Curtis, looking from one to the other to the other. None of them responded. Curtis looked at his hands, forlorn. Nigel looked up at me, tears building at the corners of his eyes, but Victor sat stony faced and silent. His face gave nothing away, nor did he meet my gaze. "Fine." I stormed off, not looking back; clenching my hands into fists at my side.

People blurred past me as I ran, some turned to stare, but most didn't notice me at all. I had less than ten minutes to get to the tunnel before the Guards caught me, and I was glad when I arrived at the Wall in record time; having run the whole way. Panting, I stood bent over, staring at the Wall with my hands on my knees, trying to catch my breath. I looked at the people milling around me and I didn't recognise a single face. I realised I recognised nothing in my vicinity, which meant I must have overshot my mark by at least two hundred meters. I had only minutes to spare, so I took a chance and headed right, down the designated pathway between the bunks and the Wall, keeping my left hand touching it at all times so I wouldn't miss the tunnel opening.

The Wall still thrummed with life and it was as though it was trying to communicate with me but we didn't speak the same language and I couldn't understand it. The warmth radiating from it was soothing. It made my fingers tingle and the resulting ripples travelled up my arm and over my entire body. After a couple of minutes of jogging, a familiar deep niche came into view up ahead. I grinned, delighted that my spontaneous decision led me to where I needed to go. I picked up my pace, rushing towards the niche and the tunnel right by it; eager to get inside it.

As I drew level with the niche next to the tunnel, a pair of hands pushed me sideways and strong arms wrapped themselves around me. They pulled me into the niche so that I looked out into Hell and he put a hand over my mouth to stop any sound from escaping.

"I am sorry Violet, but I cannot let you do this. You are too important," Victor said, appearing in front of the niche. Then he ran ahead towards the tunnel. I could see most of Hell from my position, and I watched as he paused in front of it, his long white hair whipping behind him. He took a deep fortifying breath and ran headlong into the Wall.

Twenty Guards suddenly appeared, brandishing their spears at the space where Victor had just disappeared into. The arms around me tightened and pulled me deeper into the dark niche, so I could still see what happened on the outside, but the darkened space made it difficult for anyone to see inside it. One of the Guards calmly walked through the Wall and reappeared holding Victor by the scruff of his white t-shirt.

"Look what we have here," he said to his comrades. The other Guards laughed humourlessly.

"We will be generously rewarded for this capture." One Guard cackled.

"You will rot, Mister." Another Guard shouted in Victor's face.

I struggled to free myself, but the person wouldn't let me go. The grip held fast even when I bit hard onto its palm. Two other Guards each grabbed one of Victor's arms and marched him away. I tried screaming, but no sound came out. I could do nothing as the Guards dragged Victor between the bunks like a criminal, and after around fifty feet, the Guards disappeared along with Victor. He wasn't supposed to go through the tunnel. It should have been me. I was the one who was supposed to get caught; I was supposed to meet Him.

I turned and sobbed into the strong chest, releasing the emotional pain of my disappointment and guilt over Victor's capture in a river of tears. When they abated, I looked up at my captor, into Curtis' deep green eyes and I burst into a fresh set of tears.

"Why did you let him do that?" I asked, sobbing harder still into his white t-shirt. "It should have been me."

"It should never have been you. Victor made some good points." Curtis answered.

"Good points?" I asked incredulously. "I don't care about the good points he made. I put myself here Curtis, and you and Victor just took away my only chance. Do you think this tunnel will never stay here, kept open for anyone to just walk inside?" I asked, my tears abating as a strong sense of determination gripped me. "I'm going through. Now that they have caught Victor, they won't respond in time, they'll be too busy."

I spun around and walked towards the spot where the Guards caught Victor but Curtis grabbed me around the waist, put his hand over my mouth again and dragged me deeper still into the niche.

"The Guards aren't that stupid?" he asked. "They will be watching this area. They know we are friends with Victor and they'll be trying to capture us too."

My body slumped back against his chest, sinking into his embrace, in absolute defeat, as more tears teetered at the corners of my eyes. Suddenly, a deafening noise — a siren — wailed. It ricocheted loudly inside the little niche and bounced back into Hell.

I stared out into the crowded space. People stood up from their bunks and looked around confused, with their hands over their ears, for the source of the ear– piercing sound. Guards, in their familiar Gladiatorial garb, long thin spears and shields, sprouted up everywhere and started to herd everybody back to their bunks. Most of the Guards used excessive force, punching and manhandling the spectators back to their bunks. Some shoved and prodded the people with their spears. Whereas, a fewer number of them gently guided the Souls back, without raising their voices and with no show of violence.

Curtis tightened his grip and drew us deeper into the niche. His back connected the back of it, meaning we could go no further inside. I rested my head onto his chest and let the steady beat of his heart lull me into a more relaxed state. With that rhythm I could forget the situation we were in, but then the sound of the siren pierced my mind again, and I started to panic again. I gently pulled his hand away from my mouth. "Where's Nigel?" I whispered, panicstricken.

"He stayed with Mrs Scott. He said he was too scared to come with us." Curtis replied.

I nodded, relieved to hear that Nigel was okay.

FIFTEEN

THE CAPTURE

"Macus! Get ready!" Astinal's voice rang in my head, waking me from a pleasant dream. My eyes snapped open at the call but the remnants of the dream still lingered at the periphery of my mind. Isobel had been cuddled against my side, her short black hair sticking up at odd angles having been tousled in her sleep, and candlelight was reflected in it. I ran my hands through the silky tresses, massaging her head as she slept soundly. Not a frown disturbed her perfectly sculpted face, but every once in a while a small smile broke free, giving away the tone of her dreams. I used to love lying with her like this. We couldn't do it every day, but the time we could spend alone was perfection.

I untangled myself from the thin, sweat-soaked sheets — alone — and sat at the edge of my elaborate four-poster bed; its sweeping chiffon curtains draping around me. Rubbing the sleep from my eyes with one hand, I covered my mouth with the other, yawned and stretched. My coarse chest hair tangled in my fingers as I scratched my bare chest and heaved myself off the bed using one of the intricately carved, wooden bed posts for support. A basin in the left-hand corner of the room furthest from the door beckoned me and I splashed cold water on my face, hoping it would wash away the blissful dream which still played on my mind so I could carry out my duties without distraction. My clothing lay in haphazard piles on the floor, so I walked around the room gathering them and dressed. I grabbed my spear which leant at the end of my bed, and helmet — which sat on the wooden chest at the end of the bed — and headed for the door. A mirror stood next to my desk, opposite the bed and I stopped short in front of it. Dark circles had developed under my eyes over the last few weeks, and my dishevelled hair was a result of my restless sleep. My eyes slid from the mirror to the framed portrait next to it — Isobel. I shoved my helmet onto my head to hide my unkempt appearance and pain-filled eyes and strode through the door ready for the day.

Astinal had obviously thought today was going to be an important day, as he woke every Guard an hour earlier than usual; I was the last Guard to enter the Altar room. I waded through the thick crowd, trying to get to my usual place at the altar — at Astinal's right-hand side.

"What is this all about?" I whispered into Astinal's ear when I reached him.

"Today is the day, I know it," he replied, frowning up at me.

"How can you be so sure?" I muttered quietly. If anyone else had questioned him, he would have unleashed his wrath upon them, but we had been such good friends for so long that he forgave my insubordination and shrugged in response. He then turned to the crowd, readying himself to address them.

"Okay, men." He called everyone to order, and every single man in the room quietened and faced Astinal. "As you know, we were ordered to keep an eye on our faithful Souls; two groups in particular. The leader in Hell, Violet Deneuve, and her followers, Nigel Baxter, Victor Steele and Curtis Jones, and the leader in Heaven, Mary Deneuve, and her friends Jeff Blake and Sophie Lane. You have done a great job in watching them and reporting back to me but I have it under good authority that today is the day when they will strike." No one in the room spoke. The silence hung heavy in the air. "Now I want you to keep your eyes peeled, and if I order you to go somewhere, go without question. Only I will tell you where to go.

Do not take orders from anyone else." He looked around the sea of helmets, briefly looking at each Guard in turn. "You know what to do. Dismissed."

Everyone in the room banged their spears on the ground and called, "Yes Sir," before filing out of the room.

I turned to Astinal, but he had put his hand up to his temple and was speaking to someone not present in the room. I sighed and filed out of the room along with everyone else, heading to my first post — to watch Violet.

When I reached my post, she was already awake, and was sitting at her bunk surrounded by her friends. Maybe Astinal knew something he wasn't telling me, as this early morning activity was unusual for them. Every other morning, I was forced to wait for her friends to gather at her bunk, but today it looked like they had been awake for a while.

My eyes fluttered around the room, scanning the nearby faces, looking for any disruptions, but I steadfastly refused to believe anything of note would happen today. Any flurry of movement or loud shriek from the Souls jarred me to the bone, my head snapping to the source of the sound, only to find a child playing or other such mundane activities happening around me.

After a while, Astinal appeared in front of me and made his way over. I heaved a sigh of relief — finally my watch ended. I was glad to leave and get back to the sidelines. I hated being out in the fray, it reminded me of my time here and those were not memories I wished to relive.

"Any news?" He asked me.

"They awoke early and have been together since I started my watch," I replied.

"Anything else?" He asked, looking around the cavernous space.

"No." I replied, simply.

Astinal grunted and walked away, keeping one eye on the foursome as he did so.

I walked away from him, closed my eyes and visualised the Viewing Room, when I opened them, I faced the wall of flickering screens each displaying several views of the Afterlife. I dragged one of the creaky swivel chairs up to the middle of the console table, directly underneath the screens, and sat staring up at them. A button on the console released a keyboard from beneath it. I tapped a, now, familiar sequence of keys and a view of Violet's bunk appeared — the image encompassing every screen in the room. Violet still sat on her bunk in the same position in which I had just left her, but Curtis and Victor were not with her. Only Nigel stayed, but they spoke little. After a while, Nigel shuffled to his own bunk and left her alone. She moved from her bed to the floor and sat cross legged, appearing to meditate. She looked serene and beautiful and my heart ached as the remnants of this morning's dream permeated into my mind. With difficulty, I dragged my eyes away from the screens to the keyboard and tapped another memorised sequence of keys. This time the view of Violet's bunk only appeared on one screen, at the bottom right-hand corner, and the view of Mary's bunk took up the remaining screens.

Mary was at her bunk, alone, sitting on the floor in the same position as Violet. she was also meditating, and as with Violet, her friends were not with her. Using the joystick embedded into the console table, I panned around to nearby bunks and her friend, Sophie, sat at her own bunk and the one-legged man, Jeff, at his. He was lying on his back with his arm draped over his calm face. The unusual solitary behaviour made it seem as though both Mary and Violet were expecting something to happen, as they had been accompanied by at least one of their friends at all times since they had arrived. I frowned at the screens in front of me, racking my brain as to why the twins would be acting this way.

The hours ticked by and the targets stayed at their own bunks, but the usual camaraderie between them wasn't present; a closeness between them which I had grown accustomed to and still expected to see today. The lack of it made me uncomfortable and solidified, in my mind, Astinal's earlier warnings.

I sat at the console watching them and after hours of sitting, watching and waiting, a sudden flurry of activity sprouted at Violet's bunk. I quickly tapped out a sequence of keys to rearrange the screens so Mary and Violet's view each took up half of them. Curtis had come up to Violet and was whispering something in her ear. He helped her up from the floor and they both sat on her bed and talked. After a minute, she leapt up from her bed and stormed off, but Curtis grabbed her arm and pulled her back. His hands travelled to her waist and my chest constricted when she didn't push him away but leant her head lovingly on his shoulder. My breath became laboured as their closeness became clear and my heart ached to be in Curtis' position. She raised her head from his shoulder and they spoke again but Victor and Nigel made their way over and interrupted them. At their words, Curtis and Violet spun around and glared off into the distance. I panned around, Mrs Scott and two of her men were ambling over to Violet and her friends, her back bent over double so she stared at the beige tiles as the two men guided her to Violet. This was highly unusual. Mrs Scott hadn't been away from her bunk for centuries. Everyone usually visited with her. That was how it had always been. I followed Mrs Scott's path with the joystick until she drew level with Violet and stared at the screen as they spoke. One of her men brought over two wooden cups with steaming liquid inside, gave one to Mrs Scott and the other to Violet. The other brought over her ancient rocking chair which she had owned since I had known her.

I glanced at the other half of the screens, Mary, Jeff and Sophie stood together again. I glanced at the clock and noticed it was almost time for the afternoon meeting. I tried to keep one eye on each half of the screens, not wanting to miss anything and as the clock struck four, Violet stormed off. I didn't have to follow her with the joystick, I already knew where she was going. What surprised me more was that Mary and her friends left Mary's bunk. I followed their path with the joystick, I needed to know where *they* were going. At the edge of the screen, a head of familiar dirty, matted hair, a red ball in hand, peaked over a footrest. I needed to see Astinal. He was right.

I jogged over to the Altar room, desperate to relay the news to Astinal. I was the last to reach the room for the second time today and Astinal had already started the meeting. He hated anyone who interrupted him, but this was too important. As I fought my way through the thick crowd, Astinal stopped talking and stared at me. The Guards turned to see what had distracted him and parted, making an easy pathway for me, leading me straight to him.

"You were right. It has started," I panted in his ear, when I reached him.

He glanced at me, but carried on where he left off. "Today has been a good day so far, keep it up."

"Violet is heading for the Wall. Mary, Jeff and Sophie are making their way to Stuart Willis, and you stand here as though nothing is amiss," I hissed, finally catching my breath.

"Turi, gather twenty of your best men and head to Section Eight," he called to a tall Guard standing at the front of the crowd. I instantly recognised him as the Guard who had brought Stuart Willis to us.

"Yes, Sir," Turi called back, he turned and pointed to twenty of his men who filed out, spears held out in front of them at the ready.

"What about Stuart Willis?" I asked in a low voice.

"We will deal with him later," Astinal promised.

Astinal continued his meeting, the Guards stood in rapt attention, but my mind was in turmoil, worrying about what would happen to Violet. Maybe I shouldn't have told Astinal anything, I must have misunderstood her behaviour. She must have just stormed off because everything had gotten too much for her, but deep down I knew her destination. I had to do my job and stopping her was only part of it.

The Guards in the room banged their spears in unison and filed out. The sound brought me back to the present. I hadn't noticed the meeting had ended nor heard a word Astinal had said. I glanced over at him, he was still standing at the head of the altar facing the door on the other side of the room. His eyes were closed and a deep frown furrowed his brow.

"If they find her, Macus..." he trailed off, frowning deeper.

"I know," I said, looking at the floor.

"We need to see Stuart Willis," Astinal announced, striding from the altar. He disappeared through the door before I reached him, and the absence of his footsteps led me to believe he took the easy route to Stuart Willis' bunk. I closed my eyes and pictured Stuart's bunk, and when I opened my eyes again, I was standing next to Astinal. He was towering over Stuart, his face red with rage. Stuart was perched at the far edge of the bunk, quivering with fear; I had arrived just in time.

"Astinal," I murmured.

Astinal drew back from Stuart, his face fading back to its normal colour.

"Tell me what they asked you?" Astinal asked calmly.

Stuart's eyes darted between Astinal and myself, as sweat beaded on his brow and slid down the end of his nose.

"Answer him," I growled. Stuart shuddered and sputtered, choking on his own spittle. I didn't have time for this, I needed this interrogation to end so I could make sure that Violet was unhurt.

"Th-the-they asked-" he faltered, coughing harder. "They asked why I was following them, Sirs," he choked out. "I don't know how they knew. I didn't tell them. I was trying to be, to be-,"

"To be what? Useless? Incompetent? Stupid?" Astinal spat.

Stuart cringed back away from him, fear showing in his expression. "I-I-I-I," He stuttered.

"You are useless," Astinal growled. I banged my spear on the ground once and Astinal unclenched his fists and rolled his shoulders to calm himself. "Did you tell them it was us who asked you to, so obviously, spy on them?" We took the silence and the sweat now running in rivulets down his face and neck as an affirmative response.

Astinal tsked and disappeared.

"Understand, you are only still here because of me," I said ominously. "Do not anger him again, as next time, I will make sure I am not here to protect you." I closed my eyes and readied myself to disappear and find Astinal. I didn't have to search for long, his cry of anger drew me closer to him than anything else could have. I found him in the Altar Room, surrounded by Turi and his twenty men, and in the middle of a circle of spears was Victor Steele standing frightened. He was trying, but failing, to keep every spear point in his eye line at once.

"Where did you find him?" Astinal shouted, his face redder than I had ever seen it and a vein throbbed in his temple.

"We found him at Section Eight, he was trying to get through," Turi answered gravely. "What shall I do with him?"

"Take him to Holding," Astinal ordered, and when they didn't leave fast enough, he roared, "NOW!"

The Guards in the room beat a hasty retreat, prodding Victor with their spear points to move him faster. We stood in the now empty room, the shouted command echoing several times, before fading, leaving the room in a heady silence. Astinal was breathing deeply — in through his nose and out through his mouth — and after a minute, he turned to me and said sharply. "Ring the alarm."

My eyes widened at the command. No one had sounded the alarm in centuries. I remembered the last time someone rang it. The people who guarded the afterlife then had run around, and gathered up anyone who looked even remotely guilty, admonishing, hurting and taking most away to Processing. I had not understood what was happening at the time, and I had feared for my soul, but I was lucky enough to have escaped their watchful eye. That day started an unprecedented chain of events. Isobel...

I shut my eyes and prayed it wouldn't end as it had the last time. I walked around the altar and hesitated. "Are you sure?" I asked pleadingly, knowing the outcome once I rang the alarm. "You know they will hound us after this is done?"

"Let them, I have no other choice. You know the orders," Astinal said coldly.

I knew where the button was, and without taking my eyes from Astinal's, I slid my hand under the altar and ran my finger over it for a second, wondering who had had the unfortunate job of pushing it the last time. I swallowed hard, hoping that Astinal changed his mind, but as the precious seconds ticked by, he said nothing. His face darkened, and he looked sharply at me, wondering what was taking me so long. I pressed the button I had always known lay beneath the altar, but never dreamed of pressing, and a deafening siren rang through the Altar Room and from experience, I knew it was ringing throughout the whole of the Afterlife. Teams of Guards would now be shepherding the Souls back to their bunks and noting who was missing as we had trained them to do.

Violet hadn't been in the Altar room when I came in. I had expected them to have captured *her* at Section Eight and I was more than a little surprised to see Victor, surrounded by spears, in her place. I thought for sure I would see her. She must have hidden or not gone to Section Eight at all. Did I get it wrong? I knew one thing, I would not rest until I found her and knew she was safe, then I would tell her everything and persuade her to stop this madness.

SIXTEEN

TAKEN

"When should we approach the Guards?" I asked, looking around me in search of a plumed helmet over the sea of heads. I tucked a strand of my long black hair behind an ear and took a sip of the tea that Sophie had just made. Sophie would never tell me where she got the tea from, so I just gave up asking, but it's bolstering effects did wonders to clear my head. No Guards were in sight, they must still be at their meeting. Sophie said they were always absent for at least ten minutes, and it had barely been five between our interrogation with Stuart Willis and returning to Sophie's bunk.

"Soon," Jeff replied, a cup also cradled in his hands.

"It will have to be," Sophie said. "I can't take any more of this. Did you hear what Stuart said?"

"Yes, I was right next to you," I muttered. "I can't believe the Guards set him up to watch us. He said two of them had approached him, I wonder which two?"

"I don't know. I believed him when he said he didn't know, but I'd sure like to find out," Jeff said.

We sat in silence for another five minutes, each of us terrified of making the first move. Every sip of the tea gave me renewed confidence. I knew what I needed to do, but the way to Him was clouded. Jeff and I gave Sophie our empty cups, and she stashed them, along with the cooking implements, in the usual hiding place. I was about to suggest going back to Stuart's bunk and questioning him again, when a deafening siren blared throughout the room. We each jumped at the sound and several people nearby screamed. Half a second later, hundreds of Guards appeared around us. I didn't even know that many lived here.

"Calm down, Souls. Calm down." One of them shouted. "There is nothing to be afraid of, this is simply protocol." A second and third Guard picked up the refrain, and the sound of their joint voices rose over the wailing of the siren, but no one seemed to listen to them. The unaccustomed sound frightened everyone, and a wave of panic reached a fever pitch as the wailing progressed, driving men, women and children to their knees, hands clasped over their ears to block the assaulting sound.

Panic stricken, I leapt up from Sophie's bunk and spun in a circle, looking for the unknown clue which had started the siren. All I could see were Guards shepherding the souls back onto their bunks. Sometimes it was easy, as some stayed kneeling right beside their bunks, but some strayed from their designated bunk spaces, seeking solace from neighbours and friends. A Guard strode over to us once he noticed our little group.

"You need to remain at your designated bunks Souls, move out," he commanded sharply.

"We've done nothing wrong. Can't we be together to comfort one another?" Sophie asked timidly.

"I will not ask again, back to your individual bunks," he shouted. It was as though the siren quietened whenever he spoke, but blared again once he finished speaking so his words were clear enough for us to understand.

"But-" I said, but a knock at my temple from the butt of his spear stopped me mid sentence.

"Not them!" A voice called, and once the stars dissipated from the periphery, I saw another taller Guard run up to the shorter one in front of us and whisper harsh words into his ear. Their words didn't drift over, but the first guard turned to me looking sheepish.

"I am sorry for striking you," he said. His cheeks flushed, even though his face held a scowl to mask his embarrassment. He walked away, heading to another bunk to admonish someone else.

The second Guard came up level with us. He was so tall, he towered far above Jeff's six feet. He glared at the retreating Guard's back, hazel eyes blaring. "I am sorry about my partner's use of force but I would like to invite you to go to your own bunks, as we need to tally up the numbers to make sure no one is missing."

"Why would any of us be missing? What's happening?" Sophie shouted at him, but he had already turned away and the siren swallowed her words.

I made my way over to my bunk. "What are you doing?" asked Jeff fiercely. "We should stick together."

"We don't want to draw too much attention to ourselves. I'm sure we are the ones who caused the siren to go off when we talked to Stu. Do you not find it odd that not even five minutes after we came back from questioning him the siren blared? It's too much of a coincidence." I said.

Disregarding what Jeff said, I stalked off and lay on my bunk, facing away from them, whilst watching the carnage unfold in front of me. People ran around in a panicked state, and Guards chased them, catching them by any means necessary. The Guards carried those who had strayed too far from their bunks, back to them. Some were carried fireman style, unconscious and bleeding profusely from serious head wounds and I would bet my life they had borne the brunt of a blow to the head from a spear, as I had.

I lifted a hand to my head and fingered the lump which was forming at my temple. My head throbbed but I would show no one I was hurting. I closed my eyes, trying to empty my mind, to spirit myself away to another place but the combination of the blaring siren and the ever-growing headache made it near impossible. I lay by myself for a long time, listening to the screams, both from the sirens and those around, ricochet around me. Most people had listened and retreated to their bunks, afraid of the Guards and their willingness to use their full force against them. After a while, Jeff left Sophie's bunk and made his way to his own — he had clearly given away any thought of rebellion.

The sirens quieted, but I had become so used to the intrusive sound I took a while to figure out the residual ringing came from inside my head and not from the siren itself. Someone nudged me. I turned towards the touch and saw that Jeff stood over me.

"We should confront them now," he said hurriedly, but the ringing in my ears blocked his words — his lips moved, but no sound reached me.

"What?" I asked, shoving my little finger in my ear, trying to dislodge something which would enable me to hear. "I can't hear you," I said, sitting up on my bunk.

Something must have shifted inside my ear as I sat up, because sounds came rushing back. The buzzing of many whispered conversations, the anguished cries of pain or sorrow — I couldn't tell the difference between the two anymore — and the scuffing of feet as people ran to and from the surrounding bunks. I noticed that the lights had dimmed and wondered how long it had been since I left Jeff and Sophie. Large groups of people huddled together, some of them were patching up wounds with bits of t-shirts or trousers. Broken bones surrounded me. Arms hung limply from shoulders and legs held at odd angles and I wondered how they would be mended. Other groups simply sat close to each other offering silent comfort. The Guards had disappeared, leaving us to recover in the aftermath of the utter chaos the siren caused. They obviously didn't care whether we congregated now. They must've accounted for everyone.

"Mary, we should confront them now," Jeff repeated, more forcefully this time, now sitting next to me. Sophie waddled over, clutching her stomach, with a grimace of pain on her face. I moved to make space for her between us, and Jeff and I each put a comforting arm around her shoulders.

"How are we going to do that?" I asked sceptically, looking around once more. "They've all disappeared."

Jeff shook his head. "I don't know, but we have to do something."

"This is awful. They can't treat us like this," Sophie sobbed. I tightened my grip on her shoulder, squeezing her to me to comfort her further.

"The Guards never usually act this way when they take a Soul from their bunks," I began. "This is carnage."

We sat in silence taking in our surroundings. I thought about the headache which was forming at my temple, the task which had been bequeathed to me, how stupid I was to accept it, and the life I had led. How sheltered had I been and how naïve was I to think that something better lay beyond life? Everybody around me looked miserable and in pain. This was supposed to be my salvation but I realised that I was in the wrong place for it; I had been sent to Hell when I should have been sent to Heaven.

I closed my eyes and willed the tears that had built up behind my eyes not to fall. A blurry image of my twin sister floated behind my eyelids. Certain features sharpened the more I thought of her. Her tousled short black hair and bright, sparkling green eyes — identical to mine — which held so much mischief and life, swam in front of me. I lifted a hand to my face to wipe away the errant tear which escaped. I missed her so much, and I knew nothing would stop me from getting back to her — my other half.

The slap of sandals against the tile floor pierced through my clouded brain and I instinctively knew they were coming towards us. I looked up and the taller Guard, with the hazel eyes, from earlier strode towards us.

"You need to come with me," he said calmly, once he reached us, gripping his spear so tightly that his knuckles had turned white.

"Why?" Sophie asked, tearfully. "Why should we have to do anything you say when you treat us like animals?"

"Please come with me," he sighed, kneeling, so he was at our eye level. "I do not want to use force, but I will if you make me."

"We actually wanted to talk to one of you and ask why you were following us," I said, folding my arms and scowling at him.

"If you do not come with me," he said, ignoring my question, and standing up and towering over us again. "I will have to make you come." When we didn't respond, he banged the spear on the ground and five more Guards appeared, flanking him. "This is your last chance," he warned.

None of us moved, we each glared at the Guards surrounding us with defiance in our eyes.

"So be it." One Guard's hand shot out from the formation and grasped Sophie's upper arm, she shrieked in pain and tried to wriggle free. At the same time another Guard grabbed Jeff's upper arm, and one grabbed mine, digging his nails into my soft skin. I did not cry out, but winced and struggled against his tight grip.

More Guards appeared around us, and several of our neighbouring bunkmates screamed and pointed at us in fear. They whispered behind their hands to each other, but none of them made a move to defend us; we were on our own. Jeff was bigger than Sophie and I, so three Guards surrounded him and tried to subdue him. The Guard who grabbed me, twisted my arm around my back, attempting to dislocate my shoulder, and it was only then did I scream.

Sophie surrendered. "Please don't hurt me," she pleaded. "I will come along quietly." One of the Guards jabbed the butt of his spear into her stomach, which drew a strangled cry from her mouth. I cried out, tried to run to her but the Guard's grip on my arm was too strong. Our eyes locked, fear induced tears shone in her eyes and a second later she disappeared along with the two Guards holding her.

Jeff had stopped struggling and hung limply in two other Guard's hands, his head slumped against his chest. I assumed they had knocked him out, yet the Guard's grip was still tight on his arms. They disappeared a second after Sophie. I looked up into the tall Guard's helmet, burning an imprint of his hazel eyes into my mind, vowing to meet him again and hurt him, like he hurt my friends. Our eyes locked. I tried to extricate myself from the Guard's firm grip but he twisted my arm further around, resulting in more pain than I had ever experienced throughout my entire sheltered life. My vision darkened around my periphery, and I shook my head to clear it, afraid I would lose consciousness from the pain. A tense silence filled the room as the Guard and I locked eyes for a further minute. I couldn't tell what he was thinking, his expression was robotic. I blinked back tears, but when I opened my eyes again, I was surrounded in darkness. The pain in my shoulder had abated, and I could move freely. No Guards surrounded me. No sound emitted. I was alone.

SEVENTEEN

THE GLASS CUBE

"It's all my fault. I should have listened to Mrs Scott." I sobbed into Curtis' chest, renewed tears saturating his already soaked t-shirt.

"You didn't know this would happen Violet. None of us could have predicted how this would turn out and we all wanted to find out where the tunnel led. Curiosity touched us all — a deep desire to uncover the unknown — you were not the only one dreaming of finding out the truth." His hand travelled to my back and rubbed it in soothing circular motions.

I didn't speak for a moment, the image of Victor being taken away swam in front of me, but it didn't induce tears. It, instead, brought with it a renewed strength and a resolve to find the truth. I tried to push away from Curtis to wipe the tears from my face, but he still held his arms around me, I sighed.

"We need to do something, we can't just keep hiding here, let me go Curtis," I said struggling to get out of his grip.

"Mrs Scott told me to keep you safe, and that is what I intend to do," he said, pulling me back against his chest.

I looked up into his eyes. "Why do you always do everything Mrs Scott says?"

"Because she saved me. I owe her." He stared back into my eyes.

"What did she save you from, Curtis?" I asked, cocking my head.

"Myself," he mumbled, not breaking eye contact. His gaze hypnotised me. I wanted to look away, but it was as though nothing else existed in that moment apart from the pain in his eyes. "David's disappearance troubled me," he continued. "I was desperate for answers and I was frantically searching for them, but they were out of my reach." He finally looked away.

"But what does that mean? You're being very cryptic. Just like Mrs Scott." I said, scowling at his vagueness.

He frowned before answering. "I searched for David in places I shouldn't have. Luckily Mrs Scott stopped me before it was too late." He sighed, closed his eyes and rested his head on my shoulder. "You mentioned your Father persuaded you to come here, what did you mean by that?" He said, changing the subject.

"I don't know why I said that." I whispered.

"You do, otherwise you wouldn't have said it. Come on Violet, it's just the two of us." His grip tightened around my waist, pulling me closer into his embrace.

I hesitated, I had never spoken of my Father to anyone other than my twin sister, and even then the conversations had been few and far between, and cut short if she ever said a bad word against him. "My Father was controlling and manipulative. He forced me to view the world as a cesspit of debauchery and sin. He turned me against my Mother, and tried to turn me against my sister, but that was a much harder job. He made me think that there would be something to uncover here, and if we made it, we should try to find out what lay beyond life."

"We?" Curtis asked.

"My twin sister and I. She is here somewhere. I hope she is here somewhere." I put my head back against his chest.

"Why did you go along with it?"

"Because I love him."

Neither of us spoke for five minutes. I didn't dare reveal anything more of my past, and Curtis somehow knew not to ask anymore questions.

"I like Mrs Scott," I muttered, into his chest.

"I like her too." I felt him smiling into my shoulder.

"But I know she's hiding something from us," I said.

I wouldn't have noticed anything out of the ordinary in Curtis' behaviour if he hadn't been so close. So when his body stiffened, I pulled away from him.

"What are you hiding from me?" I asked accusingly. "What do you know?"

Curtis didn't meet my eyes, he instead pulled me back to him and rested his forehead on my shoulder again.

"Curtis," I said, putting my hands on either side of his face and forcing him to look at me. He still didn't meet my eyes. "Curtis," I said louder, still holding onto his face. He finally looked at me pleadingly.

"She told us not to tell you," he whispered.

"Us?" I asked disbelievingly. "Who is 'us'?"

"I can't... she didn't want us to tell you." He looked away, ashamed.

"Is it about the Wall?" I asked. Curtis didn't respond, instead he closed his eyes looking defeated. "Curtis, please answer me. Is it about the Wall?" Again, he didn't respond. "Well, I am going to find out." I noticed his grip had loosened, so I spun away from him, and before he could stop me, I had run beyond his reach. I had only run two steps out of the niche, when Guards appeared, surrounding me on all sides, holding their spears at my face. One tip grazed my cheek, breaking through the top layers of skin and blood trickled down my face and onto my white t-shirt.

"Violet Deneuve, we have been sent here to detain you." A Guard said, and I recognised him to be one of the Guards I'd noticed watching me. He towered far above me, his deep hazel eyes looked warmer than any other Guard I had come across — except for the dark-eyed one — but none-the-less, I panicked. I spun around to check on Curtis, praying he still hid in the niche but he was standing just outside it, also surrounded by Guards. "Please come with us Violet. We will not hurt you." The hazel-eyed Guard said, holding out a hand.

I didn't take it, afraid the gesture was a trap. Instead, I held my arms to my side, trying, but failing, to keep an eye on each Guard and spear. Curtis yelled and as I turned, he collapsed to his knees, his arms wrapped around his stomach, struggling to breathe.

"We do not want to hurt you, but if you carry on in this manner, you will end up like your friend." The hazel-eyed Guard said, scowling at me. Defeated, I raised my right hand and held it out for him to take.

"Good," he said, clasping my hand in his. I took a deep breath and closed my eyes. I instantly regretted my decision because when I opened them again, I knew I was nowhere near the Wall anymore. Nor were there Guards around me that I could see or sense. The room I was in was devoid of light and I stood on a cold, hard surface. The clunking sound of a heavy lock clicked behind me and I spun toward where I thought it had issued.

"Hello." I called into the darkness in a trembling voice. "Is anyone there?" Louder this time. When no one responded I assumed the person had locked me in the room from the outside.

I kept my eyes wide open and prayed for that minute source of light would erupt somewhere which would enable me to see my surroundings, but to no avail. The darkness stayed true, leaving me with the echo of my beating heart drumming in my ears, and the amplified sound of my breathing to keep me company.

I stood stock still for five minutes, not daring to move a muscle, but once I rationalised with myself that I was alone in the room, and that if anyone was here, they would have made themselves known when I called out, I took a hesitant step forward ready to explore my surroundings. The first step was the hardest, as I couldn't be sure a sudden drop into a bed of nails or a lake of fire I had always been threatened with, would appear in front of me. My foot landed on hard ground, the same consistency as the ground I had been dropped into. The second step was easier and the third easier still. I put my hands out in front of me and waved them around to stop myself from bumping into anything, but jumped as my hands came in contact with a cold surface three steps later. I stroked, prodded and tapped the surface and concluded it was glass.

Keeping one hand on the glass, I walked around the space. I reached a corner and felt around for any imperfections, a latch, or anything that would help me escape. I only found a small blemish on the glass which I assumed the previous occupant made. Keeping the blemish as a marker, I walked around the enclosure, keeping track of its size. I realised that I was in a glass cube which was around nine feet by nine feet. I jumped, once, on the spot trying to touch a ceiling, but my hand touched nothing but empty air. Unfortunately, I had found no weaknesses, no way of escaping, nor was anyone here to help me.

The darkness enveloped me leaving me disheartened and frightened. I crawled to a corner and sat with my arms around my legs and my chin resting on my knees. I closed my eyes and thought about the previous events which led me here. How had the Guards known exactly where I was? They had appeared within seconds after I left the niche. I didn't have a chance to get far before they surrounded me.

"She told us not to tell you." The echo of Curtis' voice reverberated through my skull, teasing me. What had Mrs Scott told Curtis and the others that she couldn't have told me? I lay in a foetal position with my back to the glass and closed my eyes. My body was too tired to stay awake and I felt myself fall into a fitful sleep.

Blaring lights jerked me awake along with the same siren which had sounded in Hell the day the Guards took me prisoner. I scrambled to my feet and crouched low, swaying on the spot from exhaustion. I raised a hand to my face to shield my eyes against the bright lights, and waited for them to adjust. Once the echoes of the siren abated, the room fell into an uneasy silence, and when my eyes finally adjusted, I was surprised to see a sea of Guards surrounding the glass cube. They filled the entire space the cube didn't cover, and although they held their spears at their sides in a resting position, their presence still unnerved me.

When the Guards made no move to attack me, I looked around. Three steps encircled the cube, raising it above ground level so I had a good view of the Guards and the room. I stood up, my legs numb from the foetal position I had curled into. The Guards didn't react to my movement. They stood stock still staring vacantly at their individual middle distance. When I was keeping track of the Guards who watched me, I had thought I knew how many lived here, but I couldn't have been more wrong in my estimation. Hundreds of blank faces faced me; more than I could count.

Through the glass panel to my left, the Guards finally stirred, creating a pathway in the middle of the group leading straight to the cube. I backed away from them and the bone-straight walkway, bumping into the glass wall on the other side, trapped in the prison.

A guard appeared at the head of the pathway, too far away to see any distinguishing features, just a visored helmet, shielding unidentifiable coloured eyes. He slowly walked towards me, his spear banging on the floor at every other step. The rapping sound entered the glass chamber and echoed around it. He stopped at the bottom of the steps, looking straight into my eyes and I gasped when I recognised his bright blue ones underneath his helmet; the same Guard who had stopped me on my first attempt at getting through the Wall.

"Violet Deneuve, I hear you have been creating an uprising." He smiled, his eyes gleaming beneath his visor. "You have made a grave mistake."

A guard to his left handed him an object. I couldn't make out what it was at this distance, and was too afraid to approach the Guard to get a closer look. Instead, I pressed myself back further against the glass panel to get as far away from him and the object as possible. Still grinning, he pressed his thumb against the object. I had no time to think, breathe or react. The glass panel disappeared from beneath my fingers and I fell backwards into the sea of Guards behind me.

I tried to regain my balance by planting one foot firmly on the cube's floor, but the other foot had already passed the threshold and pawed at empty air trying to gain purchase, but I was too late. My knee slammed against the second step. With the speed of the fall and the angle at which my knee connected with the step, the subsequent sickening crunch, as my kneecap shattered on impact, signified a broken bone. My world turned black for an instant, and when my vision returned, it was hazy and discoloured around the edges. My tiredness had delayed my reactions, and it was a few seconds after the impact when I screamed out in pain. Somehow I stayed clear from the Guard's reach — for now — so I knelt on my crushed kneecap, breathing through the pain, and waited for my vision to sharpen.

A hand grabbed one of my arms and my fight-or-flight instincts kicked in. I elbowed my would-be captor hard in the face, his helmet cracked with a snap and I wrenched free from his grip. I struggled to my feet, and tore away from the Guard, hobbling blindly into the middle of the cube as fast as my crippled form would allow.

A foot connected with my shins and I pitched forward onto my face, on impact I bit hard on my tongue and a rush of metallic blood filled my mouth. I spat out the excess blood and a tooth flew out with it. Still dazed from the fall, I push myself weakly onto my good knee, attempting to stand. Failing, I started to fall but a pair of hands caught me in mid air and lifted me up into their arms. I glimpsed the Guard's coal black eyes right before my body shut down, defeated.

EIGHTEEN

TORTURE

I sputtered against the onslaught of water on my face. Surprised, I tried to lift my arms up to wipe away the excess water which was now dripping into my eyes, down my neck and soaking through my paper-thin t-shirt, but my arms barely lifted three inches before they stopped short and lifted no further. A telltale clinking sound caught my attention but my waterlogged brain didn't recognise it. I looked down at my arms and I was shocked to find them chained to the armrests of a simple metal chair bolted to a flagstone floor.

I looked up from my chained arms. I was in a large room lit by hundreds of candles, some ensconced on the walls, but most were placed haphazardly on short pillars dotted around the room. The light from them reflected off the raw stone floor, polished to a sheen by the thousands of feet which had scuffed across it in the millennia it had existed.

I faced an elaborate altar. It held the same amount of candles on it as were dotted around the room, so everything behind it was cast in eerie shadows. Five Guards stood behind it and I recognised their eyes which gleamed beneath their visored helmets. The Guard in the middle — in the place of honour — had the familiar bright blue eyes which had instilled an air of despondency in me whenever I thought of them. The Guard to his right had the coal black eyes, and the one to the left was the one who took me from the Wall; his hazel eyes shone clearly through his helmet in the soft flickering candlelight. The two Guards at each end were the tallest and broadest Guards in the room, twice the height and breadth of the hazel-eyed Guard. They reminded me of the Guards I had encountered at the archway in Purgatory and surmised that they would be one and the same. The shafts of their spears were as wide as lampposts, but their hands clasped around them comfortably. Their swords hung so low, their tips brushed the floor, five feet long and as wide as my hands.

"You have been causing quite a stir amongst the souls, Miss Deneuve." The blue eyed Guard said, leering at me. I shrunk back as far as the chains would allow me in my chair. "Please do not be afraid, Miss Deneuve, we will not hurt you, as long as you cooperate." He stepped away from the line up, walked around the altar and strode to me. Fear rippled through me, and my breath came in short, painful gasps. I tried to push myself away from him, but my feet slipped uselessly against the polished stone floor. When the Guard reached me, he shoved me back against the chair and held me down as new chains materialised out of thin air and slinked around my ankles, snaked around my legs and bound me more securely to the cold, uncomfortable chair.

"I told you Miss Deneuve, if you cooperate, we will not hurt you," he whispered, leaning close to my ear.

The chains continued to travel up my legs wrapping around my shins as the chains around my wrists sprang to life and snaked up around my arms, cutting deep into my skin. The sound of metal scraping against metal sounded much like chalk on a chalkboard and grated in my ears. From the way the Guards behind the altar grimaced, it clearly disturbed them too.

My eyes found the dark eyed Guard's, his hand still clenched around his spear, but I could see trails of blood running down his arm where his nails had dug into the soft flesh of his palm. I whimpered and gritted my teeth in pain as the chains dug deeper into my skin, tearing through it and sending rivulets of blood twisting down my arms and legs. I groaned, and he looked away, deep frown lines furrowing his brow. I thought the pain would never end, but as swiftly as the chains sprang to life, they stopped.

"Have you had enough Violet?" The blue-eyed Guard taunted, circling my chair.

"What do you want from me?" I asked them. "I have done nothing wrong." A false courage rose in me allowing me to speak.

The blue-eyed Guard chuckled. "What are you planning on doing here?"

"What am I planning on doing here?" I asked. "What do you mean? I died, I plan on being dead. What else am I supposed to do?"

"No, no, Miss Deneuve." He strode back over to the altar and snatched up a single piece of brown parchment paper and glanced at it. "I have it under good authority that you took your own life. Why was that?" He asked, striding over and shaking the piece of paper in my face.

"I–I–," I stuttered.

"Don't have an answer?" He drawled, not even waiting for me to recover.

"How do you know how I died?" I asked in a small voice.

"Oh, we know how everyone died. Take, for example, your dear friends. Would you like to know how they died, Violet?" he teased.

I shook my head vigorously, my short black hair whipping at my face. "No," I pleaded. "If they wanted to tell me, they would have done so themselves."

"Have it your way..." he said.

He turned to face the altar. "Nigel. Oh, poor Nigel. His death had been slow and painful." He turned back to face me, grinning evilly. I squirmed in my seat, shaking my head from side to side. "His father. Would you like to know what his father did to him?"

"No, please, I don't want to. Please, don't tell me," I pleaded, squirming harder still.

The tears fell.

"His father was a drunk," he continued. "Beating Nigel, starving him and chaining him up like a forgotten dog."

"No, don't tell me anymore. Please." I sobbed, my head drooping against my chest in defeat.

"Oh, and let's not forget Victor," he paused. "He shouldn't have died, but I guess when you get old, organs get weaker. He was bound to die from the shock, no matter how fit he was on the outside."

I didn't respond this time, I remained hunched in my seat, unmoving, with tears falling onto my lap. My, still drenched, head dripped profusely, adding to the pool of water gathering between my thighs.

"I will ask you one more time, Miss Deneuve. Why are you here?" Astinal asked.

"I don't know what you are talking about," I whispered.

"Suit yourself." He turned away from me and walked back to the altar, but before taking his place at the centre, he stopped at the brute at the end of it and whispered something in his ear. The Guard had to almost bend double to hear the words. I would have looked comical had I not been in such dire straits.

My tears flowed freely, it pained me to listen to that kind of information about the people whom I had grown to love. The blue-eyed Guard stopped speaking and the Brutish Guard nodded once. His heavy footsteps shook the floor along with the loosened chains. The sound of their metallic scrapes, rebounded around the room along with the heavy footfalls, which reverberated through my body. The blue-eyed Guard took his rightful place behind the altar and fixed his gaze upon me. I tore my eyes away from him and hung my head, not wanting to betray my depressive thoughts to the gallery of men before me, but I was sure that the shaking of my shoulders told all.

The footsteps receded. A door opened behind me and slammed shut, leaving the room with a tense air. Two minutes later, the door banged open behind me making me jump, and the creaking of un-oiled wheels soon followed. I didn't dare look up from my lap, afraid of what I would see. The creaking drew closer along with an occasional rattle of objects. The noise drew level with me and out of the corner of my eye, a metal trolley — much like the ones used in operating theatres — stopped next to me. When I looked up, my eyes widened in shock at what the trolley held. My sobs came even harder as a fresh wave of fear washed over me.

An assortment of medical implements — three syringes full of thick, green alien liquid, scalpels, pliers, and a myriad of other sharp instruments I couldn't name — sat on the trolley.

"What are you going to do?" I asked, my words coming out in choked sobs. I fixed my wide eyes on the blue-eyed Guard, silently pleading with him.

"I told you we wouldn't hurt you if you cooperated, but you haven't." He tore his eyes away from mine, and stared at a spot behind my right shoulder. I craned my head around and followed his gaze and my eyes bulged at the sheer size of the man who stood behind me. From a distance the two gigantic Guards who stood at the end of the altar didn't look so enormous, but up close they towered far above me.

The Guard turned and grinned, his mouth full of broken, yellowed teeth and a pink puckered scar marred the left side of his face, starting from his eye and ending at his chin. His black eyes were bottomless and held a meaner quality than the dark-eyed Guard's eyes. He wore a pristine white leather apron, covering the entire length of his body, from his neck to the tips of his sandalled toes. He picked up a pair of thick black leather gloves, the size of a child's jumper and snapped them on, covering both forearms up to his elbows. He pushed the crude trolley, so it stood in front of me and the instruments, again, rattled on top of it.

"Last chance to answer my questions, Miss Deneuve." The blue-eyed Guard said calmly, rubbing his hands together. "What do you plan to do here?"

I stayed silent, my eyes fixed onto the metal instruments on the trolley before me. Each of them looked sharp and likely to cause me unimaginable pain, and whenever the trolley moved, the razor sharp edges glinted ominously in the candlelight. A massive hand reached out and snatched up a scalpel. I followed its path and watched as the hand deftly twirled it between its massive sausage-like fingers. The

Guard traced it down the side of my face, following the same scar-line which marred his face. I flinched involuntarily, even though he hadn't broken any skin. The blue-eyed Guard had stopped speaking, and it was then that I realised that he would do nothing to stop this.

The brutish Guard lifted the scalpel from my face, twisted it in his fingers and thrust it at me. I jerked my head away from the sharp tool, dodging the attack. He grabbed my hair, held me in place and retraced the same path but this time he pushed hard on the skin, breaking through and hitting bone to my chin — I screamed.

"Ha, see, now we are twins," he barked in my face, his putrid breath washing over me, but nothing could have distracted me from the pain on my face. I clenched and unclenched my fists as the Guard used the scalpel to draw patterns and nonsensical imagery onto my flesh. He wasn't a great artist, his lines were erratic; some deep, sending shock waves of pain through my entire body as it scraped over sensitive nerve endings. At other times, the cuts felt like little pinpricks. I would never know which kind of cut would come next, and no matter how hard I tried to hold back, I screamed at every one of them. I screamed even when the scalpel wasn't tearing through my skin. The pain was too much to bear, but the Guard only laughed at me and carried on. He had become an expert with the scalpel by now.

"Please, stop." I whimpered between sobs. The tears hadn't stopped flowing since the torture had started and little snot bubbles popped whenever I exhaled too hard. I raised my head to plead with the Guards behind the altar. The blue-eyed Guard frowned at me, his eyes holding no emotion; I wouldn't be able to get through to him. I looked over to the hazel-eyed Guard and his eyes were wide and glistening, as though he couldn't look away if he tried. The dark-eyed Guard had closed his eyes. I couldn't tell what he was thinking. I wanted to call out to him, but I didn't know his name. I wanted him to save me but it would be impossible. "I can't take it any–AHHH!" My words merged into a long scream as the blade slid along my left inner thigh, creating another long, deep cut. The blood flowed freely, dripping over the chair seat, dripping off the ends of my fingers, down my legs, and pooling beneath my feet.

"Stop." A Guard shouted over my screams and my head snapped up at the sound.

The Brutish Guard stopped cutting me half way down my inner thigh. The grin faded from his face as he turned to the blue-eyed Guard with a confused grimace on his face.

"But why?" he asked, stupidly.

I clenched my eyes and mouth shut, and ground my teeth together trying not to scream out loud. A needle pricked my inner elbow, but I was too weak to protest. I sat, shoulders slumped in defeat and as the needle's contents entered my body, I relaxed. The effects were rapid. The pain melted away from my body and the tension left my muscles. When I opened my eyes and looked at my previously ravaged body, I could see the rips in my clothing but no open wounds were visible beneath them, just pinkish scar tissue which gradually turned to my natural skin colour right before my eyes.

"Miss Deneuve." The blue-eyed Guard addressed me. He had his arms folded and a scowl on his face. "Are you ready to talk?"

I remained silent, feeling braver and stronger than when I was first brought to this room, and my false courage boosted my will to defy his regime.

"Miss Deneuve," he sighed exasperated. "Do we have to go through this again?" When I didn't reply he continued. "Why did you kill yourself and your sister?" Again, I didn't respond. "We know of your past and by the looks of it, your present and future are looking just as bleak." He gestured to the room. It took my whole being not to respond. I knew he was trying to bait me. He was bluffing. I had to stay strong.

"Violet," he shouted, making me jump. "I am not the enemy here, you are fighting the wrong battle."

I remained silent, maintaining eye contact the entire time.

"Why were you at Section Eight this afternoon?"

"Section Eight?" I asked, silently cursing myself for speaking.

"So she speaks," he mocked. "Yes, Section Eight."

"Do you mean the Wall?" I asked.

"Yes, the Wall — Section Eight — what were you doing there?" He asked, losing his patience.

I had lost my resolve. My courage had run out. I shrunk back in my chair and refused to speak further. I had taken the bait and answered one of his questions, but he would never answer any of my own in return.

"So be it," he sighed. "I warned you Violet. It does not have to be this way."

I watched as the burly Guard picked up a small metal toothpick — three inches long and fifteen millimetres wide — and twirled it in his long, fat fingers, grinning. He grabbed my left hand and stretched out my clenched fingers. He ran the toothpick under my middle fingernail, seemingly cleaning out the dirt beneath it, but then he shoved it deep under my nail until it re-emerged in the middle of my finger. At first I didn't register what had happened. I had watched what he had done, but the pain didn't register until half a minute later.

My screams pierced the tense atmosphere, the pain overwhelming. I would have preferred it if he had cut off my finger. I secretly wished he had. My yells ricocheted off the walls, the resulting vibrations reverberated through my whole body but somehow concentrated on my mutilated finger, intensifying the pain. My brain became cloudy, and vomit seeped out the corner of my mouth and spilled out onto my already stained and torn t-shirt. The dark-eyed Guard's pained face was the last image I saw before my brain finally and mercifully shut down.

NINETEEN

MRS SCOTT'S WARNING

Her screams resonated in my head, long after the last of her echoes had abated. The chains around her arms and legs slinked back into their holdings — underneath the armrests and behind the front chair legs, respectively — freeing her from her confines. The Brutish Guard who had administered the torture, unceremoniously injected another green syringe full of the healing herb concoction into her arm; a recipe we had stolen from Mrs Scott centuries ago and which we still used for precisely this purpose to this day. Her face softened as the medicine took effect. The pain melted from her face and her body became so relaxed she started to slide off the chair. She stirred feebly but didn't wake.

"We will have to try again later," Astinal said, a scowl on his face.

The Brutish Guard made a move to grab her, but my shout stopped him dead in his tracks.

"Stop!" Anger vibrated through my entire body. "I will take her." I strode from my place behind the altar, and when I reached them, attempted to shove the Guard out of my way, but merely pushed against an unmovable mass. Instead, I strode around him, picked her up, hoisted her light frame over my shoulder and strode out of the Altar room. Footsteps followed me, jogging to keep up with my fast pace but I didn't turn to see who dogged my heels.

I kept up the fast pace, eating up the distance between the Altar room and the Holding Room where she was being kept. When I reached the right door, I dashed into the already open doorway, slammed the door behind me and locked it from the inside. Fists hammered, and angry, muffled shouts leaked through the well-sealed door. Ignoring them, I headed to the raised platform in the centre of the room where she was being housed. The glass which usually caged her wasn't present allowing me to climb the three steps and walk straight into the small space.

I gently lowered her to the ground, careful not to bang any part of her body on the floor. I looked at her peaceful face, stroking her short hair away from it. She looked so much like my Isobel. It ached to be this close to her. She reminded me of *her* so much that I had no doubt in my mind they were the same person.

Throughout my time in Hell I had seen reincarnation happen too many times. When identical people end up here who had led the same lives — died on the same day, at the same hour, minute and second as the previous vessel — it was hard not to believe in it. The hammering on the door brought me back to the present. I sighed, stroked her face once more and rose to leave. I walked down the steps and to the door. I looked back as the glass gracefully rose around her, sealing her inside her transparent prison. My face reddened, ashamed that I had been a part of her torture, even if inadvertently.

I grasped the doorknob but I couldn't gather the courage to face the onslaught waiting for me on the other side. I stood frozen on the spot, my forehead resting on the door, vibrating from the blows from the Guard's fists on the other side. I shut my eyes, but immediately regretted it. Violet's contorted face swam in front of me, and the fear and pain etched into her features seemed more pronounced in my mental vision. My anger came back in full force. How could Astinal condone this? Had he lost his mind? Even Turi had been perturbed by his behaviour. He had our unconditional loyalty. He didn't need to do anything outlandish to prove his leadership to any of us.

I flung the door open and faced the ten Guards standing outside it. The first three had their fists up ready to bang on the door again.

The surprise on their faces was enough to cheer me up a little; though I didn't show it.

"Move," I commanded. The Guards, used to my quiet demeanour, scrambled to get out of my way at the sound of my voice. I stalked away, my head held high and a deep frown on my face, but once I had left their eye line, I smirked.

I strode through the maze of white hallways searching for Astinal. He had refused to meet my gaze when we had been in the Altar room with Violet. I knew he would avoid me after the incident, but now he had disappeared. My first point of call was the Altar room. I hoped he was still in the room and the search could then promptly end, but I knew he would have moved on. I know that he would be attempting to preoccupy his mind with more important tasks rather than dwell on the dire situation we had found ourselves in.

As I suspected, the room was empty and the only evidence of anything untoward occurring was the faint blood stain on the floor in the middle of the room. I wondered who it was that had cleaned it up. I imagined Astinal on his hands and knees scrubbing away at the evidence of Violet's torture and laughed out loud. Astinal would never demean himself like that, not now that he had the power to command others to do his bidding.

Without a backwards glance, I left the Altar room and headed to the Viewing room. I could have easily transported myself there but the long walk helped me clear my mind. The flickering screens were the only source of light in the room, and the swivel chair creaked loudly as I sat on it and scanned the screens, looking for any immediate threats. I pulled out the keyboard from under the console and tapped out a sequence of keys. A chilling view of Mrs Scott's bunk faced me. A mass of souls crowded around her bunk and neighbouring bunks and stared at her as she sat in the centre of the group on her ancient rocking chair. I remembered the last time a gathering like this happened and the consequential deaths. I shuddered. This didn't bode well for us.

My fingers moved before I had registered what I was doing and before I could stop myself, the view of Violet's bunk came up on the screens, even though I knew she wouldn't be there. It had become a force of habit to search for it whenever I came into this room. I found that I couldn't leave the room until I had seen her on screen and made sure she was okay. After staring at her empty bunk for longer than I cared to admit, I changed the view back to look at the entire Afterlife. I carefully searched for Astinal through the crowds, but it was like looking for a needle in a haystack. All the Guards looked the same from my vantage point. This was useless. I sighed as an overpowering urge to change the view back to Violet's bunk came over me, but I wrenched myself away from the console table, knowing this room didn't hold the answers I needed.

I strode through hallways, searching earnestly for Astinal, knowing he was close, but not knowing where. I reached out to him telepathically, but received no response. Through my wanderings, I bumped into Turi.

"Turi," I called, jogging to catch up to him. He had just come out of his sleeping quarters. "Have you seen Astinal?"

"No Sir," he answered. He paused and looked ready to say something more, but instead stiffly walked away.

I thought his behaviour seemed odd, but I didn't have the time to dwell on it, I needed to find Astinal right now. On impulse, I made my way to his personal chamber, and when I reached his door, I found it was locked. He never locked it. His door was always open. I had found him.

I knocked on the door, but no one answered. I knocked again, louder this time. "Astinal, let me in. It's me Macus." I called through the door.

The sound of shuffling feet emitted through the door and the lock clicked. The feet then shuffled away from me. I pushed the door open and peered around it into the dimly lit room. His chamber was much larger than mine. He had a large four poster bed in the middle of the room — raised on a wooden platform — covered in luxurious furs, and piled high with pillows and cushions. Inch thick red carpet covered the entire room and embossed, cream coloured wallpaper covered every wall. An enormous chandelier dangled from the middle of the ceiling, but none of the candles were lit. The glow from the dying embers in the grand fireplace facing the bed was the only source of light. I couldn't see him at first, but as my eyes adjusted to the dim lighting, I spotted him sitting on the floor in the far corner of the room, hidden in the shadows. His head resting between his knees.

"Astinal?" He didn't respond, but remained unmoving in his corner.

I trod over to him and sank next to him, sitting in the same position. Our arms brushed against each other as I shifted to a more comfortable position. He didn't move, and neither did I. We just sat in silence, waiting for the other to speak.

"I am sorry Macus," he finally mumbled.

Remorse was the last emotion I expected from him. Indignation and rage — emotions which I was used to receiving from him — but not remorse.

"I–," I faltered. I was at a loss for words.

"I had to," he said, finally looking up. His eyes held a far away look. "I had to." He put his head back in his lap. "Please do not hate me," he finished, clenching and unclenching his fists in an attempt to keep his emotions in check.

I hesitantly put my arm around him, pulling him close, and to my surprise he didn't push me away, but welcomed the awkward embrace.

"I know you did," I sighed, not knowing what else to say. I was still angry at him, but I knew he wouldn't have done anything to intentionally hurt me. Deep down, I knew he was just following orders, but it didn't mean I wasn't still upset.

"You have to understand," he began after a while. "There was nothing I could have done. They expected me to take action. This is how we do things here," he paused. "From watching her today, I now know why you think she is Isobel." I flinched, unused to hearing her name spoken by another voice. "But if she keeps this up, I will have no other choice but to hand her over."

"Hand her over," I said firmly. "That is what she wants. We stopped her last time, what if we made the wrong decision? We cannot make the same mistake this time around."

"What if she is...?" He trailed off, not wanting to finish his sentence, but the look on his face told all.

"That is the risk we will have to take, she needs answers and we need them too. I have been thinking about this over the last few days and I've come to the conclusion that it has to be the only way forward," I said.

"You're right," Astinal said. "I can't go on with these ludicrous rules which I follow blindly. They have kept us in the dark for too long. Things need to change."

"Are you going to tell me why you couldn't read me in on this situation?"

"They were watching my every move, Macus. They knew she was coming back before we did and they wanted to test me. They needed to know who I was loyal to, and if I caved into your demands, they would have thought me weak and unseated me. Who would have looked after her then?"

"Who are they?"

"I can't tell you because I don't know. I am just as in the dark about the inner workings of this place as you are."

"I mean, come on Astinal. I didn't die to work, I died to get peace. Otherwise I would have stayed, but without you by my side..." I trailed off with a painful faraway look in my eyes.

"When I saw you here so soon after I arrived, I gathered you had a hand in it. You were a legend." He grinned.

"I couldn't do it without you. You always had my back and life without you seemed pointless." I paused, thinking of the three months I had lived without Astinal. Centuries had elapsed since those memories crossed my mind and dredging them up now was more difficult than knowing Isobel still lived. "Why Stuart Willis?" I said, changing the subject to something I could handle.

"He was easy to manipulate, and he didn't deserve the status he was given here." Astinal toyed with his laces.

"You can't dictate where people go Astinal, no more than I can."
I said.

"I know, but I can make sure they get what they deserve when
they've cheated the system." He glanced at me.

"What did you offer him?"

He shrugged. "What he wanted."

"Which was?"

"Drugs."

"Humanity's vice. What kind?"

"Does it matter? Offer them what they want and they will be putty
in your hands," he said, rubbing his hand over his face exasperatedly.

"Did you ever plan on giving him anything?" I asked, scoffing.

"Of course not. Are you mad?" He replied, with a small smile.

"So you used him?"

"I gave him a taste of his own medicine. Something people feared
to give him when he lived." He said flatly.

I paused thinking of what he had just said. "How do you think
we should do this then?"

"We should let her meet Him, but be present when they meet
so we can find out who He is and what He wants," Astinal replied.

"Okay, do you think she will handle it?" I asked, concerned.

"After seeing her limits today, I am sure she will be able to handle
anything we throw at her." He finally looked up at me and smiled
weakly.

I smiled hazily back, still unsure as to whether blindly dumping
her into this possibly dangerous situation was the right way to find
the answers we all needed.

"She will be fine, Macus," Astinal said. "Have faith in her. We had
no choice last time with Isobel. This time we have the power to stop
this and restore a semblance of normality to this godforsaken place."

"Astinal, you blasphemer," I mocked.

Astinal barked out a laugh and the atmosphere lightened
considerably.

"Come on, we can't sit here all day. We have responsibilities to
keep and havoc to wreak." I winked at him.

I stood up and offered him my hand. He took it and I helped him up. Grinning, we faced each other, hands still clasped. On impulse, I embraced him. He stiffened, unused to the physical contact, but surrendered to my embrace. He slapped me on the back once before breaking away and smiling up at me.

"What do you need to do now?" I asked as we made our way to the door.

"I will see what the other Deneuve twin is doing," he replied. "Keep an eye on everything. Go to the Viewing room and if you see any meetings, send Turi. Oh, and you have my permission to use force on anyone who steps out of line."

"I was just there, and there was a huge gathering at Mrs Scott's bunk, and you of all people should know what this could potentially mean." I glanced meaningfully at him.

He stopped walking and nodded. "Keep an eye on her. We do not want another riot we can't control."

I nodded, remembering the incident he was referencing. I was equally eager to avoid another revolt.

"I will call if I find out anything you need to be apprised of," I said, opening the door. "Please answer this time."

"I will," he promised and clapped me on my back once more before I disappeared.

The wall of screens shone in front of me when I opened my eyes. They were still trained on the whole of the Afterlife. I was pleased that, on the whole, everything looked calm, and the Guards were doing an excellent job of keeping the peace.

Bracing myself, I typed in the coordinates for Mrs Scott's bunk on the keyboard and hit enter. Mrs Scott sat on her rocking chair, still surrounded by a large group of souls. Her audience had increased since the last time I had looked, numbering in the low hundreds. Several Guards stood on the periphery, hands clenched around their spears, staying close in case anything happened. I turned the sound on, afraid of what I would hear, but adhering to my orders.

"We need to do something." A man hissed loudly at the back of the group.

"*Calm down, George.*" *A lady next to him nudged him in the ribs and glanced nervously at the Guards closest to them.* "*We don't wanna draw any more attention to us, do we?*"

The man's face turned red, he scowled, but didn't speak again.

"*We did nothing. I don't understand why they are treating us this way.*" *A woman piped up, she was sitting at Mrs Scott's bunk. I recognised her from the last time this happened but couldn't remember her name. She hadn't played a key role, but she wasn't just a bystander either.*

"*Yeah, we didn't do nothin'. Why they gotta treat us so bad?*" *A teenager to her left agreed.*

Several souls spoke at once. Their words were lost in the din, but occasional words drifted away from the fray — 'horrific', 'preposterous,' and 'travesty,' — to name but a few. I kept my eyes trained on Mrs Scott, knowing she would put an end to the commotion, and soon enough she raised a hand and the shouts instantly ceased. Everybody waited on bated breath for her to speak — myself included.

"*Most of us know why this has happened,*" *she began.* "*Those of us who have been in this situation before can only wait for the outcome.*" *She paused, taking a sip of tea from the smooth wooden cup she had been cradling in her hands.* "*For those of you that have not had the pleasure of experiencing this, prepare yourselves for a change. For there will be a change none of us could have predicted, and it will affect every aspect of life here. I believe we will finally get the answers we have all been craving.*" *A greedy glint flashed in her eyes. Her hand, which held the tea, shook violently, sloshing the steaming liquid all over herself. One of her men shuffled over to her and laid a hand on her shoulder, calming her instantly. He refilled her cup but didn't move from her side; a comforting hand still resting on her shoulder. She mumbled something I couldn't hear and took a sip of tea; taking a moment to compose herself.*

"*It is now just a waiting game,*" *she continued after a couple of minutes.* "*There is nothing more we can do at this time, and unless you want to be taken away, I suggest you leave me be and make your way back to your own bunks.*" *She nodded towards a group of Guards who were making their way over to them. Turi strode at the head of the group, leading them with stoic grace, butting the end of his spear on the ground at every other step.*

"Break it up." He called over to them. "Back to your own bunks, we will tell you when you may converge again."

He stood over them, glowering at anyone who didn't move quickly enough. His entourage was prodding stragglers not so gently with their spears. Once the visitors had left and Mrs Scott was alone, Turi turned to walk away.

"You cannot stop her, she is stronger this time," she prophesied. "There is only a matter of time before she wins. We all know it." He turned to face her.

"No one can predict the future." Turi answered.

"Tell Astinal I say 'hi'," she said, ignoring his last statement. "And to come and visit me some time. I miss our talks." She grinned at him revealing a mouth absent of teeth, but full of gums. She set her cup on her bedside table and closed her eyes. She crossed her hands on top of her abdomen, wordlessly dismissing him.

He stayed a heartbeat longer, then banged his spear on the ground. He and the Guards disappeared one by one, leaving Mrs Scott alone on her rocking chair.

The door opened behind me, Turi walked in and collapsed heavily into the chair next to me, causing it to shake and squeak violently. We didn't speak for a while, instead choosing to stare at the screens in front of us, which was still trained on Mrs Scott's bunk. She was still sitting in the same position as when Turi had left, and using the joystick, I zoomed in closer to her face. Her eyes moved rapidly behind her lids, then she suddenly opened them and looked straight at us; looking right into the invisible eye staring at her.

"She freaks me out," Turi finally mumbled from beside me.

I tore my eyes away from her hypnotic grey-green eyes and looked over at him. "She has been here longer than anyone. She knows things we don't," I said, turning back to the screen. She had closed her eyes again and I was glad for it. "We cannot underestimate her."

"She is still creepy," Turi muttered, reaching over and using the keyboard to zoom out of the current view so it displayed a wider area.

My eyes roamed across the screens, looking for other clandestine meetings. I turned back to Turi when nothing caught my eye; he was glued to the screens looking for the same meetings I had been looking for. I had taken no notice of him until Astinal recently made him the leader of a small group of Gladiators and the way he led his group was a testament to his leadership skills; I saw him going far here.

"What do you want, Macus?" he asked, not taking his eyes off the screens, but smiling slightly.

I smiled at the familiar way he addressed me; we would definitely become friends. "Nothing," I muttered, looking away from him. We sat in a more comfortable silence after that, but I still stared at the screens taking nothing in.

"I know we haven't spoken to each other much, but that was atrocious," Turi said after a while.

"What?" I asked, turning to face him once more, unsure of whether I had missed the prelude to that statement.

"What Astinal did." He sighed, finally tearing his eyes away from the screens and looking at me. "I didn't think he would stoop that low." He shook his head.

"You have to put yourself in his position. How else could he stop her from turning everything upside down?" I countered.

"I don't see how you can even stand him after what he did," he scoffed. I frowned, not understanding him. "I know about Isobel–"

"Do not speak of her," I said coldly, already re-evaluating our tentative friendship.

"I don't mean to overstep my bounds Macus, but come on, we were all present, and everyone in that room knew of your past," Turi said incredulously.

I shook my head, closing my eyes against the torrent of truth which was being shoved at me. "You do not know him like I do Turi. He did what he thought he needed to do, it's as simple as that."

"Okay." Turi shrugged. "If you are fine with it, then I am fine with it."

"Did you hear what Mrs Scott was saying to the others, or did you come too late?" I asked, changing the subject.

"Too late," he mumbled, staring back at the screen.

I recounted what Mrs Scott had said.

"She knows." Turi said, licking his lips. "She always knew, even when we were 'normals'."

"She was always bizarre. Astinal loves her though, that is why he allows her free rein, but he never told me what she did for him," I said.

"She freaks me out," Turi said, chuckling. I chuckled along with him. Soon it turned to a full-on laughing fit and once we started it was hard to stop. It was nice to release some of the pent up tension I had built inside me recently. I wasn't even sure why we were laughing but by the end, I was clutching a stitch at my side and wiping tears from my eyes.

"I needed that," I said once my laughter had subsided.

TWENTY

WHERE IS MARY?

I ran through a maze of wide, white corridors — split down the middle by a thick red line — my long black hair whipping wildly behind me. An eerie voice echoed, repeating the phrase: "Keep to the left. keep to the left."

I ran headlong down the corridors — a strange sense of déjà vu increasing at each turn — panting from exertion and fear. I was desperate to stop and take a breath but knowing if I stopped I wouldn't be able to run again.

I turned a corner and several black doors stood on either side of the corridor. As I progressed down it, they each opened of their own accord. Inside each doorway was a deep black interior, and in the darkness I knew, tall, skeletal, grey, alien-like creatures stood waiting. They would be at least ten feet tall, towering far above my meagre height. I could hear their breathing through the sombre openings as I ran past, and the sound urged me on.

A sudden growling behind me made me jump. A loud snap of sharp, canine teeth caused the air to ripple just above my bare ankles, giving away the creature's proximity.

I skidded to a halt. Up ahead a black void had appeared, and there was nowhere to go but into it; there were no black doors, just an endless sea of white leading to the darkness beyond. I couldn't turn back towards the growling behind me, nor take shelter in one of the many doorways I had passed. As though on cue a scraping sound erupted behind me. A huge,

214

grey, skeletal, dinner plate sized hand clawed out of a doorway, clawing into the doorjamb. It created a crater in the floor as it pushed itself to its full height. I needed to get away from this corridor and the only way out was inside the black void. I ran again, my legs cramping up and my lungs afire. I could hear more creatures emerging from each doorway but I felt their fast footsteps vibrating through the floor as they ran towards me. It pushed me to run faster; I needed to get inside the void.

Fifty feet. Forty feet. Thirty feet. The void seemed to be the only thing in the corridor, taking up much of the space the closer I got to it. Now and then the canine creatures snapped at my heels, reminding me of their imminent threat.

Ten feet. Five feet. I launched myself into the air. An invisible force inside the void pulled me into its depths and I braced myself for the collision with the warm earth which greeted me the last time I jumped into a void like this, but nothing came. The void — which, as its nature determined, held nothing, not even oxygen — had trapped me. I would die from the lack of oxygen. It was only a matter of time.

A siren pierced through my brain. The sound confused me as there had been no siren the last time I was in that corridor. A tiny pinprick of light appeared and grew brighter and wider until I burst through it and gulped down lungfuls of sweet air. The sudden rush of oxygen made me dizzy and it took a second for me to adjust to my new surroundings.

I fluttered my eyes open. A bright light lit up the whole room and it took me a moment for my eyes to adjust and figure out where I was; the glass cage. A hazy figure walked towards me. I sat up from my foetal position on the cold ground in the middle of my glass cage. I pushed my long black hair out of my face and watched, with apprehension, as the figure drew nearer. It stopped a metre away from me, standing stock still. One hand held a wide spear and under its helmet bright blue eyes stared directly into my emerald green ones.

"Mary Deneuve, it's a pleasure." A deep voice said, kneeling beside me. "How are you feeling today?"

I didn't respond, scared that this was a cruel trick. I was afraid that if I spoke I would entice him to administer some form of painful punishment.

"I will not hurt you," he continued. "Do you know why we brought you here?"

I shook my head. "No." The word came out in a croak.

He set his spear beside him. "I am sorry we had to detain you in this manner." His voice was cold, his eyes held no warmth, which made his apology redundant. "But I didn't want you causing too much trouble." He looked at his hands.

I swallowed hard. "I don't understand what you mean," I said.

"It doesn't matter." His words sounded bitter, and when he looked back up at me, he seemed to brace himself for what he was about to say next. "Your sister is fine."

"Violet?" I asked, shocked. I drew myself up to my knees and clutched at his hands. "She's okay? Thank God," I breathed, a warmth washed through me as I understood his meaning.

"Do not thank God, thank me," he spat.

I shrank back from him, puzzled by the sudden change in tone, afraid I had overstepped an unknown line.

"Sorry," he said, looking away. "I didn't mean to scare you."

"Where is she?" I asked in a small voice, once I was sure he had calmed down.

"She is safe. You will be with her soon," he replied, picking up his spear and getting to his feet.

"Please don't leave me," I shuffled towards him on my knees, looking up at him imploringly.

"I have to go, Miss Deneuve. We will provide answers in due course." He turned to leave.

I watched numbly as he climbed down the steps and the glass walls – which I hadn't noticed had disappeared – rose up, locking me in my prison again. He walked out of the room without a backwards glance, a determined set to his shoulders. His spear banged loudly on the floor at every other step.

For some reason, I trusted what the blue-eyed Guard had just told me. I was ready to see my twin sister again and get the answers we had been seeking for the last twenty-one years.

The details of my dream crept back. The blinding white corridor burned in my retinas and the air rippled around me with the echoes of the skeletal creature's breathing, making me shudder and hug my knees to my body in abject fear. The light in the room faded, leaving me, again, in complete darkness, with only the remnants of my dream to keep me company.

The door behind me opened. I looked back and watched as Astinal strode in. He stopped short at the doorway frowning at the scene before him. Unconcerned, I turned back to the screens in front of me.

"Making friends Macus?" Astinal teased.

"Yes," I replied. "Got a problem with that?" I turned back to face him, arching an eyebrow in question. Astinal had taken off his helmet and laid it in the corner of the room along with his spear and shield. He ran a hand through his soft brown curls and sighed.

"No," he responded, pulling a third, rarely used, wooden chair up to the screens and sitting between Turi and myself.

I continued to stare at his profile long after he had sat, trying to gauge his reaction and his purpose here, but as always, his face was impassive and difficult to read. Turi coughed, trying to ease the tension.

"Found anything interesting?" Astinal asked, setting his elbows on his knees and getting down to business.

I cleared my throat. "There was a gathering around Mrs Scott's bunk which Turi and his men dispersed, but not before I heard what she had to say." I paused trying to remember her exact words. "She told them a change like nothing ever before will happen. There is nothing we can do to stop it. We will have to wait. She seemed confident."

Astinal grunted in response.

"Um yeah. And err, she said to say 'Hi'," Turi muttered, his face reddening.

Astinal smiled in response but said nothing.

"And she said to come by and see her." Turi added.

Astinal smiled wider, almost grinning, Turi took the smiles as encouragement.

"And she said she missed your talks." Turi said with a small smile.

Astinal let out a bark of laughter.

I grinned at Turi, glad he was able to cheer Astinal up a little. The weight of his responsibilities were great, and he needed every excuse to let off steam.

"I do miss Mrs Scott," Astinal finally said, not looking at either Turi or myself, but keeping his gaze fixed on the screens in front of him. He would occasionally tap out a sequence of keys on the keyboard to change views, so that he had a clear picture of what went on in the Afterlife. After a while, Astinal sighed and sat back, rubbing his eyes.

"I thought the siren would have caused a bigger stir than it had, especially with the older souls," he commented, rubbing his face in his hands and then running them through his dishevelled, curly, brown hair again.

"The last time the siren sounded, there hadn't been an organisational system in place, and that was why it was a disaster," Turi said, shaking his head.

"I try not to think about it," I muttered.

"I am sorry I had to do that, to dredge up all those memories Macus," Astinal said. "There was nothing more I could have done. It was only afterwards, when we spoke, that I realised I should have left them to their plan."

"What do you mean?" Turi asked, puzzled.

"As my number Three, I guess we should apprise you of the details," Astinal paused. "We are going to meet Him."

"Him?" Turi exclaimed. "Him?" He didn't have any more words left in him, his mouth hung agape, shocked into silence.

"Yes, Him," Astinal affirmed, putting a hand on Turi's shoulder. "I will need you by my side on this one. Can I count on you?"

Turi nodded, his words still failing him.

"Good," Astinal nodded and looked at me. I nodded at him. There was no question of my loyalty. I would stick with Astinal through thick and thin. "Good," he repeated.

"How are we..." Turi trailed off, unsure of how to finish that sentence.

"Violet is the key," Astinal said. Turi frowned, not understanding.

"Miss Deneuve," Astinal said, and when Turi still looked dumbfounded, Astinal added. "The short black-haired woman I asked you to watch."

"Oh," Turi breathed, understanding who Astinal was talking about. "I didn't know you knew names. Do I have to know names?"

I shook my head at him. "Not right now."

"I only know the names of the important ones," Astinal stated. Turi nodded, acknowledging Astinal's statement.

"So what will Violet do?" Turi asked.

"Violet will demand to meet Him and we will take her to Him," Astinal explained. "We will tell them that we couldn't ignore her demands."

"Okay," Turi said, giving Astinal a questioning look.

"He can't blame us if we say she demanded to meet Him," Astinal said, frowning at Turi when Turi still looked confused.

"I would think we would get in more trouble for following the demands of a Soul. Would he not think us weak for pandering to her insanity?" I asked Astinal, trying to deflect his anger and make him see sense.

Astinal shook his head. "It will be fine, and any resulting punishment would land on me, so you don't have to worry." A finality to his tone implied the end of the conversation. Turi and I both turned back to face the screens. During our short conversation, a group of people had gathered at a bunk. I didn't have to zoom in to know it was at Mrs Scott's.

"They are at it again," Turi sighed, standing up. "I will deal with them." He quickly gathered his things and left the room. He had his fingers to his temple ready to gather his fleet of Guards.

I zoomed in on the screen at Mrs Scott's bunk. Five-seconds later a group of Guards appeared in the bottom right-hand corner of the screens and made their way over to her. The crowd quickly dispersed, afraid of retribution, leaving Mrs Scott alone. I turned the sound on.

"I thought we warned you not to have visitors for a while," Turi said.

"I do not control them, they come to me for guidance." Mrs Scott replied hotly.

"Tell them to leave next time," Turi said. "You know the rules, you have been through this before."

"I cannot tell them to leave any more than you can keep them at their bunks," she replied. One of her young followers came up to her and handed her a cup of tea. "Would you care to join me in a cup?" She gestured for Turi to sit at her bunk. Another follower came up to Turi, handed him a steaming cup to him and guided him onto her bed, leaving him little choice but to take the cup and the seat offered to him. He looked surprised at the turn of events but took them in his stride.. He motioned for the rest of the Guards to stay back and took a sip of the hot liquid. Turi stared into his cup, and Mrs Scott stared at him.

"Did you speak to Astinal?" She asked.

"Yes, I did. I relayed the message and he... laughed." Turi said, his face reddening beneath his helmet.

"I would have expected nothing less," she said. "He needs cheering up nowadays. He is too stern. The pressure of the job has gotten to him."

"Who would have thought the pressures of anything would get to you in the Afterlife," Turi paused and took another sip. "When I died, there was nothing to worry about. We didn't have a care in the world, but now..." he trailed off.

"There will be a change," she said. "Something catastrophic akin to Isobel's time." Turi flinched. "I know you are listening, Astinal." She looked straight up at the unseen eye from which we were observing through. "Let it be. Trust that this time will be different." She looked to Turi.

"I had better go," he said, awkwardly handing his half-empty cup to one of her followers and standing up to leave.

"Everything will change for you too, Turi," she called to his retreating back. He didn't reply.

When he reached the rest of the Guards, he commanded them to return to their duties, said he would brief them later and disappeared. I half expected him to come back to the Viewing room, but after five minutes I knew he had gone elsewhere. I was surprised to see how dark it had become and knew it was almost time to turn in.

"It is time for the nightly meeting. Will you attend?" Astinal asked, breaking the heavy silence.

"No, I will turn in for the night," I replied, getting up to leave. "I will see you in the morning,"

"Don't do anything stupid, Macus," Astinal warned.

I stopped short halfway out the door. I turned to say something back to him, but thought better of it and snapped the door shut behind me.

TWENTY-ONE

THE KISS

My eyes snapped open and the skin on the back of my neck prickled, warning me of another's presence in the room. I tried to ignore it as no one had come to see me in what felt like weeks, but, in reality, it had, most likely, only been a few days. I stood up, stretched and started my morning routine which I had developed since my incarceration.

I started by walking around the nine-by-nine foot space first, testing the glass for any new weaknesses, hopeful, but knowing nothing would have changed since the previous day. But before I had walked halfway around it, I stopped short, and sniffed the air, whilst keeping my ears open for any foreign sounds.

A faint exhale of breath issued close by and the even fainter scent of lavender wafted over to me bringing with it a sense of peace, but I started to panic nonetheless. Someone was in the room with me.

"Who's there?" I called out, my voice croaky from under-use.

The person didn't respond. I stood frozen, my back to the glass, afraid to move.

"I know you're there," I called again into the darkness, hoping this time the person responded. Its breath hitched in its throat, then exhaled deeply. A silence bloomed, in which a war waged between us. I was adamant not to speak again, hoping if I waited long enough the stranger would crack and break it.

"I am sorry for scaring you, Violet." The voice pierced the darkness, making me jump.

"Who are you?" I asked, after a few seconds. When it didn't respond, I asked. "Why are you here?"

"I don't know." The voice said, chuckling.

I frowned, staring at the spot from which I thought his voice issued. It had an odd effect, as though it was pulling me closer to him.

"I know you," I whispered. The air became tense. He had obviously been waiting for me to recognise his voice. "You're the Guard that came to me and warned me 'they' were watching."

"It seems you didn't listen." The voice chuckled.

"I don't need your help," I muttered.

"Evidently." His words hung heavy in the air as I looked around my current surroundings.

I folded my arms and pouted at the tone of his voice, refusing to respond and show him how his words affected me.

"Sorry." He said meekly.

"Can we get some light in here, I've been living in darkness for so long. I fear I may go crazy?"

As though at my command, a dim source of light appeared far above me. I looked up at it, shielding my eyes, and once they adapted to it, a small ball of light took shape, floating in mid air.

I looked back to ground level, and saw that he was sitting cross-legged on the floor of my prison. His spear was at his side and his back straight as an arrow. His coal-black eyes bored into me beneath his visored helmet, but when I made eye contact, he shifted his gaze away. He remained seated, unmoving, staring at a distant spot over my shoulder, as though afraid to meet my eyes again.

His eyes finally snapped to mine. "You asked for light."

"Thank you," I replied sincerely. I peeled away from the glass and stepped over to him; it was his turn to look up at me. In one swift movement I sat — mirroring his stance — and leant forward, looking deeply into his eyes. They widened in surprise. I sat waiting for him to speak and reveal his purpose for interrupting the solitary lifestyle to which I was becoming accustomed to.

He reached out his right hand and took my left one in his. I was brought back to the first time we talked and remembered the strange tingling sensation which spread through my body when our skin touched. I remember it had felt as though it hadn't been our first meeting, and the way his eyes held such love — then and now — was disarming. His hand, calloused from years of work, was twice as large as those of the tall, hazel-eyed Guard; if that was even possible. His hold was comforting. His thumb caressed my middle finger where the metal toothpick had pierced through, and even though the physical wound had healed, I still held the emotional pain from my round of torture with the Brutish Guard.

I tried to pull my hand out of his and it was almost out of his grip, but his reflexes were too quick and he snatched my hand back into his palm. He didn't need to speak for me to understand his emotions, his eyes told all. They were full of pain and sorrow, such pity and fear. I didn't know how to respond but I gathered that he needed more comfort than I did.

"It's okay, you couldn't have done anything," I said, squeezing his hand.

He looked away. "We could have avoided this situation, why didn't you listen?"

I didn't know how to answer that question without revealing my true purpose here. I didn't trust him yet, and I was afraid that he would tell the blue-eyed Guard my plan if I confided in him.

"What did you want to happen?" he asked, breaking the silence. "Did you want to hurt me Violet?" He turned his gaze back to me, his eyes accusing.

"I don't know you," I retorted. "I don't even know your name. I've never met you before. How can you ask if I've done all this to spite you?"

"We have met before, you just don't remember." He replied cryptically.

"Enlighten me," I said, taking both of his hands in mine, knowing the contact would ease his pain.

"I can't say."

I sighed, letting go of his hands.

"This has happened before, the last time we were together," he said, averting his gaze again. "But you died." I folded my arms sceptically.

"I've heard this before from Mrs Scott," I said. "But I don't understand. How was I supposed to be here centuries ago when I died only a month ago *and* I've only been living for twenty-one years?"

"The longer you are here, the more you realise what happens in the world."

"Seriously? You make no sense. This place annoys me. Just say what you mean, dammit!" I shouted at him, my voice bouncing off the glass.

He winced at the tone of my voice, but I didn't care. If that was what it took for him to give me concrete answers and not shirk my questions, then so be it.

"You are a doppelgänger. You have been reincarnated from, who I knew as, Isobel," he explained.

"A what?" I breathed, shocked; still dissatisfied with his explanation.

"Your name was Isobel," he paused. "It's strange. It's as though I am watching history repeat itself. But with you, the circumstances are different. You have your sister now, a twin. You didn't have this before. She is the key that will help you."

"A woman lived here called Isobel, who looked exactly like me and lived the same life as I did?" I asked.

"Yes, she tried to find Him but failed. The Guards tortured her in front of everyone, to make an example of her. I guess it worked because we have had no issues since that incident." He replied.

"Which Guards? You?"

"No, of course not, I would never hurt you." He said imploringly.

I nodded, accepting his words. "So her name was Isobel. Mrs Scott never told me that."

"Yes, Mrs Scott was there." He looked at his hands. "But she did nothing to stop Isobel from getting tortured, and she did nothing to stop it this time around either." He looked bitter, but I couldn't understand why.

"She tried to warn me, but I wouldn't listen to her. I went to the Wall, anyway" Neither of us spoke for a while. My hands found themselves in his again and his gentle touch calmed me. He finally looked up at me and smiled, and I couldn't help but smile back; it was infectious.

"So I failed then, but you think I will succeed this time?" I asked.

"Yes, you have your sister, and you have us."

"Us? Who is 'us'?"

"The Guards. We are on your side. We will help you."

"Which Guards?" I asked. "How can I trust you when I do not know you or your name?" I added, as an afterthought.

"I am sorry. You remind me so much of her, I forget we haven't been formally introduced. My name is Macus." He put a hand to his chest in greeting.

"Macus?" I asked, never having heard the name before.

"Macus," he repeated.

"Macus," I whispered. "Okay, so who are the others?"

"I will tell you the most important names. The ones who will help you in your mission," he started. "Astinal is the leader—"

"The one with the blue eyes?" I interrupted.

"Yes, the one with the blue eyes," he chuckled. "And Turi. He has grown in the ranks since you've come, and he has become a key member. He will help as well."

"So Astinal, the blue-eyed Guard, and is Turi tall? Does he have Hazel eyes?" I asked, Macus nodded in response.

"I've met him before. He was the one who took me away from the Wall."

"Section Eight," Macus corrected.

"Right, Section Eight," I repeated. "And your name is Macus. I am Violet," I told him, forgetting he already knew my name.

"Hello Violet," he said, staring deep into my eyes. I blushed and looked away, embarrassed by his heated gaze.

"Have you met Him?" I asked, changing the subject.

"No," he said abruptly, shaking his head empathetically.

I nodded, understanding I wouldn't get any more from him on this subject.

"Have you read the Bible?" I found that I needed to know more about him. He felt so familiar to me, but I knew nothing of him.

He scoffed. "No, I have been around long before your people made up the 'Word of God'." He rolled his eyes, so he didn't see how he hurt me. "You need to forget it. We do not know Him and have never met Him. That is why we are doing this. It is time. We all feel it."

"Thank you for this," I said. When he frowned at me, I continued. "For speaking to me like a human, I mean. And for understanding that I need answers too." He grinned back. "So we were together?" I asked shyly. "What was I like?"

"You were..." He paused for thought. "Spirited, determined and driven. I guess as you are now, but you didn't have the support you have."

"But you don't know me. How could you know what I am like?"

"I see her in you. I knew her better than anyone, I am sure. No one knew her like I did. She opened up to me and showed me her true self." He furrowed his brow in pain.

"I would have liked to have met her," I whispered.

I sat and stared at him, memorising his features.

"I knew you were coming." He began after a while. "We know of all the Souls who make it through Purgatory and of those who succumb to the trials."

I motioned with a hand for him to carry on.

He licked his dry lips. "I followed your progress and helped you in Purgatory."

"Were you the female voice which guided me?"

He laughed. "No, but I did use her voice to guide you."

"I see." I took a moment to envision the trials I had gone through to get here and a deep throbbing pain in my head warned of another headache. "Why does my head hurt all the time? It started when I first came back from Section Eight."

He took a deep breath and closed his eyes. He seemed to be battling with something inside him. He finally sighed. "Something was planted in your temple. Don't ask me what." He said quickly when he saw the incredulous expression on my face. "That is how we communicate. The Guards and I, I mean."

"Can we take it out?" I asked.

"Some have tried, but they didn't last long afterwards."

"Really?" I blanched.

"When I was in your position, I witnessed many people take out the chip — I guess you would call it — from their temples, and within a few hours Guards came and took them away."

"So I have to leave it in?"

"I am afraid so."

"Thank you for being honest with me, but what you have told me has raised new questions rather than answer those which I have asked you."

"I am sorry I can't be of more help, Violet. I am in the dark about many aspects of life here. I am also expected to grit my teeth and bare it."

I don't know what came over me, I took my hands out of his and caressed his wrists. My hands travelled up his arms, stroking them as they went. They reached his shoulders, and I cupped the back of his neck, gently massaging it. He looked deep into my eyes, his still held the pain of the dredged up memories and my heart ached for him. I rose to my knees and pulled him to me so his head rested on my chest and hung my arms around his neck. He stiffened, not used to such close contact, but soon relaxed into my embrace. His arms snaked around my waist, pulling me closer so my legs straddled his waist and I sat in his lap. He nuzzled his face into my neck, but pulled back immediately afterwards.

"What's that?" He asked, pointing at my chest.

I had completely forgotten about it. I took out the emerald pendant and showed it to him.

"She wore one just like that," he whispered.

"Mrs Scott gave it to me," I whispered back, turning the pendant so the light shone inside the stone. "She told me it was once hers, and she would have wanted me to have it."

His eyes were fixed on the pendant as though he was at a loss for words. He reached out a hand and traced the lines of the stone with the tip of his index finger, hypnotised by its intricate patterns. He tucked it away beneath my t-shirt and rested his head back against my neck, inhaling my scent as though he was saving it into his personal memory bank for a later time. I smiled, glad to have been able to penetrate the thick shell he had built around himself.

"Thank you." He breathed into my neck.

"I don't understand," I said.

"What don't you understand, Violet?"

"Why do I feel this way? I barely know you but I have this tightening in my chest as though I love you."

"Because you do love me. At least you did…once," he whispered. "I suppose her memories are merging with yours and it's her feelings she once had for me that are coming back."

I pushed myself away from him and looked into his face. The frown I had always seen him wear had disappeared and his eyes had lightened from the coal black I was accustomed to, to their apparent true colour. They were a pear green colour at the outside of the pupil and merged into a bright silvery grey on the inside, but the colours mixed together to create a new hybrid colour beyond description. My breath caught in my throat.

I leaned my head down — my eyes caught in his hypnotic gaze — unable to look away. Our noses touched. His hand snaked up my back and rested on the back of my neck. He tilted my head and pushed it down to meet his lips. They met once. Twice. Soft, short kisses that left me wanting more. I pulled my head back and looked into his eyes. They had changed colour again. This time they had turned a shade darker and the lust shone vividly in them.

He reached up and captured my lips in his, this time kissing me longer and harder. His tongue darted out of his mouth, brushing against my lips; exactly how I had fantasised. I opened my mouth, permitting him entrance and moaned when our tongues met; tentative at first, but then harder as the kiss deppened. His kisses became desperate, and he clutched my body to his as his hands roamed across my skin; his fingertips memorising every dip and curve.

He broke away and pushed me roughly from his lap.

"I am sorry," he apologised, breathing heavily. "I have to go." He made to stand up, but I grabbed his arm, attempting to keep him close.

"Don't go. Please," I said.

He pried my hand off his arm, his eyes looked apologetic. "I have to."

He launched himself to his feet and strode from my cage. The glass sank into the ground as he walked past and rose up as soon as he had left the confines of the prison. I watched as he walked away, my fingers brushing my lips where the echo of his kiss still lingered. The light faded the further he walked away as though he was taking it with him, and then the door snapped shut behind him, leaving me again in my darkness alone.

I wiped tears from my face, which had fallen without my notice, angry for allowing myself to feel but knowing this was just the beginning. I wondered where this journey with him would take me.

I strode away from the Holding Room, angry at myself for letting the encounter get out of hand. I had no idea upon entering that room that the meeting would become so intense. My lips still burned from the unexpected contact, and I ran my tongue across my lips, savouring her taste.

I closed my eyes and mentally transported myself back into the glass cage with her. I replayed the whole scenario in my head, and I still couldn't believe it had escalated as it had done and she had been so willing. The feel of her body pressed against mine and her warmth radiated inside of me. I shook my head, trying to dispel the improper thoughts which had come forth for the first time in centuries. Why did she have to come back? I had moved forward with my life. The pain had receded to a dull ache, far from reach, but meeting Violet had dredged up the past and stirred up my long-forgotten love for her.

I hadn't been paying attention to where I was going. I had let my feet lead me to where I needed to go. I found myself in the Altar room and was surprised to see several hundred Guards surrounding me. Time had slipped away from me and my eyes widened in surprise to find that it was noon and the midday meeting had already begun. Luckily, this meeting would be a quick briefing and Astinal would soon dismiss the Guards to patrol again.

I craned my neck and looked over the crowd to the Altar, Astinal stood behind it speaking to the congregation. I weaved my way through the crowd, eager to get up to him and confess what I had just done.

"Keep on doing what you have been doing. Just do more of the same," Astinal said Vaguely. He didn't look like his usual self. He looked distracted.

I frowned up at him and when he finally spotted me in the crowd, he shook his head sadly and sighed.

"Dismissed." He lazily waved a hand to the crowd, and the Guards trooped out, confused and muttering amongst themselves.

I didn't leave with the other Guards. Instead, I fought my way against the torrent, desperate to reach Astinal, and I was not the only one who fought through the tidal wave. To my left I spotted Turi making his way, with difficulty, towards the altar too.

"What was that about?" Turi demanded, when we had finally reached Astinal. The remaining stragglers who hadn't left, glanced around at the outburst and the wave of Guards halted for a moment.

"Get to your posts," I called over to them, restarting the wave.

We waited until they had all left the room and the door snapped closed behind them before speaking. "Astinal, what has gotten into you?" I asked. I pushed my own worries aside. I needed to concentrate on Astinal and find out what had changed since we last spoke.

Astinal didn't speak for a minute; refusing to look at Turi or myself

"We're just trying to help," Turi said, looking genuinely worried.

"I think we are making a mistake," he finally said, his face reddening in rage. "We have to follow the rules. They have put them in place for a reason. We can't go on with this insane plan." He paced back and forth behind the altar. "Where have you been, Macus?" He added angrily.

"I have been with Violet," I admitted, looking down at my sandals.

"She is Miss Deneuve," he said coldly. "How is she?"

"She is fine, Sir," I replied, shooting him a reproachful look. "Awake."

"Good," he nodded. "Get Travis and Trevor," he said to Turi, turning away from us as a sign of dismissal.

"Who?" Turi asked, throwing his hands in the air in exasperation.

"I think he means the two big Guards," I whispered to him out of the corner of my Mouth.

Turi snarled at Astinal but marched out the room, muttering angrily to himself.

"Astinal, we can't back down now," I pleaded, once Turi had left the room. "We have come so close. We all want this." I grabbed his arm when he didn't respond and wrenched him around to face me, but still, he didn't speak.

"Have they gotten to you? What did they say?" I asked, panicked; grabbing him by the shoulders and shaking him.

"Don't you think about how much they know and how much *they* watch us?" Astinal asked, his temper rising with every word he spoke.

"I had never thought of it," I confessed, half-shrugging.

"Do you remember when we died? We always questioned the Guards and their motives. How did they disappear and reappear at will? How did they know of every action we made?" He wrenched free from my grasp and resumed his pacing. "When we gained these positions, we were apprised of the secrets we questioned. Now we are the guards, but what if those who gave us these positions are listening to what we say and do and have done all along?"

"If that is the case Astinal, we are in too deep. We can't back out now." I sighed. "If they have, indeed, been listening to every word we have ever said, I am afraid they already know what we are planning."

"We don't need her to go forward. We need answers and we can get them on our own."

"Everyone needs answers," I said. "We owe it to everyone who was involved last time. Think of Mrs Scott. Think of all those people who died or were tortured. We owe them justice.

Astinal didn't seem convinced. He worked everything I said over in his mind and I watched him as his mental cogs turned. He chewed his lip in concentration, a deep frown marred his brow. Then he screwed his eyes up in frustration.

"Okay," he conceded, frowning up at me. "I am not happy about this, but we have come this far, so we may as well continue."

I nodded, glad he was back on track.

The door opened and Turi walked in, still scowling, accompanied by Travis and Trevor; the Brutish Guards. Only four 'mega-glads' existed at that moment and I don't know why these two were assigned to us. They stalked up to the Altar flanking Turi.

"Travis and Trevor Sir," Turi snapped. He turned to leave, but I grabbed his wrist. He fought hard against me but it was a battle of strength, not wills, and I won.

"Stay, Turi," I said. "You will not regret it."

He saw the sincerity in my face and stopped fighting. He scowled at Astinal and crossed his arms across his huge chest but stayed.

"Wait outside," I gestured towards Travis and Trevor and they filed out of the room. "We are on the same side, we need to stick together." I looked between Turi and Astinal, they didn't make eye contact with each other. "At least shake hands," I said, exasperatedly.

They reached out their hands and let them touch, but immediately let them go as though their hands were on fire.

"Good," I nodded. "Let's do this."

Without waiting for a response, I closed my eyes and visualised Violet in her Holding Room, and when I opened them I was facing the cube. She stood inside it in a defensive stance, her eyes darting around the room. I could see why. I wasn't alone. The entire room was filled with Guards surrounding her glass prison on all sides.

TWENTY-TWO

WHO'S CALLING?

I lay on my back, in the same position I was in when Macus left, legs curled under me and my arms splayed outwards. "Macus," I said his name out loud, savouring the foreign sounds on my tongue and found I liked it. "Macus," I said it again for good measure, memorising it; hopingI would be saying it more often in the future.

I thought back to our conversation, and even though some parts unnerved me — specifically that I am a doppelgänger and have lived this life before — I trusted everything he had told me. Mrs Scott already told me this, but I only truly believed it when Macus confirmed it.

"I thought Mrs Scott was trying to manipulate me," I said aloud to myself. I hadn't been ready to believe it then, but I was ready now. He told me this time it will be different as Mary, and the Guards were on my side; Macus, Astinal and Turi. My resolve had waned when I first arrived. I had become complacent. I was happy with the friends I made, and the life I was living amongst my equals, but being put in this prison and being tortured, I now knew I was ready to be that woman. I was ready to be my doppelgänger who led an identical life. This had to be why I put myself here – what I was born to do – and I could not wait to meet Him.

As I stared wide-eyed into the darkness, willing the little orb of light Macus gifted me to return, I relived my actions with him. I had never allowed myself to let go with anyone before, not even with Mary or my father.

"Why did I kiss him?" I asked myself. "Why did I let him walk away?"

The darkness pressed into me. I had gotten used to the light and when Macus left, it seemed he took more than the light with him; he took a piece of myself. My heart ached to be near him again. To watch his eyes change colour with his emotions as I stroked away his worries and held him.

"I-" I started to say. "No Violet, stop talking to yourself," I said, punching the side of my head in frustration. I stood up and paced the perimeter of the cube, a ritual I routinely practiced since my incarceration. The glass brushed against my finger tips, and it made me feel connected to the world. Sitting in the dark, with only depressive thoughts for company could drive anybody insane. I needed to feel something solid and real in order for my brain to calm down, and the simple act of movement helped me think clearly. From what Macus said, it would only be a matter of time before I would meet Him — I would demand it. I craved it.

I walked faster around the glass cube, my thoughts running amok in my brain. My calming strategy wasn't working, as my thoughts were too disorganised, and they kept slipping through my fingers every time I tried to grab hold of them, making any coherent organisation near impossible. I needed to get out of here, do something which would further my path. Running in circles, thinking the same things over and over again, would never help me.

"Let me out of here!" I shouted to the blackness, frustrated by the lack of contact between myself and other people. I would have preferred to have been back in the room with the Brutish Guard. At least then I would have had someone to interact with. The snippets of time which I had been granted to be with other people since I had been in this prison were too few for my liking. I needed other people around me. I needed company. I needed my twin.

"Get in your room now you two." His voice cracked out from the other room.

I vaguely remembered wondering what we had done this time, but recently no clear reasons came forth. He lurched into the living room, his large frame taking up the whole doorway.

"Why are you not in your room like I told you?" He unbuckled his belt.

I grabbed my twin sister's hand and ran to our room, slamming the door shut behind us, praying he wouldn't follow us inside. A sigh of relief escaped when the lock clicked outside of the room, but in the same breath I sobbed out loud; we were trapped. We shuffled to the corner of the room and cuddled together. At least we had each other.

I punched the nearest glass panel and the telltale crack warned me of a broken bone. Wincing at the pain, I examined my hand. Two of my fingers glowed red and when I prodded them, a sharp jolt of pain ran up my arm. I sank to my knees and cradled the broken hand to my chest, cursing myself for being so rash and unthinking.

A minute later, the familiar siren blared. The lights flashed on, which caught me unawares. I jumped to my feet, accidentally banging my damaged hand against my leg. I gritted my teeth and blinked as waves of pain washed over me and unwanted tears threatened to fall. I looked around the perimeter of the cube and a sea of Guards surrounded me on all sides.

"You know what to do, Miss Deneuve." A deep voice called out at the back of the crowd.

I scanned the sea of helmets looking for the one which held the bright blue eyes of my tormenter. I found him at the back of the crowd leaning against the wall next to the door. His arms crossed over his chest, with an air of superiority hanging over him like a storm cloud — Astinal. I could now put a name to those hauntingly blue eyes and I glared at him.

The glass sank into the ground, leaving the pathway clear. I strode from the cube, glad to be out of its confines and vowing to myself never to be inside it again. I walked down the three steps with as much dignity as I could muster — given the state of my tattered clothing and general appearance — and as soon as I reached the last step, I hit the unmovable wall of Guards. A hand shot out and grabbed my upper left arm but I wrenched myself free of its grip.

"I can walk by myself," I spat at the Guard who had manhandled me. He backed away with his hands held up in surrender and I walked down the rest of the makeshift pathway, which the Guard had just made, to Astinal, with no one else touching me and my head held high. All the while, I surreptitiously scanned the crowd for Macus, but I could not spot him.

When I reached Astinal, he swept a hand out in front of him, gesturing for me to walk ahead. I took this as a peace offering and strode ahead but was annoyed when he matched my pace and walked alongside me. The door swung open and the way forward was revealed in a clinically white hallway, with black doors on either side, much like the one I saw in Purgatory. I kept glancing around, hoping Macus was close by but saw no sign of him. This worried me, and made me question whether he had been truthful when he had visited me.

I didn't need Astinal to guide me. My feet led me the right way at each turn, as though I had walked these hallways before. A door swung open ahead of us and we both strode through the wide opening at the same time without braking pace. It shut behind us, permitting no one else to enter.

The room looked unchanged. The elaborate altar sat at the front of the room and the same metal chair sat in the middle. Chains lay hidden underneath the arm rests and behind the front legs, which I knew would bind me to it soon. The hundreds of candles still dotted around the room and looked frozen in time as though they had burned at the same height for centuries.

Four Guards stood behind the altar. The two gigantic Guards at the two ends, and the hazel-eyed Guard, who I now knew to be Turi, stood to my left. A small smile played on his lips, much like the last time I sat in this room, making me feel slightly more comfortable. Macus stood next to Turi. He smiled shyly at me and I smiled back. He seemed to remember himself, drew his body to his full height and stared off into the distance. A gap big enough to fit another person lay between them for Astinal; the definite leader of the group. He strode past me and took the remaining spot.

I hesitated before sitting down in the chair and as I predicted, the chains came to life and slinked around my wrists and ankles; snaking tightly up my arms and legs, and binding me to the chair so I couldn't move an inch. The chains held my right arm to the armrest, and waves of pain from my injured hand made me lose consciousness for a second. I took a deep, steadying breath and looked up at the panel of Guards in front of me. My head held high with pride and my lips pursed in a tight line. Macus gave me an imperceptible approving nod.

"How are you feeling today, Miss Deneuve?" Astinal asked once I made myself as comfortable as I could in my designated chair.

I refused to answer him, knowing he was only toying with me before he would strike.

"Very well, Miss Deneuve," he sighed. "Have it your way." He gestured to the Brutish Guard at the end of the line up and he slouched out the room. The candles shook violently as his footsteps reverberated around the room and the atmosphere instantly turned heavy. Everyone present knew what the Guard went to fetch, and the squeaking wheels preceded the Guard's heavy footsteps. I flinched hard at the sound as it brought back horrific memories of the last time I was in this chair; memories which I thought I had successfully pushed into the darkest corner of my mind.

The door swung open noiselessly, and the trolley appeared beside me; the Guard's huge hands fingered the deadly instruments which were neatly laid out on top of it. My eyes followed his huge hands, travelled up his bulging arms to his thick neck and our eyes met. He grinned at me. The same broken yellow teeth showed through his dry, chapped lips and I cringed away from him.

All the memories came flooding back. The way he had so obviously enjoyed hurting me. The way he laughed manically whenever I screamed, and when he pouted when Astinal told him to end my torture. I needed to do something so I would never have to experience pain like that again. I had been brave then, but I was not sure how much more pain I could endure.

I looked back at the panel of Guards in front of me. I licked my lips, and hoped my strategy would work.

"I want to see my sister," I demanded, my voice shakier than I hoped it would be. "I know she is here."

"Do you, now?" Astinal jeered. "I suppose we can arrange that," he said, nodding to Turi and Macus. "But first you have to answer our questions."

"No!" I shot back. "I want to see my sister and then I will answer your questions."

"We can't do that, I'm afraid, Miss Deneuve." Astinal shook his head sadly.

He motioned to the Guard standing next to me. The scrape of metal on metal grated on my ears as he snatched up a corkscrew from the trolley. The Guard grinned and twirled the implement between his fingers. He picked his fingernails with the sharp end and mimed piercing his middle finger with it, grinning at me and raising his eyebrows suggestively. I stared at him wide-eyed as he balanced the corkscrew on my forearm. He started to twist until he created a small hole in it. The pain was already bearable. I thought if I breathed through it, I would be able to handle it, but it appeared I thought too soon.

The Guard twisted the corkscrew with more pressure so the metal disappeared into my arm. It scraped against my sensitive nerve endings, sending shocking waves of pain through my entire body. Then it hit bone, twisting no further. The Guard grunted as his progress was halted and frowned down at the instrument. He tried twisting it again, harder this time, but he couldn't move it past the blockade. He snarled at me as though I had actively impeded the corkscrew's progress. He scratched his head in a comical manner and frowned at the object as though he was willing it to move with his mind. A sharp cry of frustration escaped his lips, and he slammed his hand onto my arm. The pain was explosive. The corkscrew shattered my bone and ran straight through the metal armrest, trapping my arm securely to it.

I stared in horror as blood bubbled from the wound, ran down my hand and dripped onto the floor. I clenched and unclenched my hands as my stress levels rose, but it only made the pain worse. Tears spilt from my eyes, but no sound escaped my lips. Why had I been so emotional since I had arrived? It was as though my walls I had so carefully created in my twenty-one years of living had crumbled when I died and I had suddenly allowed myself to feel.

"Please, no more." I sobbed. "I will answer your questions. Just stop hurting me." I glared at the panel of Guards in front of me through tearfilled eyes, but I couldn't see their expressions through my blurry vision.

"Very well, Miss Deneuve," Astinal said. "I am glad you have seen sense."

"Will you then let me see my sister?" I asked, mumbling.

"Of course, we are not animals," Astinal replied.

My vision slowly cleared and Astinal smiled. He opened his mouth to speak, but no words came out. His eyes widened and his mouth hung open in shock as his attention was drawn away to something within.

A wave rippled in my head and I froze on the spot. I closed my coal black eyes and my hand clenched tightly around my spear shaft. It was as though an aerial had switched on in my head but was tuned to a station that hadn't been turned on in centuries. A crackling erupted in my mind and a disquieting voice rang out immediately after it.

"Bring her to me." A deep rumbling voice I hadn't heard in centuries, vibrated through me, making my whole body shake. "If that was your plan all along, bring her and her sister to me."

The ripple faded, and the crackling disappeared. I unfroze, took a deep shuddering breath as Turi and Astinal did the same. We each looked at each other; our surroundings momentarily forgotten.

"Erm, can I carry on Astinal?" Travis asked in a slow drawling voice. Trevor stood next to me, staring at us with a half-puzzled expression on his face.

"No," Astinal snapped. He composed himself and drew himself up to his full height. "Stand up, Miss Deneuve."

The chains slinked back to their original position, so she was free to stand, but with her injuries she wouldn't have been able to do it by herself.

I strode over to her and reached for a syringe full of green liquid on the trolley and brought it to the inside of her elbow. She flinched away from me, but I grabbed her arm and brought the syringe to her skin. She looked up at me, her eyes wide with fear.

"What are you going to do?" She asked.

"It's okay," I said gently. "This will make you feel better. Like last time."

I prodded around for a vein, inserted the needle and injected the green liquid inside her. Warmth seeped through her as the concoction ran through her body. The wound was healing, pushing the corkscrew out of her body in the process. We watched as the object twisted itself out of her arm, scraping against the metal chair all the while, and clattered to the floor.

"How did it do that?" She breathed, flexing her newly-healed fingers.

"I don't know," I admitted, just as surprised as she was. I had expected the wound to heal enough for me to painlessly extract the corkscrew out of her arm, but the green concoction was much stronger than I realised.

"Thank you."

I looked at her, hypnotised by her eyes. "No problem."

"If you are done, we have to leave," Turi's voice invaded our little moment.

My cheeks burned, and I watched as her cheeks reddened and we both quickly looked away at the same time. She stood from the chair on shaky legs, and I grabbed her arm to support her.

"Where are we going?" She whispered.

"To see Him," I whispered back.

"What?" She asked me.

"We are going to see Him," I said again, assuming she hadn't understood me.

"God? The Devil? How?" She asked. "Where is He?"

"I don't know who we are meeting," I said. "But it is as though a beacon has been lit inside of me and I need to get to it." I finished, shrugging.

She nodded but said nothing more. I guided her towards the door with my hand at the small of her back and we strode out of it together, side by side. I let my feet guide us and we passed through empty corridors I had never been to, but which jolted a memory deep inside of me. I glanced back, and Turi and Astinal were keeping pace behind us. Turi grinned nervously at me, but Astinal simply nodded, giving nothing away. Travis and Trevor were not with us; it was just the four of us heading to Him. This was definitely a sign of things to come.

TWENTY-THREE

HIM

I strode down the white hallways — my short black hair sticking to my forehead in the rivulets of sweat coating my body — with Macus at my side. Our arms brushed against each other's, but neither of us flinched away from the touch. Instead, I longed for our touches to linger. I longed to hold his hand and connect with him physically, but this wasn't the time to think of such trivialities. The walkways brought forth memories of Purgatory and unlocked deeper ones which unnerved me because they brought with them a dark ominous cloud. My doppelgänger's memories must be seeping into my consciousness and fusing with my own, blurring the barrier between mine and hers so I couldn't tell which was which.

I tried to embrace the change, hoping it wouldn't hurt me, and also hoping they would morph me into the being I needed to be to reach my goal. I knew I needed to tap into her strength because without it I would fail to reach my goal. I was nervous to meet Him. What if He was completely different to what I pictured in my head? That was a strong possibility given that nothing I had experienced in the Afterlife had resembled anything I had been taught throughout my short life on Earth.

What would He look like? Would He have red skin, horns and cloven hooves? The picture seemed absurd to me, cartoonised and fabricated by fanatics and the media to scare the masses.

After striding along several nondescript white corridors, the atmosphere changed. The air suddenly turned heavy, oppressive. Something or someone wanted to forewarn us of its nearing presence. It worked. My head lolled on my shoulders and my pace slowed. The palpable power overwhelmed me; it was as though I was walking through molasses. Someone much stronger than us was nearby — it was Him.

"Be strong Violet," Macus whispered next to me. His words cleared away some of the fog, which filled my mind with misdirected second thoughts and dark, distorted images of the hurdles I had to jump over to get to this point — the Wall, Purgatory, my death. Right behind me, the phantom strangled breathing of the grey skeletal creatures I encountered when I first died sprouted. The manic laughter of the little girl — Mary-Jane — who I met on the long staircase rang in my ears, and the imagined pain of the recent torture flooded back to me with full force. I willed these dark thoughts out of my head, and clutched at Macus' arm. The physical contact and his calming demeanour drove me back to the present and helped disperse the negative thoughts which currently filled my head.

"He's inside my head, Macus," I whispered, my lips trembling.

"He's inside all our heads, Violet." Astinal surprised me by answering. "We have to fight Him."

"Why are you doing this? Why are we now on the same team?" I asked confused, glancing over my shoulder at him.

"I realised we have been following unwritten rules for a long time — centuries — but now I am ready to find answers," he said calmly. "It took your reappearance to realise that blindly following the unheard commands of an invisible man was insanity."

"Are you sure He is a man?" I asked.

"I am not sure of anything," he said simply.

I let his words wash over me; his assuredness calming me further still. I allowed my mind to become still, my thoughts to align as they had never done before. Images, which I had never seen before, raced through my mind. They seemed familiar, as though I had actually lived through them, but deep down I knew I hadn't. Isobel's thoughts and memories were indeed fusing with my own.

The tiled hallway was magically replaced with new magical surroundings, as a forest came into view right in front of my very eyes, and gigantic redwoods stood rod-straight all around me. As I walked on in, what I knew to be, the white hallway, but the lush green forest kept up pace. A bubbling stream ran to my left. Streams of dazzling sunlight broke through the canopy of leaves, dappling the nature around me with its soft golden kiss, and through a thicket of trees a clearing materialised.

A hand grasped my arm in a tight grip, but the physical contact did not dull the scene.

Ten small log huts stood in the circle, each facing a fire pit lined with huge, grey stones. A wisp of smoke rose in the air and carried with it a tangy scent. A high-pitched squeal broke through the calm, and a toddler streaked from the doorway of one hut into the doorway of another. A woman with short black hair and green eyes emerged from the first hut sighing, her hands on her hips. A tall man with long blonde hair strode towards her from the second hut with the laughing infant squirming in his arms.

"I don't know what I am going to do with him," she said, smiling up at the blond haired man.

"Children," he muttered, shaking his head and kissing the woman's forehead lovingly.

"Isobel!"

A sharp pain in my left palm jolted through me and the scene faded until the beige tiled corridor took its place once more.

"Violet, are you okay?" Macus asked, standing in front of me, his hands grasping my upper arms.

I put my right hand to his chest. He took my hand in both of his, bringing it to his lips. I brought my still burning left hand to my face and examined it. The red birthmark I had seen on Mrs Scott's palm stood in stark relief against my white palm; in the same shape and shade as hers.

"I'm okay," I said, leaning into him, folding my hand to hide the new imperfection. "I…we are…I don't know how to explain it."

"What happened? What did you see?" Astinal stood to my left. I hadn't noticed him standing there, my only thoughts were on Macus in front of me.

"I saw a forest, and huts, and Isobel," I licked my lips, looking up meaningfully at Macus. "A small child and a tall, blond man were with her. Someone shouted her name, but I didn't see them. You shook me awake. But the strange thing was, I didn't have my eyes closed, but I could see this vision so clearly. What do you think this means?"

"I don't know. I have never heard of something like this happening before," Astinal replied. "Make sure you tell us if anything like that happens again."

I nodded, afraid to speak. We carried on walking and the corridors smoothly changed from the white tiles to a rough earthen floor. Up ahead an archway loomed, but the pitch black interior allowed me to see nothing beyond it. Our pace quickened. We ignored oppressive air, our joint strength pushing us towards Him. We strode beneath the archway and emerged into a circular chamber. A door, devoid of a handle, keyhole, or anything which would allow entry, stood before us. Turi and Astinal moved to stand at either side of Macus and I. All doors in this place opened of their own accord, but this one stayed resolutely shut.

"What do we do now?" I asked, in a hushed voice.

"We wait?" Turi's answer was unsure.

"We need to get Mary," Macus said with certainty. "Our numbers are not complete."

I didn't question him, but trusted him implicitly.

"Astinal, care to do the honours?" Turi asked, looking around at Macus and myself.

I turned to Astinal, he nodded once, unsmiling, closed his eyes and disappeared. The imbalance was plain without him. None of us spoke, instead soaking up the silence and peace, and waiting. Waiting for Astinal to return with Mary. Waiting to meet Him. Waiting for the change we knew would inevitably come. We stared at the handleless door, waiting for it to open.

The siren sounded — a sharp, jarring sound — for the first time in two days. The bright lights came on half a second later, waking me from my doze. I pushed my long black hair from my eyes and tucked an errant strand behind an ear. Through the unaccustomed bright light — much like the first time — a lone figure walked towards me, and from his stance and stride I knew it would be the blue-eyed Guard. He appeared in relief — a halo of light behind him making him look ethereal — on the other side of the glass. I pushed myself away from him, tiredly dragging my body along the floor, trying to distance myself from him.

"Don't be afraid, Mary," he said gently. "Come with me."

The glass disappeared, and he strode into the cube holding out a hand for me to take. I didn't, afraid of a trap. I didn't trust him, no matter how kind he was, because in my eyes he was the kind of evil who acted kind at one moment but could turn on you in the same beat. He reminded me a lot of my father and I was more afraid of him than of any other person I had ever met.

Everybody at church says we are lucky to have a father like him," Violet said.

"I don't think we are so lucky," I pouted. "Do you honestly like him?"

"I love him, Mary." Violet sighed, lovingly.

I sighed darkly. I didn't want to voice my doubts, as I didn't want to upset my twin sister, but I thought the complete opposite of my Father. "What do you think about Mother?"

"What about Mother?" She spat out the last word. "She does nothing for us. She stays locked up in her room, and never speaks. It's as though we don't exist. Mother means nothing to me."

"You can't mean that Violet." I cried, shocked.

"I mean every word," she said. "I love Father and I'd do anything for him."

I shook my head, baffled at the way she saw our distorted family.

"I will take you to your sister, like I promised." He knelt in front of me and took my hand in his. He smiled and closed his eyes. A rush of air passed through me, and I watched, wide-eyed as my prison disappeared and a myriad of images flitted by. When they stopped, we were in an earthen hallway, a heavy air around us, and I braced myself against a wall, retching.

"It helps if you close your eyes. I am sorry I should have warned you." The blue eyed Guard said sheepishly.

"Where are we?" I asked, when the bile had settled in my stomach.

"We are near Him," he replied.

He grabbed my upper arm and steered me down the earthen hallway. I was happy to have his support. With my blurred vision and my wobbly knees, I needed it then. I gave myself over to him, trusting in his guidance to take me where I needed to go.

I felt her before I heard her. I felt whole, my broken soul had finally found its other half. I sank to my knees as footsteps rushed towards me. Familiar arms wrapped around me, the scent of her filled my nostrils. The familiar shape of her body pressed against mine as she embraced me.

"Violet," I whispered, clutching at her desperately.

"Mary. Oh, Mary," she breathed. Her tears hit my shoulder at the same time as mine hit hers.

"I hate to break this up, but this is not the time for a reunion." I looked up, and the hazel-eyed Guard, who had taken me from my bunk, stood over us.

"Right," I said, composing myself.

The dark-eyed Guard held out a hand to Violet, she took it and didn't let go.

"What's going on Violet?" I asked, confused.

"We are meeting Him, Mary. These Guards are helping us," she replied.

A ripple of confusion passed between the tall men surrounding us, but I knew exactly what she was talking about.

I nodded. "And they are...?" I asked.

"This is Macus," she said, pointing to the dark-eyed Guard, whose hand she still held. "This is Turi," she said, pointing to the hazel-eyed Guard. "And this is Astinal," she gestured to the blue-eyed Guard; the one who had taken me from my prison. I nodded to each of them in turn.

"Where are Sophie and Jeff? Where did you take them?" I pointedly stared into Astinal's eyes, challenging him.

"We needed to keep them out of the way so nobody else would get influenced by their combative behaviour," he answered, maintaining eye contact all the while.

"The last time something like this happened, there was death and destruction like you've never seen before," Macus added. He looked down at Violet and she nodded in agreement, gazing lovingly into his eyes.

"Are we ready?" Macus asked her.

"Only if you are." She grinned at him.

I frowned, but knew this wasn't the time to question their budding relationship. We turned and faced a wooden door I hadn't noticed until now. It had no handle and intricate carvings covered it the entirety of it. We waited a beat in deafening silence and then the door creaked open.

"I am glad you have finally made it. Enter." A deep, fear-inducing voice echoed from the depths of the doorway.

Our collective breath hitched in our throats. We braced ourselves for the cumulation of our separate paths being drawn together; our destinies fusing into one. There was no turning back.